I Love You…Like Crazy

By

Erin Mack

Table of Contents

Chapter 1
Chloe

I have always considered myself as a reasonable, some might even say a boring adult. I rarely make decisions without weighing out all the options. I am a huge fan of the pros and cons list when making any decision. That is why I am so confused about how I ended up at this point in my life, driving in the freezing cold at 10 miles per hour on an icy road in the middle of nowhere Minnesota.

At the beginning of December, I received a phone call from my great-aunt, Betty. Growing up, we would spend a few weeks during the summer visiting Aunt Betty in Minnesota. Minnesota was always a breath of fresh air during the oppressive summer heat in Arizona. I would always look forward to the visits for more than just the weather, though. Betty was a little on the cooky side of life but that only made for some of my best childhood memories during those summer vacations.

Naturally, when Betty called and randomly invited me and my daughter to move to Little Falls, I carefully weighed all my options, NOT! My life in Arizona was a dumpster fire at best. The only good thing about my life was my beautiful daughter, Phoebe. We needed a fresh start, one where I could build Phoebe the life she deserves. At the time I felt like Betty's call was divine intervention guiding us here. Fast forward to me moving to the middle of a frozen wasteland, and I am starting to feel the inspiration is less than divine.

A serious flaw in this life-altering plan that I jumped at, with not one pros and cons list being made, was the fact that I have never been to Minnesota at any time other than summer. Did you know frozen boogers were actually a thing? I do now, sadly, through experience. We have only been here a few days, and in those few days, I don't think the temperature has gotten higher than zero degrees.

It is New Year's Eve, and my plans have consisted of not getting out of my pajamas. I am going to unpack and watch movies with Phoebe all day. The best part of this plan was that I would be staying indoors all day, enjoying the comfort of a heating system cranked on high. In my book, it was totally worth the extra expense out of my budget to have extra heat. You know what they say about a good plan? Well, I don't know what they actually say about a good plan because I rarely have one. Betty just called and told me she would need a ride home from the salon because her car would not start.

I bundled Phoebe up in the cutest snowsuit I could find on Amazon because, of course, Arizona is never in the season to sell something to wear that is appropriate for these temperatures. We are currently on our way to pick up Betty at the beauty salon for her weekly curl and set appointment. Little Falls is a small town and rarely has any traffic, which I am very grateful for as I fishtail through town.

I pull up in front of the salon grateful for a spot close to the front door. I am waiting in the car, dreading having to get out of my car to walk 20 feet from my car to the blessed heat of the salon. Finally deciding, the sooner, I go inside to retrieve my aunt, the sooner I can get back home and back in my pajamas. I turn the car off and open the door. The wind whips into the car, and it feels like I am being stabbed in the face by dozens of tiny ice swords – a super pleasant sensation. I hurry to get out of the car and move quickly to unbuckle Phoebe from her car seat. Phoebe is the happiest baby I have ever been around. She is all smiles and giggles. The only skin that is showing is her face, so I throw a blanket over her head to protect her face from the wind. I rush to the door with Phoebe giggling the entire way. She probably thinks we are playing a game instead of trying to survive the horrific winter.

I open the door with a little too much force, and it slams into the wall. The bell attached slams into the glass door, announcing my less-than-graceful entrance. Everyone in the salon goes dead silent and stops what they are doing and just stare at the spectacle that is currently unfolding before their eyes. The receptionist hurries over to help me shut the door. Although I opted to change out of my pajamas I only changed into sweats. I have a parka on, with my sweatpants tucked into my Uggs. I look like I could be related to an Abdominal Snow Creature with only my face peeking out. This is a great first impression. Phoebe's giggles break loose again, helping to break the awkward silence.

"Sorry about that, the wind seemed to help me out with opening the door." I remove the blanket covering Phoebe's face. She is all smiles when she sees me.

"Oh dear, come here. I want you to meet someone." I can hear my aunt calling for me from the back of the salon.

"Sorry if I am late, Betty. The roads are awful out there, and I had to go slow," I say as I try to explain the delay.

"Oh, hush darling, you are right on time. I could hang out here all day. The gossip is always right on the mark, and Stella takes such good care of me."

"Hi, I am Stella; it's nice to meet you. Your aunt has not stopped talking about her amazing niece, who just moved here. It is nice to put a face with the stories now." A woman that was about five foot tall and dressed like a punk rocker princess stated. Her hair was in a stylish bob cut but stood out by the bright purple color.

"Yeah, we just moved here. I am looking for a fresh start in life, and my aunt was kind enough to invite us to stay with her while I get back on my feet." I have no idea why I keep talking. I never share personal details about my life, let alone with someone I just met five seconds ago.

"I might be biased, but I think you will love it here. I was born and raised here and could never see myself living anywhere else but here." Stella turns to put the finishing touches on my aunt's hair.

There is something about Stella that makes me want to be instantly friends with her. I can bet that she is fun to hang out with. I haven't had a girl's night in so long. I can barely remember what it feels like to cut loose and enjoy a night out. The nights of hanging out with friends seem to be far in my rear-view mirror at this point in my life.

"I bet you haven't had much of a chance to meet anyone in town. You should totally come out and hang out with me and my friends tonight. We are going to the Thirsty Moose to celebrate the new year. It will be so much fun!" Stella is almost bouncing up and down with excitement as she talks about her plans tonight.

"Oh, thank you that is really nice of you to think of me, but I won't be able to make it. I have Phoebe. I have no one to watch her. I would be down for hanging out tonight if I had a sitter." Even though it is a legit reason not to go it still sounds lame using my child as an excuse.

"Now you listen to me, child, you are going out tonight. I am more than capable of staying with Phoebe tonight. She will be in bed sleeping the entire time you are gone anyway. You need this time to go cut loose and meet some new people." Betty has this 'don't question me" expression plastered on her face.

"I can't ask you to watch Phoebe for me, Betty."

"Good thing you are not asking; I am volunteering. Now that is settled, Stella who else is going to be there tonight." Betty turns her attention back toward Stella.

Why is it I feel like I was just put in the corner for a timeout, and there is no getting out from a night with complete strangers.

Stella looks amused by Betty putting me in my place, "So the regulars will be there. Everyone was able to get work off tonight. Bubba, Henry, Ralph will be there tonight. They are the singles in the group. Then the couples will also be there. Max and Jane, who are recently engaged. Harrison and Ginger are also planning on coming. Noah and Emma were able to find a sitter for Lola, so they are in too." Stella turns to me. "I need to connect you with Emma. I bet Phoebe and Lola would have the best time together."

Stella just spewed out a lot of information. I am still stuck on the part where she is pointing out everyone's relationship status. I want to immediately tell her that I do not care if they are single or not, it makes no difference to me, but helpful Aunt Betty jumps in first.

"Oh, I am a little jealous. That does sound like a fun group of kids. I am tempted to say we sneak Phoebe into the Moose so I can tag along, too." I can see wheels turning in Betty's mind that sneaking my baby into a bar is a feasible idea. That alone should have me saying no thank you to the offer to babysit tonight.

Stella beats me to the punch, though. "Betty, you know, calling us kids is kind of funny, seeing we are all now functioning adults." Stella seems amused by Betty and her antics.

"Please, you are all still babies. I can't believe you and the three boys are still single. Maybe I should come tonight to help you all find your mates."

A laugh escapes before I can stop it. "Betty, I see you are still reading your weird romance books about shifters. I am pretty sure Stella and the others do not need help finding a mate." I cannot believe we are having this conversation in the middle of a salon and no one is batting an eye at the weird direction it turns. "Listen, Betty, why don't you go out tonight and enjoy your New Year's Eve? I will stay home with Phoebe." Is it wishful thinking that she will take the bait, and I will be off the hook for tonight?

"Nice try, sweetie. You are going." Betty says, giving me a stern look. "And for the record, there is nothing weird about my books. I just finished a series about men that shift into sharks, and it was very informative."

Stella is giggling under her breath as she removes the cape from around Betty's neck. "Betty, you have to give me the name of that series. Jane is terrified of sharks. She might enjoy a good love story about a shark man."

"She can have my copies, and I marked all the good spots!"

Stella turns to me with a big smile on her face, "Okay, well, it looks like Betty is not going to let you off the hook tonight and you are stuck with going out tonight. Do you want Bubba and me to swing by and pick you up?"

I am trapped, and we all know it. I look down at Phoebe who is all smiles as she is babbling. How did I just lose this battle with my elderly aunt and a punk rock princess? "Okay, maybe I can stop by for a little while tonight. I can drive myself, though, just in case I need to duck out early for Phoebe."

"Yay!! I am so excited. Everyone is going to be excited to meet you. You will love them all. They are a bunch of weirdos, but they are the best of the best at the end of the day." Stella beams when she talks about her friends. I am not sure, even before my life imploded in Arizona, if I ever had friends that I would endorse with the same excitement. "Okay, Betty, try to stay out of trouble, and I will see you next week for your next appointment."

"Pish posh, trouble, me? I am sure I do not know what you are talking about." Betty has this twinkle in her eyes. I wonder if it has always been there, and I never noticed. Betty pays and makes the rounds as she says goodbye to everyone in the salon. I throw the blanket back over Phoebe's head, and I hurry back out to the car. I buckle Phoebe in the car seat and hurry to jump in the driver's seat to start the car. Betty is putting on her seat belt when suddenly she turns to me to start round two of meddling for the day.

"So, what are you wearing tonight? How are you going to do your hair? I think you need to leave it down."

I pull out of my spot onto Main Street. "Betty, are you sure you don't mind watching Phoebe tonight? I feel weird asking you to watch her. We just moved here, and I don't want you to think I am dumping my responsibilities on you."

"Child, are you crazy? I love that little girl. I would not have offered if I did not want to watch her. The more important elephant in the room that needs to be addressed is that you need to get back in the saddle and put yourself out there again. Enough moping around about that loser who wormed his way into your life. He wasn't worth your time then and certainly not worth your time now."

"I am not hung up on my ex." It comes out weak and defeated, but it is true. I could care less about my ex, but the scars he left behind are a lot harder to move on from.

"I know he hurt you by what he did to you. I will never understand how he could walk away from you and Phoebe, but you cannot continue to punish yourself. You need to start living your life again. That is why I invited you to move here. A fresh start for both you and Phoebe."

I can feel the tears welling in my eyes. I refuse to cry any more tears over my idiot ex, but Betty's words seem to be hitting me hard today. "Don't make me cry, Betty. They will freeze to my face."

Betty lets out a sharp laugh, "That's my girl! Don't worry they will thaw when you head in a warm house." She says it like it is normal that things freeze here so easily. "So, I will ask you again, what are you wearing tonight."

I lost this battle; I know it, and she knows it. I haven't dressed up for a night on the town since I was expecting Phoebe. I am mentally going through what I have unpacked, trying to rack my brain if I have anything that will work, when Betty yells out, "Child, stop! There is a stop sign".

It was then that I noticed the stop sign for the intersection was partially blocked by a truck. I try to stop, but it is too late with the layers of ice covering the road. My car starts to spin out. The incident last no longer than a few seconds but feels like an eternity until my car comes to a complete stop. I am clutching the steering wheel so tightly that my knuckles are bright white. I gasped for a breath as if I had been holding my breath.

"Betty! Are you okay? I am so sorry." I turn to look at Betty to find her smiling. Phoebe lets out a full on belly laughs. That laugh is my favorite of hers, but under the circumstances, I wish the laughing was a result of something less scary than what just happened. I sent up a silent prayer that everyone was okay. It could have been so much worse.

"We are going to have to work on your winter driving, sweetie. Although, I haven't done donuts in years. I forgot how much fun they can be."

"I am so sorry, Betty…". I didn't get to finish before my rear-view mirror was flashing the lights of a police car. Why can I not catch a break? I knew I should have never left the house today. Betty looks even more pleased with the new development when she turns to see an officer walking this way.

Someone is knocking on my window. I let out a small groan of annoyance with my lack of luck as I rolled my window down. I roll it enough to keep the warmth in the car for Betty and Phoebe.

"Mam' do you realize you just ran that stop sign?"

I am speechless when I look up to the mountain of a man who just knocked on my window. This man before me is gorgeous. He is tall and looks to be built solid. I have always been a sucker for a man in uniform, but it should be illegal the way he fills his uniform out. My eyes finally make it to his face. Crap, this will be my kryptonite. I should have avoided a closer inspection of his face. He has whisps of brown curls peeking out from under his knit hat. He has a full beard that is trimmed and clings to his sharp jawline. What really stops me in my tracks and makes me lose all train of thought are his eyes. They are the most beautiful crystal-clear green I have ever seen. I could get lost in those eyes and not be mad about it at all.

I feel a sharp poke to my right side, "You might want to wipe the drool away, sweetie, that will freeze, too." Betty starts to laugh under her breath.

Oh, right, law enforcement asked me a question: how about I act like a reasonable adult and not a lust-crazed teen? "I am sorry, officer, I didn't see it. When I did see it and tried to stop, I slid on the ice."

"I need your driver's license and registration." His tone is so matter-of-fact and cold, I am screwed. I really cannot afford a ticket right now.

I hand over what he asked for, and then he retreats to his car. He returns quicker than I thought he would. I am racking my brain to see if that should be a good sign or a bad sign. Maybe he just wrote me a ticket and wants to be done with me so he can get on with his day.

Another tap on the window alerting me that officer McHottie has returned to deliver my fate. I crack my window again.

"What brings you to town, Miss Forrester?"

Before I can answer, Betty leans across so she can see out the window. "Ralph, don't you make me call your mother. This is my niece, and she just moved to town. She is from Arizona and is not used to driving here yet. Now, can you give my girl her warning so we can get back home? We need to pick out her outfit for her hot date tonight."

I am staring out the windshield in disbelief that Betty just said all that. I can feel the blush taking over my face. The number one problem with being a redhead is that it is impossible to hide anything I am feeling, and right now, mortification is at the top of the feelings list. There are no words for this crazy woman I have uprooted my whole life to move halfway across the country for.

A deep, manly chuckle comes from the mountain of a man standing right out my door. I didn't even know a deep, manly chuckle could sound so sexy. I turn and peer up and Officer McHottie, waiting for him to throw the cuffs at my mouthy aunt.

"Alright Betty, no need to call my mom. Miss Forrester, you need to take it easy on the roads until you get a little more experience. I am just glad it wasn't anything more serious. I will let you go this time with a warning. I wouldn't want to be the reason you are late for your hot date." He leans in and looks through the window toward Betty. "Betty, you behave yourself too."

"That doesn't sound very fun to me, bye Ralph," Betty says as she waves him off like he is a nuisance.

The man is laughing as he is heading back to his car. He leaves before I can tell him that there is no hot date. Not that it should matter what officer McHottie thinks I am doing tonight. I turn in disbelief and just stare at Betty.

"Don't look at me like that child. I have known that boy since he waddled around in diapers. Now hurry up, we need to get home to pick out your clothes for a night out on the town."

This woman is exhausting and wonderful all at the same time. How is that even possible? As I pull away, I notice Officer McHottie just sitting in his car watching me pull out, probably concerned I will hit something. I hate that I am wondering If I will see him again. At the first sighting of hot man my resolve to never fall in love again is crumbling. I need to remind myself why I am living in this frozen wasteland and what got me here. That should kill any desire to run into Officer McHottie again.

Chapter 2
Ralph

It is New Year's Eve, and I've worked all day. I am dead on my feet and want to cancel my plans tonight and stay home for a quiet evening. I am starting to sound like the old man the guys are constantly teasing me of becoming. I don't mind holding the old man title if it means I can stay home and have a night to myself. I am due to meet up at the Thirsty Moose with everyone shortly, and I am having a hard time finding any motivation to get ready.

It has been a long few weeks of overtime and covering shifts for the officers under my command who needed time off. I don't really mind covering the extra shifts. Usually, most of my officers have families and want the extra time off during the holidays. This year is hitting me a little differently, though. I am burned out and need a vacation. I need an escape where I can just relax and no one is asking me to do anything for them. I have never been in a rut like this before. This is the first time in my life that my job feels like it is not enough for me.

And as much as I love my friends, sometimes they can be a lot. Over this past six months our group dynamics have changed with Max and Jane getting engaged. I am happy for them, of course, but Max is over-the-top lovey-dovey, and it can be a bit much at times. Then there is Harrison and Ginger, who finally came out of the dating closet to admit that they have been dating for months. News flash: it was not a surprise to anyone that they had been secretly dating, but we played along to make them feel better. I am happy for my buddies that they have found their person. I have never seen myself settling down with a wife and 2.5 kids, but if that makes them happy, I wish them luck.

I am seconds away from coming up with a lame excuse to duck out tonight when my phone buzzes with a text alert.

Henry: Who is excited about tonight?

Bubba: Are you bringing a date or something?

Henry: A no! Thank you for pointing out my single status.

Bubba: You make it sound like a bad thing to be single. These are supposed to be the best years of our life.

Henry: Agreed…But Harrison and Max might be onto something.

Max: I just took a screenshot of that text. It is like you are saying I am the coolest, and I am always right.

Harrison: Henry, we are onto something. You should try it. Max, you're an idiot; you are starting to sound like Noah.

Noah: Should you really be insulting the brothers of your girlfriend.

These guys have been my best friends since before I can remember. I usually love the ridiculous text messages that go back in forth, but tonight, I am not in the mood for the banter.

Me: So I am not going to make it tonight. Make sure to stay safe out there.

Henry: You have to come, Ralph!! That will leave me as the only single in the group and that sounds pathetic.

Bubba: Hello, Henry, what about me??

Henry: You don't count…You have Stella.

Max: Henry wins that argument.

Harrison: Agreed.

Bubba: You all suck. Stella is just a friend. You all realize how annoying you have been about the Stella topic lately.

Noah: I feel conflicted. Do I pick on Bubba more or do I interrogate the Chief on why he is ditching us tonight?

Henry: Why choose…when you can do both.

Noah: Ha, good point. Bubba I would put money down that you are bringing Stella tonight. LIKE YOU ALWAYS DO. Eventually, you will stop being annoyed at us for pointing out the obvious.

Noah: Old man, why are you ditching us tonight? You got a hot date, and you are worried we would embarrass you?

Me: Nope, no hot date. Just worked all day and need a quiet night in.

Harrison: That was an old man's response. It is New Year's Eve. You have to come out tonight.

Henry: There will be a lot of single women there tonight.

Me: Don't care

Max: You sound extra grumpy tonight. What's your deal?

Isn't that the million-dollar question? Nothing has caught my attention or got me excited about life lately. Well, that is not exactly true. If I were to be honest with myself, there is one thing that has piqued my interest. My traffic stops from earlier in the day. Betty's niece, Miss Forrester, she caught my attention. I have never been so instantly attracted to someone in my life. She looked ridiculous all bundled up her puffy coat and hood pulled over her head. All I could really see was her face. Her skin looked perfectly sun-kissed which was my clue she is not from around here. I could get lost in tracing all the freckles that cover the bridge of her nose stretching out over her cheeks. The look of panic that was trapped in her alluring blue eyes brought me back to reality.

I had watched as she had spun donuts in the middle of the intersection, the poor girl was probably worried she was in trouble. I had no business ogling her, no matter how much I found the blush covering her face adorable as Betty tried to put me in my place. I doubt I will see her again, and it was probably a fluke in my response to her anyway.

Harrison: Yeah, old man, why so grumpy?

Henry: If you are not dying from some infectious disease, I expect you to show up tonight to help represent the single population with me.

Me: If I am so grumpy, why are you all wanting me to come tonight. I will only be a buzz kill.

Noah: Yeah, but you are our buzz kill. So, it is settled you are coming.

Bubba: Stella informed me that we all have to be on our best behavior. She invited a friend to come tonight. She threatened that she would do horrible things to us if we were not on our best behavior.

Max: I am always on my best behavior. That threat does not apply to me.

Noah: Me neither.

Harrison: Stella loves me. I could be her favorite.

Henry: Is the friend single?

Bubba: I am already sick of all of you, and the night hasn't even started. Maybe Ralph has the right idea about staying in for the night.

And just like that, the text thread goes dead just as quickly as it started. If I don't go, I run the risk of one of them showing up at my door tonight. So, I decided I would go, make an appearance, and then come up with an excuse to duck out early. With any luck I will be in bed snoring when everyone else is ringing in the new year.

When I walk through the front door of the Thirsty Moose, I am instantly hit with regret for not sticking to my guns and staying home tonight. There is a buzz of excitement in the air, with the bar being packed tonight. The thought enters my mind of escaping out the back door and pretending that I never came. My friends might be onto something, with my grumpy old man attitude taking over more recently. The thought doesn't bother me as much as it should. Before I can put my escape plan into place, Bubba slams his hand, which feels more like a hammer, down on my shoulder.

"Nice of you to show up, Officer Grumpy Pants," he says before releasing an amused chuckle.

"How much will it cost me for you to pretend you never saw me and let me escape back out the front?"

"I am a man of principle; I cannot be bought off."

I just stare him down. Bubba is the biggest out of all of us, but I still have a convincing stare-down.

"Okay, enough with the eyes that say I am close to being tased. If you want to know the truth, I would prefer to leave myself. I am not really in the mood to be here tonight either."

"That is a quick turnaround from earlier when we were texting. What happened between then and now that makes you want to ditch out on the fun tonight," my voice is laced with sarcasm for the last part of that.

"Does it matter? You would just keep giving me a hard time. If you want to take off, I won't say anything," Bubba looks defeated.

"Hey, what's going on with you? Of course, we make fun of each other that is what we do, but if something is bothering you, I want to know about it."

"I just can't take any more jokes about Stella and me. I came to terms with it a long time ago, and it was never going to happen. Lately, it seems to be brought up anytime we text or on guy's nights. I don't need a reminder of the one thing in this life that I want, I will never have."

I know this confession cost Bubba something to say. I have never heard him admit he had feelings for Stella before. "Listen, man, I am sorry we give you a hard time about Stella, we just assumed that you would always get together. Why are you so convinced it can never happen." Despite our surroundings being chaotic and loud, we are having this weird, deep conversation that, in my opinion, is way overdue.

"We have such a long history; not sure we can overcome it. Not even sure she wants to overcome it. That is not the point, the point is the constant jabs are getting old."

"I am sorry, man; I promise you won't hear another word about it from me. Want to go find the rest of the misfits before they eat all the food?"

"I thought you were going to leave?"

"Yeah, maybe in a little while. I am suddenly in the mood for some nachos," that is a lie. I do not want nachos. I do want, however, to make sure Bubba is okay before I head out for the night. No matter how much I would prefer to be at home scrolling ESPN, I can't leave knowing one of my friends needs some extra support tonight. "Lead the way, I am sure the others of already arrived and secured the tables."

Bubba smiles, "Thanks, man. Maybe tonight could be fun?" He looks like a burden has been lifted from his shoulders, and he stands a little taller, if that is even possible. Right then, I know I made the right decision to stay.

As we walk up to the table, I found that I was right, and we were the last to arrive. Our usual spot has already been snagged and secured by others. Bubba snags the seat by Henry instead of taking his regular spot by Stella. If I had not been paying attention to Stella, I would have missed the flash of confusion and hurt that passed over her face. She recovered quickly and called me over to take the seat next to her. I move around the table to take the free seat next to Stella.

"Looks like you are stuck sitting next to me tonight, Officer Grumpy-Pants," Stella tries to hide her smirk but does a crappy job doing it.

I bump my shoulder into her, "Not you, too, I am not grumpy with you, so you cannot use the nickname."

"It is true you are never grumpy with me, but it is a good nickname. It would be a shame not to put it to good use."

"Stella, who is this friend that you invited tonight?" Jane asks from across the table.

"She is new in town, but she is great. I really hope she comes tonight. I don't want to gossip, but she has had a rough go of it lately, and she could use some fun."

"Hopefully, the guys don't scare her off, and it would be nice to add some more estrogen to the group. Might lead to more girl's nights." Emma directs the last part about more girl's nights in Max's direction, knowing how much he hates those nights.

Like the idiot he is, he takes the bait with a loud groan, "You have already exceeded your number of girl's nights. You are not allowed to add any more."

"Sounds like a challenge to me, ladies," Emma laughs while Max pouts.

The next hour flies by, and my escape plan has been put on the back burner. As much as staying home tonight was appealing to me, I am glad I came and stayed. For better or worse, these are my people, and I need them to add some balance to my life.

The dynamics of the group have changed so much recently. I am the first to admit that I hate change. I like boring and constant. It is becoming clear why my role in the group is "old man grump." It is hard to begrudge the new couples in the group their happiness. I have never seen Max or Harrison happier than they are now. At this rate, Henry will be the next to fall into the trap of love.

Stella suddenly jumps up out of her chair and rounds the table. "You came! I am so happy you decided to come hang out. I thought maybe you changed your mind." Stella throws he arms around a woman slightly taller than her. When Stella pulls away, I realize I know this woman. What are the chances that Stella's new friend is my traffic stop from earlier.

"Yeah, sorry I am late. All my clothes are still packed and…" The moment that Miss Forrester looks up and we make eye contact she freezes and stops mid-sentence.

All my friends are volleying stares back in forth between me and this woman who appears to be scowling at me now. Not sure I deserved that face. I did let her off with a warning.

"You." Is the only thing she says as she stares at me.

My reply was equally brilliant, "You."

Stella is the first to break in. "Chloe, I didn't know you knew Ralph?"

"I don't know him." She looks so uncomfortable all of a sudden. I am not sure what I could have done to her in the hours since I last saw her but there is a part of me that wants to be the one to replace that uncomfortable scowl with a smile on her face.

"Okay, sure, that is believable. Anyways, Chloe, this is everyone. Everyone, this is Chloe," Stella introduces her despite the awkward tension.

The girls all jump up and try to welcome my girl. What! Where in the world did that thought come from? She is not my girl. I don't even want a girl, let alone one that seems to hate my guts. I need a vacation from life, including my over-the-top friends who recently found love. Their crazy thoughts are starting to rub off on me.

"Henry, can you drag an extra chair over for our new friend," Emma asks as the girls start to come back to their seats.

"No need, she can have this chair," Harrison grabs Ginger by the waist and has her sitting in his lap before she can protest, not that she would. Ginger melts right into Harrison and throws her arms around his neck.

"Gross. I might not want to punch you in the face anymore for dating my baby sister, but I do not need to see any forms of affection at all. You get me. Someone find my baby sister a chair before my eyes have to be scrubbed clean with bleach," Noah is dramatically covering his eyes with his hands.

Ginger lets out a laugh, "Sorry, big brother, but this is my new spot for the night, and I quite like it. You will have to learn to deal. And for the record, Max is the dramatic one in the family, not you."

"Rude, kid. I prefer spirited, not dramatic," Max says with a big smile on his face, not at all offended by Ginger's statement of facts.

"Ok, you all need to behave yourselves so we don't scare Chloe off." Stella turns to Chloe and winks at her before continuing, "Let me introduce everyone to you, Chloe, and don't feel bad if you don't remember everyone; there are a lot of us."

With Ginger now taking up residence in Harrison's lap that leaves the open seat right next to me. Lucky me. Chloe sits down but carefully avoids any contact with me, which is quite the feat in a crowded bar. We are all squished in tight tonight.

"So, the big baby with his eyes closed is Noah. This his twin brother is Max. Their baby sister is Ginger. Noah is married to Emma. They have the daughter Lola that I told you about. Max is recently engaged to Jane. Ginger and Harrison recently started dating.

As you can tell, her brothers are very supportive." Everyone laughs, but Stella continues with introductions, "That leaves our resident bachelors in the group Henry, Bubba, and Ralph. That is everyone."

As Stella would introduce someone, they would wave their hand, letting Chloe know who Stella was talking about. That is everyone except me; my arms are crossed over my chest as I scowl in no specific direction.

"Oh, wow, that will take me a minute, but I am sure I will get it straight." Chloe looks overwhelmed by all the new faces staring at her. "Thank you for letting me crash your night out, not that Betty gave you much option, Stella."

"No worries, I love your aunt. She is one of my favorite regulars. I want to be her when I grow up. You never know what she will say next."

"I would have to agree with you, Stella. You never know what she will say." Chloe gives me a side glance, then quickly looks away.

"I am going to get a drink from the bar, Chloe, want me to grab you something?" Henry is always the polite gentleman, but it is pissing me off that he is directing his attention toward Chloe right now. So much so that I actually let a growl slip out under my breath, but Chloe still heard it.

She momentarily turns to me with wide eyes but finally addresses Henry, "Sure, that would be great, but I would rather join you if that's okay?"

Henry looks amused by my reaction, jerk. 'Of course, let me lead the way." Henry places his hand on Chloe's lower back as he directs her toward the bar. I know I am staring, but I can't help myself. If I thought Chloe was adorable this afternoon bundled up in her coat with her face peeking through, well, this version of Chloe is breathtaking. She is wearing jeans that hug her every curve. The dark purple fitted sweater is making her blue eyes almost have a purple tint. Her hair is this red curly mane that is untamed and a little wild like I suspect Chloe is. I can't believe she was hiding all that hair in the hood of her coat before. Bottom line I have never seen a more beautiful woman in my life while simultaneously making me want to lose my mind.

"Umm, care to explain why you are being so rude to my new friend," it's now Stella who is glaring at me.

"I don't know what you are talking about," I drag my eyes away from Chloe at the bar to focus on Stella.

"She has had a rough go of it lately. You better not scare her off with your grumpy-pants attitude."

"What do you mean she has had a rough go of it lately? What happened?" My tone is much harsher than I meant it to come out, but this weird protectiveness flooded through. This girl is trouble, and I need to steer clear of her, but at the same time want to protect her.

"Listen, bro, you need to chill. Stella is just trying to be a friend to that girl. No need to talk to her like that," Bubba looks as if he is going to flatten me if I don't heed his warning.

I turn to Stella, "Sorry, not sure what got into me. It is not an excuse, but it has been a long week. I never meant to be grumpy with you. I should have stayed home tonight. Maybe I should head."

"You can't leave Ralph. It won't be the same without you here to bring in the new year with us," Jane pipes up, adding her thoughts.

Before I can come up with an excuse that will let me bow out for the rest of the evening, I hear a girly, over-the-top giggle. I look up to find Chloe and Henry returning to the table. Chloe cannot control herself and is in the middle of a giggle fit. Her whole face is radiating joy. She places her hand on Henry's forearm and leans into him, "Henry, that sounds so amazing! Phoebe and I would love to come by sometime."

"You are welcome to come by anytime," Henry says nonchalantly as he takes his seat. Chloe makes her way around the table to sit in her spot next to me.

"What is so funny? I have known Henry most of my life, and he is not that funny," Noah says before he pops a loaded chip into his mouth.

"Thanks, Noah, you are a true friend." Henry retorts back to Noah dryly, not the least bit bothered by the comment.

"Oh, Henry was telling me about Bubbles and all the mischief she gets into."

Henry raises his hand in Bubba's direction as Bubba opens his mouth to say something, "I will stop you right there, Bubba!! Do not even think about saying anything against the majestic creature."

A while back, Bubba started a joke about Bubbles being a pregnant stripper, and the joke never died, mainly because Bubba wouldn't let it go. Bubba burst out laughing. At this point everyone is joining in on jokes about Henry and his pregnant hippo, Bubbles. I never would have thought growing up that Henry would have grown up to work at the zoo and we would be joking about a pregnant hippo but here we are. Everyone is distracted and engaged in their own conversations, and Chloe is just looking around, taking it all in.

I lean over so only she can hear me, "I thought you had a hot date?" I am a little too close, and she lets out a little gasp after I whisper into her ear.

"I never said that."

"Princess, you know it is bad to lie to the police, right." I have no idea what I am saying at this point or why I am calling her princess. The name fits her, though. She is all soft and feminine while still exuding a strong determination to do anything she puts her mind to.

"Don't call me that. I did not lie to you, officer. Betty told you I had a hot date. I never confirmed or denied my plans." Chloe grabs her glass and takes a sip, trying to avoid eye contact with me.

"So, you never had a hot date?" Why can I not let this go? Better yet, why do I care? This girl means nothing to me. She has trouble written all over her face before she can answer me, my less-than-helpful friends jump in.

"Chloe, is Officer grumpy-pants bothering you? He has had a long week and might need a nap. Don't pay him any attention," Harrison interrupts, making sure that nickname does not die.

As I turn my scowl on Harrison, Chloe tries to hold her laughter back but fails. "Oh, I like that nickname. It is very fitting for you. Better than the one I came up for him." Chloe immediately throws a hand over her mouth, and her eyes open comically wide. It is too late though; the damage is done, and I now need to know what her nickname for me is.

"You have a nickname for me, Princess?" I know without looking in a mirror that I have a cocky smirk plastered across my face at this revelation.

"Nope, not what I meant. You must have misunderstood me." Chloe is fidgeting in her seat and looks like she is ready to bolt for the door.

"I need to move. Girls, what do you say we hit up the dance floor." Stella is already moving, not waiting for anyone to respond.

"Yes! I agree! See you later, boys," Emma has no problem following Stella's lead.

"Why do I feel like I am not being invited to come with you," Max is already pouting at the thought of his girl 20 feet away on the dance floor.

"Because you're not, Max. Come on, Chloe, let's go find some trouble." Stella links arms with Chloe and drags her out of her chair. Ginger, Emma, and Jane all follow behind to the dance floor.

I can't help but sit here and pathetically watch the girls all laughing and having fun. Chloe looks like she fits right in. You would not know by watching them that she met the others just tonight.

"Dude, what is your problem with Chloe?" Henry asks, more curious than annoyed at me. "She is a nice girl, and you are making her feel uncomfortable."

"I am not."

"I agree with Henry. What is your deal with her?" Harrison is the next to jump onto the interrogation train.

"I have no deal. I told you already. It has been a long week, and I am tired, that is all. I really should go home. My company apparently is crap tonight."

"No one wants that. We are just worried about you, man. You just seem off tonight. If you would rather go home, we will all understand." Noah looks like he is being careful in the words he chooses to avoid setting off officer grumpy pants.

I take a pull of my beer, hoping to buy me some time. I turn and look out onto the dance floor. My eyes are immediately drawn to Chloe. She is pure joy and happiness when she smiles. Stella is holding court out on the dance floor, and all the girls look to be having the best time. The guys lose interest in pulling me out of my bad mood and ignore my sour attitude. I can vaguely hear parts of their conversation. Max is bringing up wedding plans. Noah goes on about the latest and greatest Lola story. Henry and Bubba jump in periodically adding their own two cents on life. All I can do is sit here staring at the dance floor, at the girl I have no business staring at.

Chapter 3
Chloe

There have been so many times today that I have regretted getting out of my pajamas and leaving the house. After getting home from picking Betty up at the hair salon, she had to give me another pep talk about coming tonight. I know I need to put some effort into making a fresh start in Minnesota successful. However, secretly, I was hoping for a few more days of hiding away from the real world.

I also don't want to admit that my run-in with a certain officer this afternoon has thrown me off balance. After my divorce, I swore men off completely. I never want to put myself in the position to be that vulnerable with someone that they have the power to destroy me. Now, as the day progressed, I couldn't stop my thoughts from wandering to him again and again.

I was becoming increasingly annoyed with Officer McHottie. Is it irrational that I am annoyed at a man for being ridiculously handsome with kind eyes? That didn't stop me from wanting to punch him in the throat when I saw him sitting at the table tonight, though. The nerve of this man. He looks even better now than he did a few hours ago if that is even possible. His curly mop of hair lays effortlessly in all the right ways on top of his head. I usually hate beards, but his beard is trimmed perfectly while not distracting from the sharp angles of his jaw line. His button-down is stretched in all the right places and the jerk even has the sleeves rolled up his forearms. I didn't realize I was a girl that had a thing for forearms but here I am, all but drooling at the sight of his forearms. Why is life so cruel? Why does this perfect specimen appear only after I vow to hate men forever?

I am very much aware that I am possibly insane. I wonder if I could get away with blaming my recent crazy streak on the weather. That sounds like a plausible defense to me, the freakin freezing temperatures froze my only two brain cells. I know why I am acting irrationally mad toward him, but I am clueless why he is all growly with me. He seems upset that I am crashing his night out with his friends.

Stella saves the day when she suggests the girls move to the dance floor. I can breathe better out on a crowded dance floor than I could sitting next to Officer McHottie. I hate myself for trying to maneuver myself on the dance floor to steal glances at him. The girl's interrogation distracts me enough to abandon my stalker ways and focus on them.

"Spill now, girl!" Stella is going to be one of my favorites, and I can already tell. She is direct and to the point.

"What?! What are you talking about?"

"Nice try, Chloe. Betty said you did not know anyone in town. You clearly have something going on with our favorite Chief of Police."

"Oh, garbage!! You have got to be kidding me. He is the Chief of Police?" I start to panic for reasons I am not quite clear about. It's not like I broke any laws or anything.

"Yeah, Ralph is the Chief of Police. Even though he is a little grumpy tonight, he usually is a giant sweetheart." Jane has a sweet, reassuring smile that calms my nerves.

"I agree. He is usually a teddy bear, but I have never heard him growl before. So that is new." Ginger joins in on the conversation.

Ginger looks younger than the rest of the group but also exudes genuine kindness.

"I wonder if the new growly side of Ralph has anything to do with our new friend," Emma looks like she is up to something. I get the distinct feeling that Emma and Stella are the ring leaders in any trouble that these girls get into.

"I agree with Emma. Spill Chloe, how do you know Ralph?" Stella is not letting this go.

"I really don't know Ralph. I ran a stop sign on the way home from your salon earlier today. I spun out on some black ice, and he was there to watch my less-than-stellar winter driving abilities. No big deal. The conversation lasted less than five minutes."

"Interesting," I do not love Emma's tone or the fact that she is bobbling looks between me and Ralph. I just met this woman, but her tone terrifies me.

I am not the only one who is worried about where Emma is going with this. Ginger must have picked up on the tone as well, "Don't even think about it, Emma, leave Chloe alone. I swear you need another hobby besides playing the group matchmaker."

"Matchmaker!!" The music is cranked up loud, and with the crowds of people surrounding us, I am pretty sure the bartender across the room still heard me yell that.

"Yeah, Emma thinks that she is a match-making extraordinaire. She often employs her evil tactics on her friends."

"Jane, how could you say that? If it wasn't for my brilliant skills, not evil, you would not be engaged right now." Emma folds her arms over her chest and huffs out an annoyed breath.

You have got to be kidding me. Is this a thing? This is her thing, fixing up her friends? I am rethinking needing friends as part of my fresh start. "Girls, I think there has been a misunderstanding. I am never and I cannot stress this enough, N-E-V-E-R going to date again. My ex-husband did a real number on me. I would really like to get to know you girls better and make some new friends, but not at the risk of a misguided attempt at trying to set me up with anyone." I am borderline hyperventilating at the thought of dating again. I need to get out of here, and I knew coming tonight was a mistake, I turn to head back to the table to grab my stuff.

Stella reaches out and grabs me by the elbow, "Chloe, hold on, we are sorry. We are sorry if we were too pushy. We have all known each other for so long that sometimes we forget we are a bit much for newcomers. Some might say we even have issues with healthy, appropriate boundaries with each other. We promise to be on our best behavior for the rest of the evening. Just stay; there is no pressure for anything other than friendship."

I look at all the women and suddenly feel so foolish. "I am sorry, too, I overreacted. Sometimes, it feels like I will never not feel broken." I look down at the ground, unable to make eye contact after my confession.

Emma throws her arm around my shoulder and pulls me for a side hug, "I am sorry if I made you feel uncomfortable. I blame the pregnancy hormones. This pregnancy has been way worse in terms of the hormonal roller coaster that I cannot seem to get off, ever. If you promise to give us another chance, I promise to be on my best behavior."

"Sounds great, I would like that." I look at my watch, and we have less than an hour until midnight then I can probably escape back home.

"I need a drink. Let's refuel, and then we can head back out for more dancing?" Jane adds timidly, probably worried I will freak out again.

We all head back toward the guys at the table. Without saying a word, the girls move seats around, putting me in the spot furthest away from Ralph. The guys don't question anything about why they are all of a sudden in the middle of musical chairs. As hard as I try to avoid eye contact with Ralph, I catch him staring at me. I take that back he looks upset by the moving of seats. Or maybe that is his normal resting grump face. Hard to tell.

"Stella tells me that you have a daughter the same age as my daughter, Lola?"

Emma does not seem phased one bit by my previous freak-out on the dance floor. Grateful she is so willing to move on without a second thought. "Yes, my daughter, Phoebe, is 15 months old. She is the best thing that has ever happened to me. How old is Lola?"

"She is almost 18 months old. She is in a fun stage in life. I swear every day she says something new or finds some new trouble to get into." Emma beams as she talks about Lola. "We should get the girls together for a play group. I bet they will be the best of friends."

Max leans over and pretends to whisper, "Chloe, you need to be careful about Lola. She has a dark side that holy water won't even cure."

"Ha, don't listen to my fiancé. He is good at a lot of things, but babysitting is not one of them. Lola was the victim, not the possessed demon child, he claims." Jane can barely finish her thought before Max grabs her to pull her into his lap. "You are a trader, and you are supposed to be on my side, Cupcake." He then proceeds to whisper in her ear so only she can hear. Whatever he is saying to her has her turning multiple different shades of pink.

No one at the table bats an eye at their public displays of affection for each other. I wonder if this is a mid-west thing? Or were my old friends, not the lovey-dovey type? Or am I just more aware of PDA now that I am firmly in the anti-love group? I am lost in thought, trying to figure it all out, when Henry interrupts my train of thought. "I got you a new drink. Diet Pepsi, right?"

"That was thoughtful of you, and yes, you got the right drink. Thank you." I take the drink from him. He lowers himself into the chair next to me. I have no physical reaction when Henry is sitting next to me, unlike when I sat down next to Ralph earlier. Luckily, I don't have time to think why that might be, and the girls are recharged and itching to get back out on the dance floor.

This time around it is nothing but laughing and fun. Stella is constantly introducing me to anyone and everyone we bump into. The guys slowly join us on the dance floor. Henry asked me to dance for one of the slow songs. I was hesitant at first but reluctantly agreed, not wanting to be rude. It is what I imagined dancing with my brother would feel like if I had a brother. Not one spark. Henry was a perfect gentleman the entire time. The conversation was good. He is funny in a non-obvious way. I start wondering if maybe this is the type of guy I should go out with, one that has no risk of breaking my heart.

A guy jumps up on the stage to announce that there is less than a minute until the new year. He encourages everyone to find there special someone for a new year's kiss. That is my cue to bow out and find a place to hide. I start to back up toward the table slowly. No one really notices my absence through the excitement flowing through the dance floor. I make it to the edge of the crowd without anyone noticing. The man on stage starts the count down.

The crowd all joins in, "10…9…8…7…6…5..." I decide to turn my back on the crowd and hide at the table when I run into a mountain. Well, not exactly a mountain. I look up to see I ran into Officer McHottie. The countdown continues "4…3…2…1…Happy New year!" Everyone is screaming and hollering all around us. Everyone but Ralph and I, we are just staring at each other. His nostrils are flared, is jaw is set, and there is a fire in his eyes. Something has him pissed, and I am on his warpath.

He mumbles under his breath, but I cannot make out what he says with everyone screaming. A split second later his hand moves to the nape of my neck under my hair. He puts his other hand on my waist and pulls me into him. Before I can react, his lips are on my lips in a bruising kiss. I freeze for less than five seconds before responding. I grab his shirt with both my hands, pulling him closer to me. The kiss is not sweet or tender like you would expect first kisses to be. Not that I expected anything less from Ralph. He kisses with everything he has and is not apologetic about it. I have never been kissed like this before. It is all consuming and feels like I am being turned inside out, and yet I feel safe cocooned in his arms.

Ralph is the first to come to his senses. He pulls back slowly, resting his forehead against mine. We are both trying to catch our breath. Reality slams back into me with a force that would have knocked me over if he didn't still have a hold of me.

"Happy New Year, Princess," and he releases me and turns to go. I watch him walk straight out of the bar without another look back at me.

I am left standing there, not sure what just happened. I bring my fingers to my lips, which are still tingling. I turn back to the dance floor and see all the faces of the people I was hoping to become, my new friends, just staring at me, silently. Yep, I am very much regretting getting out of my pajamas this morning.

Chapter 4
Ralph

Two weeks. It has been two weeks since I lost my mind and kissed Chloe on New Year's Eve. Two weeks since I saw her last. Two weeks, and I am still over the top grumpy. It seems like an eternity.

No matter how much I think about her or how long it takes to relive that kiss that endlessly plays on a loop in my mind, I know I must keep my distance. I have successfully avoided my friends. I am not sure if they witnessed my lapse in judgment, but I am not really interested in hearing their opinions about me and the fiery redhead. I have never lost control like that before. I am the level-headed one among our friends, but for some reason the very thought of that woman and I am losing my focus.

"Boss, you left the mayor on hold, line 3. If you don't pick up, he will hang up and call back. I am not really in the mood for his whining this early in the morning." Estelle, my secretary is now standing in my doorway with her hands on her hips, not impressed with my lack of responding to the intercom system.

"Funny you are calling me boss. You are the one being very bossy this morning." I don't even look up from the stack of paperwork on my desk. I am not in the mood to talk to the mayor right now or anyone, really. I was hoping he would lose interest while being on hold and move onto another city employee to bug.

"I like to give you the illusion that you are in charge. Now, pick up the phone and talk to the mayor so I don't have to." Estelle continues to stand there with her hands on her hips except now she has added tapping her foot at an annoyed rate. Estelle started at the police station back when my grandfather was the chief. Lots of officers have come and gone since then, but Estelle has always been a constant here at the station.

"Fine, you win! But you should know it will be your fault if it puts me in a bad mood."

"Not sure that it is possible to be in a worse mood than you have already been in lately," Estelle mumbles under her breath, loud enough to ensure I heard every word.

I let out a sigh of defeat as I reached for my phone. I am fully aware that the funk I have been in for the past few weeks has only gotten worse. We are two weeks into the new year, and I can't seem to shake this bad mood. I push the flashing light to connect me with the mayor.

"Hello sir, what can I do for you?" I look up just in time to see Estelle turning to leave. She must be satisfied that I will do my job, and no babysitting of the police chief is required right now.

"Boswell, why on earth did it take you so long to answer my call? I am a busy man. I am not accustomed to having to wait."

The mayor is one of the few people who address me solely by my last name. I always have the urge to tell him that we are a small-town community, and it sounds weird when he is constantly addressing me by my last name when most people just call me Ralph. But I decided the quickest way to get off this call is not to bring that up right now.

"Sorry about keeping you on hold, sir; it has been a busy morning. What can I do for you?"

"We need to talk about budgets."

"What? Why? We have our budget meeting scheduled in a few weeks. Can this conversation not wait until the meeting?"

"No, it cannot. That is why I am reaching out now. I have been informed of a fundraising opportunity."

"What type of fundraising opportunity?" I try not to groan into the phone. I know by the sound of glee in his voice I am not going to like what he has to say.

"We are partnering with the Sheriff's office and joining forces on this opportunity."

"What opportunity?"

"Before you say no or start coming up with excuses, you should know that the Fireman's Ball that was held last month brought in more money than they expected. The police station needs to step up their game."

I already know from the way he is dodging all my questions that this idea is bad, and I will hate every part of this so-called fundraiser. The dull headache that I woke up with this morning is moving toward a splitting headache.

"I am fully aware that the Fireman's Ball was very successful this year. What does that have to do with my department? I always have excess in my budget every year."

"Agreed, Boswell. No one is saying anything about how you run your budget."

"Then why the sudden need for a fundraiser to outdo the fire department?"

"Listen up, I cannot take one more meeting with the fire chief bragging about how his department is superior. I need to shut him up.

The only way that happens is if the police department steps up and does better.”

“With all due respect, we are already stretched thin and finding the time to do a fundraiser is not a priority right now for me.”

“Boswell, you better make it a priority because this is not optional. I have already agreed that the Little Falls Police department will take part. The Sheriff’s office has already drawn up flyers and started advertising.”

“What exactly did you volunteer us to do?”

“They are having a dinner and an auction. Simple enough.”

“What is our part in this?”

“I am glad you asked. You are being auctioned off to the highest bidder.”

I am no longer moving toward a splitting headache. I have arrived. My head feels like a jackhammer is making its way down my forehead.

“How do you expect me to get my single officers to agree to this?”

“By leading by example.”

“No! No way!” I am fully aware that I am now raising my voice to my boss in a borderline insubordinate tone, but I don’t care. “I am not going on a date with some random stranger because she read a romance book that stars a small-town cop, and she expects me to fill the role for her. No way.”

“That was oddly specific. Don’t make this weird, Boswell. You can say no all you want, but you are doing this whether you like it or not. The advertisement has already been printed with your face all over it. You are on the chopping block, so to speak. Just think you will be the one with bragging rights and a healthy budget when all is said and done. I will send over the contact information to your email for who you will be working with at the Sheriff's office."

Before I can get another word out the mayor disconnects the call. I am sitting there staring at the phone receiver in my hand. I am rarely at a loss for words, but I am just sitting here dumbfounded by the conversation that just took place.

Estelle comes walking back through my office door and is now standing in front of my desk. "That was fast. You are already done with the mayor?" There is a glee dancing in her eyes.

"You know, don't you?" Of course, she knows. She knows everything that happens in the department before me nine times out of ten. The smile she is currently sporting across her face confirms that I am right; she knows. "Thanks for the heads up, traitor," I yell the traitor part.

"Oh, stop pouting. You can't pull off the look, boss. Who do you think gave the sheriff's office a picture of you to use for the posters that will be hanging all over time by dinner time."

"Did I do something to you that you've betrayed me in such a way?"

"Here we go with the dramatics. Besides your grumpy mood the past few weeks you know you are one of my favorite people. I am going to be honest with you, boss. I helped the mayor with all this because I think you need a push into the dating world."

"You have got to be kidding me? You sabotaged me because you are worried about the status of my dating life?"

"Yep. And saying I sabotaged you is still being dramatic."

I am so close to blowing a gasket on this woman who I have known all my life. The only thing that is holding me back is the thought of how disappointed my grandfather would be in me. I was raised better than to raise my voice toward a woman. I take a deep breath, trying to find some calm.

"Listen, Estelle, I appreciate your concern, but I am very much content with how my life is now. I have no interest in adding another person into my life now or ever. Do you understand?"

"Okay, I hear you. Now, you listen to me. As long as I am overstepping boundaries, I am going to say my piece on this and then you will never hear another word from me on the matter again. I know your dad did a number on you growing up. I also know that he left you to shoulder the burden of secrets that no son should have to, but refusing to find love now is only punishing you, not him. He has taken enough from you, Ralph; don't let him take any more." As she did not just drop a bomb, she swiftly turned and left my office.

I am so angry right now. I can feel it radiating throughout my body. I take a few more deep breaths to try and calm myself down. I am not angry with Estelle. I had always suspected she knew about my dad and his wandering ways, but we had never spoken about it. I want to march out to her desk and tell her that she is wrong. My decision to not date or get married is not meant as a punishment to anyone. It is meant to save me the lifetime of heartache that I have had a front row watching in my parent's marriage.

As the anger starts to dissipate and leave my body, I slump back into my chair. I rest my head on the back of my chair and stare at the ceiling, wishing I had taken the day off. I would love a month off, but that is never going to happen. My only realistic option is cutting out early today. My headache does not appear to be leaving anytime soon, so I pack up my stuff ready to head out for the day. I stop, again, at Estelle's desk on the way out.

"Estelle, I am taking off for the rest of the day. If there are any emergencies, I can be reached by cell. I will be back first thing tomorrow morning." I then head out toward my truck. I should have probably cleared the air with Estelle before leaving, but I have hit my limit on serious conversations for the day.

As I make my way through town in the direction of my house, Estelle's words keep replaying in my head. Whether Estelle meant to or not, her words bring a more resolute resolve to stay away from Princess. No matter how much I want to see her again or have a repeat of that kiss we shared on the dance floor, I can't afford to give in to those thoughts. I am better off forgetting about my princess.

Chapter 5
Chloe

"Hello, earth to Chloe. Are you even listening to me?"

I am ripped out of my thoughts to find my aunt poised and ready to chuck a rolled-up napkin in the direction of my head. I shake my head, trying to lift the fog that settled over me. "Sorry, Betty. I was up late working; I must have zoned out. What did you say?" I tried to sound more carefree in my tone than I felt. I have Phoebe in her highchair, with an assortment of diced strawberries and bananas on her tray.

"What has you so distracted this morning, sweetie? You might as well spill your guts to me. What is the point of having all this wisdom and age if you won't share your troubles with me."

My Aunt Betty is annoyingly astute for someone her age, and I can't get much by her. I never told her about the kiss that has recked my focus. I should be concentrating on mine and Phoebe's fresh start. I have made some good connections, and my website is coming along. Although we are saving money staying with Betty right now I am eating through my savings faster than I planned.

"Nothing has me distracted. I told you I was up late working on my business plan and tweaking my website." Although it was not a complete lie, it also wasn't a complete truth. I keep second-guessing my choice to move to Minnesota. The pressure I feel to make sure every decision I make will be the best one for my daughter can be crippling at times.

"I know I look like I was born yesterday with my youthful good looks and all, but I am calling bull-pucky on your lame excuse. What is really going on with you? You have been off since you went out with Stella and her friends a few weeks ago. Did something happen?"

When did my dear, sweet aunt turn into a bloodhound, scenting out lies? "Betty, I told you I had a good time. Stella and her friends are really great."

"Then why have you not gone out with them since?"

"I have been busy, and they are all busy, that is all. I have been meaning to reach out to Emma and set up a play date for Phoebe and her daughter Lola, and I just haven't gotten around to it." I probably would have already done that if I had thought about grabbing anyone's numbers. After I turned around and realized that they had all watched Ralph kiss me and then walk away from me, the embarrassment took over. I hurried and gathered my stuff, making an excuse that I needed to get back home to check on Phoebe. The guys stood there, not saying a word, but the girls tried to talk me into staying. But facing them seemed too much at the time, so I rushed out without getting any of the girls' contact info.

"You are putting too much pressure on yourself to get your business started. You have no big expenses right now. You are welcome to stay with me for as long as you like. I love having you and Phoebe around."

"You have been more than good to us, and I do appreciate all your kindness but I need to prove I can stand on my own and provide for Phoebe. Does that make me sound ungrateful?"

"Not at all, my darling girl. I am proud of you and what you are trying to build for that sweet girl. But you should know that anyone who spends more than five seconds with Phoebe can see how happy and content she is. That is a reflection on you as her mother and what a good job you are doing. I just want you to be happy too.”

Her words strike my deepest insecurities that I try to hide. What if I am not enough? What if I can’t provide what Phoebe needs to be successful in this life? I am close to tears with the kind words that Betty so freely gives.

“Thank you, Betty. I really am trying to find my own happiness, just not sure what that will look like for me.”

“Well, I can tell you it starts with you leaving this house. You haven’t left the house since the party with Stella.” Betty’s spice and vinegar tone is back, and the loving elderly aunt is gone. Probably for the best, I love her ‘take it or leave it’ attitude the best.

“First of all, it is freezing out there. Why would I leave the warmth of the house to die of hypothermia?”

Betty lets out a sharp laugh. “Girl, if you never leave the house when it is cold outside, well, you would never leave. We need to toughen you up. Time to get Minnesota tuff.”

The urge to whine and protest the idea of leaving the house is on the tip of my tongue when Betty cuts me off. “I need a favor; I was hoping you could run an errand for me.”

Knowing that I will not refuse her anything at this point, seeing my daughter and I are technically squatters at her house, “What do you need?”

“I have a few friends coming over tonight. It’s my turn to host poker night. Ethal is supposed to bring the snacks, but she is on a health kick, and I don’t want any vegan-organic garbage that she tries to pass off as snacks.”

Trying to resist letting a laugh-free, I compose myself before responding. "So, you need me to get a backup treat just in case?"

"Yes, of course! I need you to head down to the Cupcake Shack in town and grab some goodies. I will call ahead and put my order in. Just need you to pick them up."

"No problem, happy to do it. Let me get Phoebe cleaned up, and we will go grab your contraband, I mean your treats." I give my aunt a side eye, pretty sure she is not supposed to be eating the high-sugar treats either. "Phoebe and I will be hiding out in my room tonight so we don't interrupt the festivities tonight."

"Are you kidding me? Why don't you join in? The group would love some fresh meat, I mean a new face to play with."

"Ha, I think you meant fresh meat. It is not in my budget right now to be crazy at poker nights. Let me get a few accounts under my belt first." Great my social calendar is now filling up with geriatric poker nights. At this rate, I can hear the call to be a lonely old cat lady coming through loud and clear.

"Want me to watch the little one while you are out?"

"Nah, that is okay. I will take her with me. Maybe some fresh air will do both of us good. Even if the air is freezing."

I hurry to clean up our mess. I can hear Betty on the phone putting her order in. Before she hangs up, she whispers something into the phone. I am fairly certain my aunt would not get me involved in anything illegal, but there is that small percentage of uncertainty. I get Phoebe dressed and ready to brave the outside temperatures. I look down at my daughter, and she looks like a puffed-up pink snowball with only her face showing. She is having a hard time sitting up in her snowsuit and keeps toppling over. Every time she falls over, she starts to giggle. I finally give up and leave her on her back as she babbles away.

She can say mama, no, boo for peek-a-boo, "ine" which means mine, and her favorite word is "ack." She loves ducks, and I think she is trying to say quack, but "ack" is all that comes out. Her vocabulary seems to grow daily. As she is trying to sit up and roll over in her snowsuit, I can't help but laugh. I scoop her up and pepper her face with kisses as she giggles. There is nothing I would not do for this girl. She puts her chubby hands on my cheeks and babbles away. I want to pretend that she is telling me that we made the right decision to move here and start over, but in reality, she probably wants her wub-a-nub that she can spot in her crib. I give her one more big smooch on the cheek, grab my purse, and head for the front door. The sooner I leave, the sooner I can get home and warm up.

Chapter 6
Chloe

I pull up in front of the Cupcake Shack. The storefront is beyond adorable. The pink striped awning that hangs over the door and the cheerfully painted window scenes are very inviting. I have tried so hard to stay away from places like this since I still have a few stubborn pounds that won't go away from pregnancy. I turn off the engine and hurry to gather my purse, get out and move to the back seat to get Phoebe from her car seat. The minute the wind hits her face, she starts to blow raspberries. A laugh escapes me; it looks like she is trying to blow the wind away. Nice try, sweetie, not sure that will work.

The minute I open the door to hurry inside, we are filled with warmth and heavenly smells. Hating that I am wondering if you can gain weight from smell alone. If that is true then I would definitely need to be rolled out of here. The inside is just as adorable as the outside. The floors are black and white checked. The walls are pale pink and have paintings of cupcakes placed randomly around. Phoebe appears to be in awe, too. Her eyes are wide open as she takes in the new surroundings.

I am pulled out of my head when a familiar voice calls my name. "Chloe, I am so glad you came in."

I looked over toward the counter to see where the voice was coming from. Behind the counter is Jane. She is holding an adorable little girl who looks to be a similar age to Phoebe maybe a little older. On this side of the counter is a very pregnant Emma. Starting to feel like Betty's whispering on the phone was a planned ambush.

"Jane, Emma, I am so glad I ran into you. Jane, I totally spaced you saying you owned this place." I move toward the counter, hoping this is not going to be awkward.

"Not sure if it came up the other night. When Betty called in her order, I was hoping you were going to be the one to come pick it up." Jane is so genuine and kind it is hard not to want to be friends with her.

Emma pipes up before I can respond. "We never got around to exchanging numbers the other night, so I am glad I popped in randomly."

No part of me believes this was random, but I am still glad they're both here. I was so disappointed that I might have missed out on being friends with them over that stupid kiss.

"I was just about to take a break with Emma and Lola, want to join us?"

I really have no excuse to hurry off. "That actually sounds really nice. I would really like that."

Both Jane and Emma looked pleased that I was willing to hang out for a little while. Jane hollers in the back that she is going to take a break. Jane makes her way around the counter with Lola in tow. Emma moves two high chairs over to the far wall, with booth seating lining the wall. Jane puts Lola in her seat and does up the seat belt. "I will be right back. Let me grab some treats for us." Before I can tell her no thank you, she is rushing behind the counter.

Emma must have picked up on my hesitant look, "Jane will bring out goodies whether you tell her not to or not. That is her love language, and she likes to feed people her treats."

"It smells so good in here; I won't deny that they probably taste just as divine, but my hips could use a carrot instead of any of the sugar delectables that are made here."

"I am going to shut you down right there, girl. You are beautiful. I would kill for curves like yours. A treat occasionally is good for the soul." Emma just smiles at me simultaneously shutting any future complaints down.

Knowing when I am beaten, I start to peel the layers off Phoebe now that we are staying for a visit. Once the snowsuit is discarded, I put Phoebe in the other highchair and buckle her in. Lola and Phoebe stare at each other. Phoebe has never been around other kids her age. Before Emma or I can say anything, the girls start to babble and giggle together. My heart melts right then and there. Jane returns with a platter of goodies.

"Sorry, I couldn't decide, Chloe. I wasn't sure what your poison would be, so I grabbed a variety to pick from." Jane places the giant platter of food on the table.

"Jane, that was kind of you. I am fairly certain by the smells coming from your kitchen you really cannot go wrong with anything in your displays."

Jane looks pleased by the compliment. Jane hands out plates. Emma digs in. She gives a sugar cookie to Lola. Then turns to me, "Can Phoebe have something?"

"Sure, she will probably make a huge mess, but I will clean it up before we leave." I hand a sugar cookie to Phoebe. Her eyes are wide open with wonder. I wish there was a way to bottle this feeling that kids so freely give. Something as simple as a sugar cookie being handed to you could cause such joy and wonder. "I need to apologize now, Jane. Normally, I break small pieces of cookie and give them to her. Not sure this will end well for the cleanliness of your shop." Before I can even finish talking, my daughter turns into a real-life cookie monster and starts shoving it in her mouth. Crumbs are flying all around her.

Mortified, the women will think I am a crap mother who hasn't taught manners to her daughter, I am seconds away from apologizing when both women bust our laughing.

"Finally, Lola is in good company. The only other kid Lola has spent time with is my cousin's kid. Lola is a tornado of messes and trouble compared to that child. This is refreshing that she has finally found her people." Emma is wiping her eyes from the tears of laughter.

I look over and realize that Lola is doing the exact same thing and created a similar mess. Lola is holding out a fist of crumbled-up cookies to Phoebe. Phoebe puts her mouth on Lola's fist of goo. Then Phoebe offers her fist of what is left of the cookie and offers it to Lola. Lola then leans forward, taking a mouthful of it.

"I think my ovaries just exploded. Do you two know how lucky you are? I want one so bad. Look how cute they are." Jane looks like she wants to join in on the cookie exchange with the girls.

"Calm down, Jane, you are getting married soon. I imagine you will be in the exhausted, never sleep, rarely shower, always covered in something suspicious club before you know it." Emma says matter-of-factly as she pops a goodie in her mouth.

I can't help but laugh at the description of motherhood that Emma just gave Jane. "Emma, you could give that description in high school classes, and it might help prevent teen pregnancies."

"I speak the truth, and you know it." She stares me down like I dare to disagree with her.

"It is true. Being a mother is the hardest thing I have ever done in my life. But Jane, even though all the things Emma said were accurate, I would do it all over again to have this little one call me Mama."

"That is it. I am texting, Max, that I want a bunch of babies right now." Jane pulls out her phone. Emma and I stared at each other and burst out laughing. The look on Jane's face is killing me. She is concentrating so much on the text.

"Okay, ignore her," Emma is referring to Jane. "Let's talk about the elephant in the room, shall we?"

"Not sure I know what you are talking about…" I trail off, hoping for some for of intervention to get me out of this conversation.

"Yes, you do…". Emma trails off like she expects me to offer up the elephant in the room.

"Okay sorry ladies, Max was being difficult. What are we talking about?"

"Umm…". I can't bring myself to talk about the kiss. They have been friends with him for so long.

"We were talking about how Chloe forgot to give us her number the other night before leaving. We need to grab it so we can do a girl's night. And there are definitely more play dates in the future for these two. They already look like best friends."

Relief sweeps through me; Emma has a smirk plastered on her face. I am not convinced that she was not messing with me, but I am still grateful for the reprieve. I grab my phone and put in the girls' numbers as they rattle them off. They also give me Ginger and Stella's number. I then give them mine.

"I will start a group thread with the other girls so they have your number, too." Jane was texting away before I knew what was happening.

"Everyone is so busy with work and everyday life that the text threads are how we keep in contact with each other. You might find the number of texts back in forth oppressive at times, but you grow accustomed to them after a while."

"Accustomed, uhh? Sounds like you will wear me down until I give in and join the texting frenzy?"

"See, you get it," Emma says with a smile.

My phone starts to ding repeatedly, alerting me to multiple messages. I grab my phone and open the messages.

Jane: Girls, the new number I added is Phoebe's number.

Stella: Yes, girl!! I was so close to calling Betty to get her number.

Ginger: Does this mean girls' night?

Stella: Pleeeeease say we can have an impromptu girls' night.

Emma: I bet I can talk Chloe into a girl's night tonight if we invite ALL the girls.

I look up, amused that Emma is texting and we are sitting right across from each other. More dings.

Stella: The more the merrier, but who else are you inviting?

Emma: Lola and Phoebe are best friends now and will need to be introduced to the benefit of a good girls' night.

Jane: This is going to be a hard sell to Max after I already asked him for lots of babies a little while ago.

Ginger: I bet the new girls will be adorable and most welcome.

Stella: IS it sad that I am not even batting an eye at Jane asking for lots of babies?

Ginger: Want me to have Harry invite him over? It will distract Harry, too, so he won't blow up my phone every five minutes after I get there.

Stella: It goes without saying that some of you have needy men.

Emma: Agreed.

The randomness that is these women is kind of wonderful. I weigh my options for tonight. I can either sit at home and hang out with a geriatric illegal poker ring or have a fun girls' night.

Me: You can count me and Phoebe in for girls' night!

Stella: YAY!! We wore you down a lot faster than I thought we would.

Emma: Let's plan 5 o'clock at my house.

Ginger: I am there.

Stella: Me too.

I put my phone down. Although I am excited for a girl's night, it is the possibility of friends who are kind and real that has me really excited. The little girls are still going back in forth, babbling to each other. The bell over the door rings out as someone enters. I am distracted trying to clean up some of the mess my daughter has made that I don't immediately look up to see who came in.

"Hey, Jane. How is it going?" A young male voice asks from behind me.

"Oh hey, Luca, I am good. What brings you in today?" Jane rises and heads toward the front. I glance over my shoulder and notice the man couldn't be older than mid-twenties, who is dressed in a law enforcement uniform. His uniform is a different color than what Ralph was wearing when he pulled her over.

"The Sheriff's office and the police department are joining forces this year on a joint fundraiser. Would you let me hang a poster in the Cupcake Shack to help get the word out?" The guy momentarily looks down at the ground before continuing, "And even if you say no to the advertisement, I was heading in for a cupcake. It has been a while since I had one. I have been out all morning hanging these posters, and a cupcake sounds like it might hit the spot."

By the end of the young deputy's rant, I wasn't sure what had him more enamored, Jane or her cupcakes. I was not alone in this thought because Emma let her giggles go freely but tried to cover them with some coughs.

"Of course, you can hang the advertisement. Anything to help local law enforcement. What does the fundraiser involve? I thought Ralph would have mentioned it to us, but I haven't heard anything yet."

"Funny you should bring up Chief Boswell…" Luca stops mid-thought to grab a poster. He turns it around so we can all see it. He apparently thought showing us would be easier than explaining.

Staring straight back out me, was Officer McHottie. He was the poster. It took me a hot second to focus on anything but his face.

Finally, I focus on the text announcing a bachelor auction. Luckily, I am not the one that lets out the gasp. Emma and Jane gasp at the same time. Luca goes on to give details to the girls while I tune them out.

I have no right to be hurt. He is not mine. What does it matter to me if he is being auctioned off to the highest bidder. In big, bold letters, it says, "MOST ELIGIBLE BACHELOR." I don't even want his attention. This is perfect, really. He can go find some teeny bopper that will fall for his ruggedly good-looking face, eyes that will pierce through you, and stupid kissable lips. Yeah, that teeny bopper can have all that; it sounds kind of horrible to me.

High-pitched screaming brings me out of my Officer McHottie funk. I look over and see Phoebe and Lola screaming, then they stop, look at each other then burst out in a fit of giggles. Then, they start the cycle all over again. I look over at Emma, who also looks like she is amused with the girls. Jane has moved behind the counter and is helping Luca with his cupcake purchase.

Emma leans over the table and quietly asks, "Are you okay?"

I try to play dumb. "My eardrums might never recover, but it was totally worth it to see Phoebe so happy and making friends."

"I want you to show up to my house for girls' night so I will let that answer slide, but we both know that is not what I was asking you." Just like that Emma stands and starts to clean Lola up.

I know I need friends like Emma, who will call me on my crap and will not let me hang out in my comfort zone of life. Now, I am rethinking that assessment. I am pretty sure that is the only pass that she will give me on that question. Jane was kind enough to hold Phoebe while I loaded the three giant pastry boxes that Betty ordered into my car. I went back in to grab my pink snowball who looked more than ready for her afternoon nap.

"So glad you came in today, Chloe. I know we can be a lot to take, but I promise girls' nights are totally worth it." Jane doesn't even hesitate and reaches out for a hug. I try not to get choked up by Jane's unconditional friendship that she is freely offering.

I step back after Jane releases me, "You guys barely know me and are so willing to accept me into your inner circle. I have never had friends like you before." I start to feel unsure about revealing so much so soon.

"I will remind you later when we are being overbearing and all up in your business that you were excited to be friends with us," Emma says with a big smile. "Now I need to get Lola home so she can get her nap in before her first official girls' night with her new bestie coming tonight. I will see you girls later." I walk out with Emma promising I will see her later.

Chapter 7
Ralph

My phone has been blowing up with text message alerts for the past twenty minutes. I can't turn it off because the station needs to be able to get ahold of me for emergencies. As I stretched out in my lazy-boy recliner, I contemplate whether I want to know what my friends are saying. My headache is a dull ache now, but I am still not sure I have it in me to respond to them. Another alert dings. Before I can grab my phone, there is pounding at my front door. I should have known if I didn't respond, they would have shown up here tonight.

I begrudgingly get up and make my way to the door. I can hear them on the other side making ridiculous comments about whether I am alive or not. I swing the front door open with more force than intended. Besides the freezing burst of air that I am greeted with, I find Max, Noah, Henry, and Harrison crowded together on my front porch. They are all carrying bags of what looks like beer and smell like the heavenly aroma of greasy take-out.

"Dude, are you going to let us in? I am freezing my butt off." Bubba is literally jumping up and down like a toddler who needs to pee.

I reluctantly move to the side and grunt that they can come in. It was a smart move on their part to bring the food and beer; otherwise, they might still be standing outside. They all start to unload the goods on the kitchen table. Noah moves through my kitchen pulling out plates like it was his place. I stand in the entryway of my kitchen, taking it all in. We all might give each other a hard time, but they are more like brothers to me than friends.

Henry walks up to me to hand me a beer. "Okay, Officer Grumpy, I drew the short straw on the way over here, so I have to be the one to tell you…" Henry trails off, unwilling to finish his thought.

"Tell me what?" I growl out as I grab the beer from him.

"Yeah, he is definitely not in the right head space for this conversation. I am tapping out. You're up, Bubba." Henry slinks back to his chair and joins in with the others who are dishing up food. I send my glare in Bubba's direction, daring him to keep whatever they have planned to say to himself. The problem is Bubba is the only one that is bigger than me and my glares and growls are not as effective on the big guy.

"Calm down with the glaring, Ralph; you look like you could stroke out at any moment." Bubba chuckles, then crams a massive bite of his burger into his large trap. Even though his mouth is full of food, I still hear the next part crystal clear, "This is an intervention, man."

It was bad timing to take a pull on my beer as Bubba informed me this is an intervention; I am lucky I didn't spray beer all over my kitchen. "A what?! You have got to be kidding me. What do I need an intervention for? How many beers did you have before you came over here tonight?"

Max is the next brave soul, "Well, you have been extra grouchy lately."

"Not true."

"Umm, it's kind of is. This is why we brought greasy food and beer. It will help you talk about your feelings in a manly way."

I now turn my glare on Harrison. Talk about my feelings in a manly way. He has lost his mind. Ever since he started dating Ginger, he has gone soft. "Are we going to braid each other's hair too?" I am not quite sure why I am being a jerk to them. They brought me food, and they are not wrong; I have been in a crappy mood. My resolve to deny my bad attitude is crumbling.

"If you don't want to talk about your homicidal mood that has taken root the last few weeks, we can talk about that kiss on New Year's Eve. We have given you a long enough grace period without any interrogation about what the heck happened that night, and we are happy to discuss that instead." Noah casually drops the kiss bomb.

That is going to be a hard pass. I can't talk about Princess, and I don't even know what I would say. I move toward the table, pull out a chair, and slide into it. Feeling worn down and unwilling to stonewall the guys anymore, I give in, "I know I have been in a crap mood for a few weeks. I am sorry, guys. I am a little burnt out at work and could use a few days off. I am sorry if I have been taking it out on you guys."

"I don't want to spook the bear, but does anyone else think that was a successful intervention?"

I pick up a cheese curd and chuck it at Henry's head. Henry opens his mouth wide and catches the curd with little difficulty. "I might take off next weekend to the cabin to clear my head, and then I will be back to my normal charming self."

"Not sure charming is how I would describe you, but I will take that over grumpy." Max joins in on the commentary as he shoves a plate toward me, which I will gladly accept.

"Sorry work has been stressing you out so much lately. Anything we can do to help?" Harrison asks between bites of his burger.

"Nah, there have just been a lot of changes lately." That was true about more than my work life. The group dynamic has drastically changed in the last six months. Max is now engaged to Jane. Harrison finally manned up and claimed Ginger. So many changes, not bad but it still is change. Noah is now expecting his second child. Before you know it all my friends will be married and popping out kids. I have to wonder where that leaves me – the fun uncle, category, I guess.

I am pulled out of my downward spiral of thought by Bubba, "Well, we all know you hate change of any type."

I just shrug because he is not wrong.

"Well, as long as we are poking the bear tonight, should we talk about what has been plastered all over town." Noah hesitantly asks.

"I have only been home for a few hours, and I didn't see anything when I drove through town." Clearly, I am missing something because when I look around at all my friends, they are all avoiding eye contact and really focused on their food. "Spill, Noah! You seem to be the only one brave enough to bring it up. What is plastered all over town?"

"I haven't actually seen it. Emma told me about it. She was with Jane when Jane agreed to hang the poster in her shop."

"Hold on one minute, Noah. Don't you dare throw my girl under the bus." The only time Max gets fired up about anything is when it is the defense of his girl. His obsession wavers between sweet and annoying. "It is not Jane's fault she is so supportive of the community her civic duty to law enforcement."

Bubba lets out a loud bark of a laugh, "I might have seen this elusive poster because I also agreed to hang it in my shop. Not sure what Jane was thinking with her civic minded brain at the time she agrees to hang it up."

Max turns bright red, I am seriously having concerns he is going to blow a gasket. "Cupcake only has eyes for me. WHAT are you implying, Bubba?!"

Everyone busts out laughing at how ridiculous this conversation is. It hits me like a sucker punch what the poster in question is about. I try to holler over their laughter to get their attention. "What is on the poster?" I am practically growling out the question.

Henry is the first one to bravely answer, "I always figured you for the type of guy to go to a bar to pick up a girl, but, hey, auctioning your grumpy self off might be our only option at this point."

Cripes, I totally forgot about that stupid fundraiser. The conversation with the mayor feels like it happened months ago, not this morning. Feeling resigned to the flood of verbal jabs that are about to be slung my way, "How bad is it? I was just told this morning that participation is not optional. My secretary picked out some random picture without me even knowing."

"I heard you have very dreamy eyes that have the girls very swoon-worthy over the chance to win a date with Little Falls's most eligible bachelor." Noah looks so pleased with my misery.

"Tell me you are joking, and it does not say that?!"

"Might be better to show you," Max pulls his phone out and pulls up the photo before turning it around to show me.

"You have got to be kidding me? I fill out the whole poster. The only writing you can read is announcing the most eligible bachelor. Cripes, this is bad."

"What is the big deal? You raise some money for the police fund, and maybe you get a cute girl to love on. This really seems like a win-win all around." Harrison states nonchalantly like I am the irrational one.

"Harrison, this is all your fault!"

"What are you talking about? How is this my fault?"

"The mayor is tired of hearing about your chief brag about how much money you and Ginger raised at the Fireman's Ball, and he is trying to out-raise you guys in money with this fundraiser."

"Sorry, not sorry. The Fireman's Ball not only raised a butt-load of money that will help so many people, it also brought me the love of my life." Harrison shrugs my outrage off like I am the one being a baby here.

"I have to agree with Harrison, and you are making this a bigger deal than it needs to be. Ralph, you think you have problems. Jane texted me this afternoon wanting lots of babies."

"Has no one explained where babies come from, Max? Need good old Bubba to explain it to you?"

"Thanks, but I am good. I am just saying Jane hanging out with all these babies is giving her baby fever. Better watch out; Stella could catch the baby fever next." Max folds his arm across his chest and glares at Bubba. Bubba then proceeds to glare back. How did making fun of me turn into this?

"Max not sure you can say babies in plural. Baby number two, who is currently residing inside the Emma Hotel, can't cause baby fever, can it?" Henry has always been the group peacemaker when we get too riled up, not sure this was the best direction to go in to bring peace back.

"Henry, not sure how I feel about you talking about my wife being a hotel for our unborn baby. But I think Max is referring to Lola's playdate that joined them in this morning." Noah carefully avoids looking in my direction.

My spidey investigator senses are going off that Noah is being weird, well, weirder than normal. No one is calling him out on it either, so I take it upon myself, "So where are the girls tonight? It is unlike Max to agree to the girls having a night without him included."

"I will have you know. Jane loves it when I crash girls' night. She misses me and it is hard for her when we do these nights apart." The sad part about what Max just said is that he honestly believes Jane is equally miserable.

"I promised my wife that we wouldn't crash tonight. Hence, plan B was born."

"Do I even want to know what plan B involves? Or better yet, why do I need to be involved in a plan B to stay away from girls' night? I never crash the night, those offenders would be Max and now Harrison." I knew I shouldn't have asked before I asked.

"Plan B is fairly obvious: come over here and torment you and bring you good food. There is also the elephant in the room that needs to be addressed: out of all the single guys in town or even in our group of friends, you were the one picked as the most eligible bachelor, a real brain scratcher if you ask me."

A valiant effort to distract me with all the dumb things that just flew out of his mouth, I am still stuck on the fact that they are not allowed to crash girls' night tonight. "So why have you been banned from crashing tonight, boys? What did you do to get banned?"

Bubba elbows Noah, "I told you he would figure it out. He might be grumpy, but he is wicked smart when it comes to BS."

"Uhh, fine, so we can't crash tonight because Chloe agreed to come tonight. Emma doesn't want anyone to ruin it for her or scare her off." Noah looks relieved the secret is out.

Well, that has my attention. I want to ask all the questions that are running through my head, but I stop myself when I remember the new resolve I found on the way home from work. I need to leave her alone. I felt that night at the bar that Chloe was a little lost and could really benefit from some friends. The girls will suck her into their world and help build her up. She deserves that.

"Really, you have nothing to say about Chloe being over at Noah's house?" Harrison looks frustrated with my lack of response.

"What do you want me to say?"

"You could fill us all in on the kiss seen around the bar on New Year's Eve? We are dying to know what is going on. And you have been stone-walling us the last two weeks. So, spill now."

"Max, you are starting to sound like one of the girls instead of one of us guys," I am stalling, and they all know it.

"You cost me a night of hanging with my girl. The least you could do is explain yourself."

Max is relentless tonight. He might have had one too many cheese curds. "How is this my fault?"

"I usually don't like to feed into the town gossip, but everyone is talking about the kiss you and Chloe shared on the dance floor. They might also be saying that you kissed the girl and ran like your britches were on fire."

"Bubba, are you kidding me? You are one of the town's biggest gossips. Britches?! Have you been talking to ladies down in the quilting bee? How do I get the rap for being the old man in the group, and you are using the word 'britches.'" I really don't want to explain that kiss to the guys or why I turned and ran from the woman who has consumed my every thought. That kiss has consumed my thoughts for the last two weeks, and at this point, I am not sure I even know the answers to their questions.

Henry has a death wish tonight, "Deflection, that is a great coping mechanism, one I am willing to allow to avoid grumpy Ralph reappearing."

"Listen, man, we are not here to make you grumpier, but the girls just wanted to make sure we didn't interrupt girls' night. Chloe seems a little shy and we are all a lot to take in when we are all together. Emma thought maybe if she got to know the group in smaller numbers, there would be a better chance of not scaring her off." Noah looks sincere in wanting to be supportive of his wife.

"Plus, everyone is afraid you might maul the poor girl again, and we would never see her again." Bubba gives it to me straight with a giant smile plastered on his face. I appreciate the straight answer for what it is, but I hate that they all think I can't control myself around her. The thought that is nagging me in the back of my mind, which is preventing me from focusing on the ridiculous banter the guys are currently engaged in, is maybe I don't trust myself around Chloe without losing control.

Chapter 8
Chloe

I pull up in front of the most adorable house. I would love to buy something similar in the future for Phoebe to grow up in. A wave a disappointment hits me when I think about all the areas that I am clearly lacking in providing for my daughter. Lola has two parents who adore her, and is being raised in this adorable house. Even in the dead of winter, when everything is dead and covered with snow and ice, this house still looks warm and inviting. Phoebe takes this moment to start babbling in the back seat, bringing me out of my melancholy.

I try to shake the feelings off. I told myself that I would give the girls a fair shake tonight and make an honest effort to get to know them if not for my own sake but for Phoebe. After seeing her with Lola this morning, there is not much I would not do to hear that laugh again. So, if that means I have to put myself out there and make an effort to leave my comfort zone, then that is what I will do. I am running a little late, though. I felt bad leaving Betty, worried that she might need help tonight. She assured me multiple times to get out and have fun. On top of that, the girls blew up my phone with reminder texts about girls night. That is how I find myself sitting outside Emma's house, trying to gather the courage to head in. The freezing temperatures are a great motivator to get my butt in gear.

I gather the diaper bag and my pink snowball from the back seat. I should really take a page out of Phoebe's playbook of life. I have done nothing but whine and complain about the weather here, but Phoebe is all giggles and smiles no matter what is thrown at her. I secretly wish, as I make my way toward the front door, that she never loses that aspect of her.

Emma immediately opens the door and welcomes us in. As I thought we are the last to arrive. The inside of the house is more adorable than I thought possible. The cozy feeling is so inviting. "Sorry we are late, I am kind of nervous that Betty's poker night is breaking multiple laws. How has she survived this long without being arrested?" All the girls start to laugh. Emma offers to take my coat, and I make my way to the couch to de-layer my snowball.

"I love your aunt Betty. I kind of wish I'll have that much fire left in me when I am her age," Stella says as she carries in a platter of food.

Emma has a smirk on her face. "I am not sure it was ever an option that you would not have that fire." Stella shrugs it off in agreement.

Emma has set out a blanket on the floor with a bunch of toys. When Lola spots Phoebe, she immediately stands and waddles over to her. "Lola is way better at walking than Phoebe. Phoebe is still unsteady. She always opts for crawling because she is faster at that mode of transportation."

"I blame Noah and his genes. My mother-in-law told me that Noah and his twin were not only walking by nine months they were running. No wonder she waited nine years to have Ginger. The twins did a real number on her." Everyone laughs at the matter-of-fact way Emma states the facts.

"Did I know Noah had a twin?"

"Max is Noah's twin. And Ginger is their baby sister. There are a lot of us but let me see if I can explain better." Jane has been over the top, genuine, and nice during any interaction I have had with her. "So, Noah and Max are twins. They have been best friends with Bubba, Henry, Ralph, and Harrison since Kindergarten. Bubba adopts Stella into the best friend group in second grade. When they are all around nine years old, Ginger arrives on the scene. She is Noah and Max's little sister. Then fast forward to college, Noah meets and marries the love of his life, Emma. Then fast forward some more, I move to town, and they adopt me into the group. I know that is a lot, but does that help?"

Lola is now standing at my knees and is desperate to have Phoebe join her. I quickly finish taking the multiple layers off my daughter. "Yes, that is helpful. That is impressive how long you guys have stayed friends and involved in each other lives." What would I give to have just one lifelong friend I could count on the way they all count on each other?

"There have been a few recent changes. Max had moved away from town right around the time Jane moved here. He was gone for about three years before deciding to move home this past summer. He wasn't home more than a hot five seconds before he claimed our Jane as his. He teeters between sweet and obsessive over our Jane." Emma is a matter of fact, about her brother-in-law being possibly crazy. "Max proposed to Jane around Christmas time.

"Then Harrison was the next to step up and claim his girl, and to no one's surprise except maybe Noah's, it was Ginger." I look over to see Ginger blushing at Stella's comment. "It was only a matter of time before those two figured it out and got together, but man, did it take forever for them to figure it out."

"Gee, thanks Stella. Should we address how long it has taken you to figure out your love life?" Jane says with more amusement than annoyance.

"Oh brother, really you're going to bring this up in front of Chloe?" Stella, on the other hand, looks annoyed.

"Girls, behave yourself. We are putting a non-crazy front up so Chloe wants to hang with us," Emma chides the girls in a perfect mom tone.

"Don't mind me. I would actually like to see your crazy side. Right now, you all seem a little perfect. I would definitely bring the group down with my crazy side." My comment has the desired effect, and they all look relieved. "And by the way, Emma, you have the mom tone down perfectly."

"You will not be surprised by this, but once you get to know the guys better, I have perfected my mom's tone on my husband and his friends with all the shenanigans they get into." At that, we all start to laugh.

"I might as well be the one to tell you. The girls are under the impression that Bubba and I are destined to be together, and we are on the slow train to figure out how to make it happen." Stella tries to play it off like what she said was no big deal, but I can tell otherwise. There is a split second where there is longing in her eyes for what she said to be true, and then it is gone.

"Forget slow train, they have been docked at the train station not moving for years," Ginger adds.

Stella is saved from further explanation as Lola expresses her annoyance that I have yet to put Chloe down for her to play with. "I am sorry, Lola, I am getting distracted. Would you like Phoebe to come to play with you?" Lola gives me a "no duh" look. Clearly, she has just as much of her mother's genes as well. I make my way over to the blanket and plop Phoebe in the middle of all the scattered toys. Lola waddled close behind me and plopped herself down right by Phoebe. The girls start to babble back in forth. From an outsider looking in on their interaction, it appears that they both understand what the other is saying. It is adorable and makes it worth braving the freezing temperatures tonight for this moment.

"Girls, this is not helping with my baby fever." Jane says as she is snapping pics on her phone. "Max was weirded out earlier by my texts asking for lots of babies. I probably shouldn't send him a picture of this, reminding him of my previous request, right?"

"You could ask him to rob a bank, and he would probably respond which bank," Emma says as she is carrying a pitcher of some drink concoction and cups.

"Ha ha, he would not." Jane is not impressed.

"I have to agree with Emma. My brother would do anything for you, Jane." Ginger passed me a plate as I returned to the couch, where I continue to watch the little girls out of the corner of my eye.

"I would agree with you, but I am telling you he is being weird about the baby topic." Jane now looks sad, which hits a little close to home for me.

Emma offers me a drink, "Normally we have some fun alcohol concoction but seeing there are babies pregnant, and I can't drink, I decided for all of you that the only thing fun we are drinking tonight would be strawberry lemonade."

"Sounds perfect, actually." I grab the drink and take a sip.

"Okay, dig in, Chloe. Normally, we have to eat fast because the guys always seem to show up, interrupting girls' night. When they show up, it is guaranteed no food is safe." Stella says it matter of fact.

"Wait, the guys are coming tonight?" It comes out more panicked than I meant.

Emma shoots a glare at Stella, "No, I promise this is strictly a girls' night. Noah promised to keep the boys away and distracted tonight."

Feeling bad that the girls might prefer to have the guys here tonight and I am the reason they are separate. It is like Jane can read my mind, "Let me stop you right there, Chloe before you start thinking the wrong thing. We are not missing the guys being here tonight. Max and Harrison have been kind of needy since they started dating Ginger and me. But honestly, I miss having girls' night. They always seem to find some dumb reason to crash every time."

"As long as you are sure you don't mind them not being here. I don't want…". I don't get the rest of my thoughts out before the girls agree unanimously that they are fine with the guys being absent. We burst into laughter at how adamant they responded.

"Chloe, does Phoebe like Baby Shark?" Emma asks as she is retrieving the remote from the entertainment center.

"Of course, it is the only way I can shower some days." Emma and I share a look acknowledging the struggle to find time to shower with a young child is real.

"Hold the phone. What are you guys talking about? What is Baby Shark?" Jane's expression would be hilarious if it was not borderline horrified.

"Jane, even I have heard about Baby Shark." Ginger adds.

"Just watch, Jane. Lola loves it. I am betting Phoebe is a fan, too." Emma pulls up the app on her TV and scrolls through her favorite list before landing on Baby Shark.

Stella lets out a groan, "Last time you played this, it was stuck in my head forever. I even got it stuck in Bubba's head. He was so mad at me when he couldn't get the catchy tune out of his head."

Soon, the screen fills with colorful sharks, and the song that haunts every parent's nightmares starts to play. The little girls immediately stop babbling and stare at the TV in a state of complete trance.

"You have got to be kidding me!" Jane's outrage would be funny if it was not so genuine. I know the song is annoying, but her outrage seems a little out of place for just hearing it for the first time.

"Don't mind Jane, she has a 'thing' about sharks," Ginger loops me in on the instant outrage.

"A thing?" Not sure I want to know but curiosity got the better of me.

"I hate them! Plain and simple! I am fairly certain that they are trying to kill me." Jane says it straight face. I really have to push down the urge to laugh.

"Trying to kill you?" That is all I can manage.

"You can see how her crazy compliments my brother's crazy?" Ginger doesn't even blink at calling Jane crazy, but the way she says it you can tell that she loves Jane despite her crazy.

"I am not crazy. I just really hate sharks. And now I find out that they have made a catchy song with colorful cartoons about the evil demons, making them seem friendly. Emma, how can you let Lola watch this?"

"Because Jane, sometimes I need five minutes to myself, and baby shark gives me that." I love that Emma is a powerhouse who is not apologetic for the way she approaches life. I envy that about her.

"Oh, my gosh, I can't believe I forgot to tell you, Jane!!" Stella is barely containing her excitement as she bounces up and down, "Betty told me about this new romance book that she read, might be right up your alley."

The conversation from the salon pops into my mind, where Betty describes a book with the main love interest shifted from shark to man. I know I am just getting to know Jane, but something tells me that she will hate this idea.

Stella proceeds to explain the book in the same level of outlandish detail that Betty provided. My head bobbles between Stella and Jane. Stella looks like this is Christmas morning and Jane looks like she is being chased through the forest with a chainsaw-wielding maniac close behind her.

All that Jane can get out after the graphic description Stella so willingly gave is, "You have ruined book boyfriends for me."

"Jane, you have a real boyfriend; you don't need a book boyfriend, remember." Ginger lovingly reminds Jane as she fills up a plate of goodies.

"I might have a fiancé, but there is always room in a girl's life for book boyfriends, and Stella ruined it."

"Okay, girls, I would say you are doing a crappy job hiding your crazy tonight. We will be lucky to get Chloe back for another night at this rate." Emma says she turns the volume down. The little girls are still fascinated with the colorful pictures, but the annoying jingle is less prominent.

"Don't hide your crazy on my behalf. It is kind of refreshing. I was starting to think you were all perfect, and that is way more difficult to live up to than crazy."

They all seem relieved by my confession. "That is good to hear. So now that you know we are all a little touched by crazy tell us about yourself. All I really know is your aunt is Betty. And you have a beautiful daughter who is quite adorable." Ginger sweetly asks. She might be the youngest of the group but she exudes maturity.

"Not much to say; I am kind of boring," I want to give the basics without giving the gory details of my past. "I was born and raised in Arizona. My family and I would come here most summers and spend time with Betty. She became aware of my need for a fresh start and invited me and Phoebe to come stay with her."

They were all staring at me like that was not enough to satisfy their curiosity, so I continued. "I am an interior designer. I am hoping to start up a business here. My website goes live next week."

"One of my regulars at the salon, well, she is more of a friend than a client, but that doesn't matter; the point is she was just telling me this week that her family wants to update their family cabin, and she is looking for someone to help her. She has small kids at home and doesn't know where to start with the project. Can I give her your number?"

"That would be perfect! Are you sure you want to recommend me without seeing any of my work? I can show you some of my mockup designs and projects that I completed back home if you want?"

"I would love to see your work, but I am sure you will be perfect for Lara and her family cabin. It is more like a mountain resort than a cabin. Her family comes from money, so calling it a cabin is a little misleading."

I am battling feelings of being overwhelmed and excited. If I can land this job that would be huge for Phoebe and me moving forward. As the excitement starts to bubble up at the idea of my first client I notice the wide eye expressions on the other girls.

Emma is the first to speak. "Are you sure that is a good idea, Stella? Involving Lara?"

My hope for my first client is quickly dashed with disappointment over Emma's reaction. I feel the need to defend my abilities to them. "This might sound arrogant, but I promise I am good. There are a lot of areas in my life I fall short but interior design is not one of them. I promise."

"Chloe, I am sorry, that is not what I meant. I am sure you are excellent. I am just surprised that Lara is looking for help, that is all. I hadn't heard about the project at the family cabin."

I feel like Emma is holding something back, but I don't feel like I can call her on it this early in the friendship.

"Of course, it is a good idea. It is a win-win for everyone involved. Let me text her right now." Before I can stop her or ask for a minute to think about it, she has her phone out, and she has a text sent off to Lara.

Not a minute later, I can hear my phone ding with a text message. I dig my phone out of the never-ending, bottomless pit of despair that every diaper bag becomes. I click opt to my messages and see a text from an unknown number, and I click on it.

Unknown: Hey, this is Lara Smith. Stella recommended you to me. I hope it is okay I reached out. We are looking to overhaul our family cabin. Trust me when I say every room is in desperate need!! Do you have time to meet up next week to talk about options and design?

I quickly add the number to my address book and shoot back a reply.

Me: I would love to sit down with you and talk design and what your vision is for the cabin. Does Monday or Tuesday work for you?

Lara Smith: Yes!! I am so excited! You have no idea what a relief will be. Tuesday at 11 am, works for me. Does that work for you? We can meet at the diner in town.

Me: Yes, perfect. I will see you then.

I am beside myself with giddiness. This might be my first client. I look up from my phone to see all the girls have their eyes trained on me. "Sorry, that was Lara. She wants to meet up on Tuesday to talk about the project. This will be huge for Phoebe and me if I can land this account." Feeling the need to explain myself to them.

"I am sure you will land it no problem." Jane is so unconditional with her kindness.

I have had the full swing through so many emotions tonight. I have a sudden urge to share more than I expected I would ever want to share with anyone. "It has been a rough couple of years, and I find myself overwhelmed by all your willingness to offer your friendship so easily." I look down overcome with emotions that I thought were locked away.

"I am not sure what you have been through or what caused the last few years to be rough for you, but when I tell you that you are stuck with us, I mean it. If you ever want to talk, we will always listen. We might all be a little unhinged in our own way, but we are fierce protectors of each other's crazy." Emma says with a smirk, easing my anxiety that I am close to turning into a basket case in front of them.

The other girls join in with their support and agree with Emma's thoughts.

I look over at Phoebe, who is happily playing with Lola. What would I give to understand baby babble to know what they are saying to each other? I am unaware that a tear slips out and down my cheek.

I wipe it away fast, but not fast enough for the girls to notice. "Uhh, I am a mess, sorry. I just haven't had this in a really long time, and maybe I never had this." The girls stay silent, probably afraid to spook me. "I hope you all know how lucky you are to have the type of friendship you all share." They all look at each other and nod in agreement to what I said.

Wanting to tell my story to someone for the first time ever, I let out a heavy breath and pray this is the right decision. "Ugh, so I was married before. We met at the end of my junior year in college. He was charming and said all the right things. He had been married before me. He claims that marriage didn't work because they grew apart and wanted different things. I was young and dumb and believed him. I know it sounds like a cliche excuse, but it's true." I feel exhausted, and I really haven't shared anything yet.

"Go on, don't stop. I promise from experience that getting the story out there gives it less power over you," Ginger says almost in a whisper. I know without asking that she has a story in her background that left its own scars on her.

I gather up my desire to get this over with and continue, "We had a whirlwind courtship and married all within a few months of meeting. My friends became his friends. Our lives just intertwined so well that I never realized it until it was too late. I unexpectedly became pregnant. It was not in the plan, but it happened. At first, he seemed happy with the idea of a baby." I pause and look at my beautiful daughter. She is sitting with her new friend, so happy and carefree. "It started off slowly at first, him pulling away. I thought the pregnancy hormones were making me lose my mind. Then it was harder to make justifications for him always being gone. He made excuses of why he couldn't come to doctor appointments, not coming home for dinner, or why weekends away for golf tournaments with his boys were more important than being home with me." I look back at the girls and find a wide variety of expressions ranging from sadness to rage.

I wish I could be done with my story here and call it good, but I know if I want to start to build real relationships, I need to stop hiding and open myself up. "By all your expressions, you are smarter than me and figured out that my husband was cheating on me. I confronted him one night. It was the day I found out I was carrying a girl. He texted me last minute, saying he could not make the scan. I was devastated and felt so alone. When he got home that night, I confronted him. I thought he would deny it and tell me I was crazy, and I felt like I was going crazy, so it would have been fitting. But that is not what happened. He admitted that he was cheating on me with his ex-wife."

I take a deep breath, fully aware that tears are flowing freely unchecked currently. I need to finish before I lose it completely. "He was cheating on me with his first wife. He had reconnected with her right after we found out I was pregnant. He then informed me that he never wanted children, and it was not fair of me to trap him in a life that he never wanted. He then felt the need to explain that his ex was the love of his life, and he never got over her leaving him. I pathetically just sat there in shock. He packed his bags that night and moved in with his ex. I never got the chance to tell him he was having a daughter." Feeling completely drained I sit there staring at my hands that were fidgeting in my lap.

"Okay, so between Emma and I, I think we would be very successful in hiding his body, and no one would ever assume it was you. We would need to leave Ginger and Jane out of our plans for murder and mayhem. They are the 'good' ones in the group, and they will crumple like a deck of cards under interrogation." Stella is full on in planning mode for the demise of my ex. I look up in time to see Ginger and Jane agree with simultaneous head nods.

"Stella is not wrong. I can bring cupcakes to the murder after-party. Just make sure I don't know about the murder. I will crumble after one Dateline interview." Jane is so nonchalantly throwing around terms like 'murder party' and 'Dateline interviews.'

I lose it, but this time, it is laughter that is flowing free. The tears are drying and I am full on belly laughing. How did these girls I just met take the single most painful moment of my life and bring light to it? My laughing catches Phoebe's attention, and she crawls over to me. She is tugging on my pants, a sign she would like to be picked up. I reach down and pull her into my arms. Phoebe instantly snuggles into the crook of my neck and offers her love unconditionally.

"I am not sure how I have lived my life so long and not found friends like you before?"

"We are kind of an acquired taste. Not everyone is up for our brand of crazy." Stella is proud of the crazy factor, as she should be.

"What about your girlfriends in Arizona? Sure, they might not jump straight to murder like we are, but didn't they at least want to kick his trash or egg his house?" Emma asks.

Phoebe seems satisfied that I am not going crazy and wants to be put back down on the floor. I watch as she speed crawls back to Lola, who patiently waits for her return. "Remember me saying our lives became so intertwined, well lines were drawn. Let's just say after the dust settled the girls, I thought my friend would rather be friends with my ex and his ex-wife, who is now his current wife. They would go out clubbing and hit up sports events. I was pregnant and no fun for a bunch of single carefree girls."

"You are joking, right?" Ginger asks in an outraged tone.

"Wish I was. I lost everything that night." I pause and rethink what I just said, "Actually, that might not be completely true. That night, I felt like I lost everything but truthfully, my ex did me a favor. I was divorced, and he signed his paternal rights over to my daughter before I even gave birth to her."

Emma, who I felt was a pillar of strength since the first day I met her, looked close to tears, "Please tell me you were not alone in that delivery room."

"I was," I rush out. "But it was okay. Phoebe and I have been a team since day one. I have found that I am capable of way more than I thought possible."

"You're my hero. And let me stress that you are stuck with us, and there is no trying to escape our overbearing friendship that we will thrust upon you whether you want it or not." Emma states with little to no wiggle room for discussion.

"That actually sounds kind of nice."

"Perfect!! Does that mean we can broach the Ralph subject now?"

"Stella! Seriously, you have no chill." Jane is shaking her head in disbelief while rubbing her temples.

"What's the problem? She agreed to friendship and all the craziness that goes along with said friendship. I am dying to know?" Stella is borderline whining at this point.

"You will have to excuse Stella. Between her and Bubba, they put the local church ladies to shame with their gossip." Emma states.

"That is not fair. You all want to know, too. I am the only one brave enough to ask." Stella reaches for her drink, not at all apologetic for her question.

Feeling like it is unavoidable if I want to move forward with these friendships. "There is nothing to say, really. Sorry to let you down on the hot gossip. There is none here."

"Okay, you opened the door, so I am more than willing to walk through it," Ginger moves to the edge of her seat with excitement dancing in her eyes. "I have known Ralph my entire life, and I have never seen him act like he did that night. He has never been grumpy with a stranger like he was with you. He is always the picture of a perfect gentleman. And can we please talk about that kiss? Oh man, it was hot. There has to be something we are missing?" Ginger struck me as the quiet one of the group. Her desire for gossip might rival Stella's need for it.

I let out a little chuckle, and she is not wrong. That kiss was hot. The single best kiss of my life. She is also not wrong in the fact that he acted all night that he was annoyed I was there. The last thing I need in my life is a man who doesn't know what he wants. Correction, the last thing I need in my life is a man, period. "I don't know what to tell you. I thought he didn't like me by the end of the night. I have no idea what I did to him for him to already hate me. He pulled me over earlier that day. Betty threatened to call his mama if he didn't let us get on our way." A giggle escapes at the thought of Betty calling

Ralph's mom to tell on him. "But he seemed more amused with my crazy than annoyed."

"But what about the kiss? And Ginger was right, it was steamy!" Jane is now leaning forward in her seat. Do they think leaning closer to me will get them a different answer? They plan murder parties complete with cupcakes, so nothing is off the table with these girls.

"You got me there. I am willing to admit that was the single hottest moment of my life, which makes it the most confusing, too. I have no idea why he kissed me. I have no idea why he calls me princess. I am just as clueless as you girls." I am finding way more satisfaction in girl talk than I have previously with past friends. There is something about these women that is special.

This is how the next few hours flow: we talk about anything and everything. The little girls have collapsed in a pile of pillows and blankets that Emma brought out and spread on the floor for them. They have fallen asleep lying next to each other. Jane starts snapping pictures, mumbling under her breath about being baby-hungry. We all try to stifle our giggles, but it is hard to when Jane looks so earnest in her desire to have a little one of her own. I would love to be on the other end of that text message so I could see Max's reaction to the baby-hungry pics she has been sending him all night. I don't know her man, but I hope he is a good one that will treat Jane right.

We all start to clean up. I am packing my diaper bag up and moving toward my sleeping baby with her snowsuit. She is out cold. Apparently, it is very taxing on a 15-month-old to have her first play date and meet her bestie in one day. She doesn't even make a sound as I start to dress her to go get in the car.

The front door opens and Noah timidly walks through the door. All the women look at the front door expecting more than just Noah. Noah raises his hands into the air like, "It is just me. Is it okay if I sneak by? I will head to my room, and you will never know I was here."

Emma shoots him a glare; she can't maintain it, and a smirk starts to form. "You can come in, babe. Girls' night is wrapping up. You have perfect timing, actually. I was just trying to figure out how I was going to get your daughter off the floor. She needs to be changed and dressed for bed. Any chance I can talk you into doing all that for your very tired and very pregnant wife?" Emma batts her eyelashes at her husband while rubbing her baby bump.

The look Noah gives his wife is one I would kill for. You can tell that he adores the very ground she walks on. No request is too much to ask. He walks across the room and wraps his arms around her as he tenderly kisses her. I look away, feeling awkward watching such an intimate gesture.

"Okay, get a room, you too. Noah, do you realize that is how you got yourself into your current situation? One sleeping baby on the floor and another one cooking?" At first, I thought Stella was annoyed by Noah and Emma's show of affection for each other, but when I look over at Stella I realize she is not annoyed but amused with her friends.

"Thank you Stella, always so helpful." Noah looks amused with his friend's objection. Noah leans down and kisses Emma on the top of the head before letting her go. He turns and makes his way to the pile of pillows and blankets that little girls are currently cocooned in.

Noah bends down to surveil the scene before him. "Hey, Chloe, it is good to see you again."

"Hey, Noah. Thank you for letting us crash at your house tonight for girls' night. Sorry, you got kicked out on our behalf."

"This is quite normal practice around here. Looks like the next generation is getting started on girls' night a little sooner than planned." We both look down at the sleeping babies.

"It was kind of adorable, I have to admit. I will bundle up mine and get out of your hair for the night."

"Wait, give me your keys and I will go start your car so you can put Phoebe in a warm car."

Without thinking, I hand my keys over. I am speechless that this man who doesn't know me or my baby has shown us more kindness than Phoebe's birth father ever showed. Determined not to break down again, I focus on getting Phoebe ready.

Chapter 9
Chloe

I spent the rest of the weekend preparing for my meeting with Lara. I really need this account to go through. Not only will it help me build my portfolio, but Stella stuck her neck out for me, and I want to make sure I deliver on my end.

"Child, why don't you leave Phoebe with me? How much trouble can we really get into while you are gone for your meeting?" Betty has been relentless in trying to get me to leave Phoebe with her for my meeting. On the one hand, it would be more professional to show up without my toddler in tow, but on the other hand, I already feel like we are taking advantage of Betty's generosity in staying here rent-free.

"Before living with you I would say that it would be impossible for you to get into trouble, but I now know better." I send her a knowing look that her sweet, elderly exterior does not fool me.

Betty lets out a quick laugh under her breath, "I am sure I have no clue what you are referring to. Now, you need to stop being so stubborn and let me bond with that sweet girl."

On cue, Phoebe hits her tray on her high chair and starts to babble away as she fists her eggs cramming them in her mouth. So lady like, never been so proud. If I didn't know better, I would think she is on team Betty right now and wants to stay with her. Shaking my head at her antics, I turn to Betty, "Are you sure you don't mind she will be awake the whole time."

"Ha, victory! Of course, I am sure. Now, don't you worry about us and get ready for your meeting with Lara. Nice girl, that one. Comes from a good family. You will love working with them."

"Fingers crossed. I hope I can secure the account. I don't have the job yet."

"Pish-posh child, don't talk back to your elders. If I say you will get the job, then you will get the job. Worst case scenario I will have to call her mother if the meeting doesn't go your way, but I am confident that we will not have to go that direction. Lara is a smart girl. She will see what so many already see in you: greatness!"

I am torn between wondering if she knows everyone's mother and being overwhelmed by her belief in my ability to do this. "Thank you, Betty, for everything. Letting us stay here, for believing in me and for loving my little girl as much as you do. If you're sure, maybe I will leave her with you. I should only be gone for an hour."

"Hot dog, that is what I am talking about. Now, what have you taught our girl about poker yet?"

"Ummm, maybe I should..."

"Your face, you are too easy, child. Obviously, I will hold off on teaching her the finer details of poker until preschool."

What have I done by agreeing to let Betty watch my child? I look at the clock and realize I have run out of time for overanalyzing my decision. I need to get dressed and get moving or I am going to be late. I clean Phoebe up and place her in her playpen in the living room. Betty lovingly refers to it as a baby jail, and she is not wrong. I hurry to my room and change clothes. I try to tame my hair but that is near impossible with the lack of time I have left to get ready. I grab everything I need for my presentation. Before I head out I kiss Phoebe on the head. Betty assures me one last time that she promises not to get into trouble while I am gone. The number of times I need that assurance from her should be a red flag for me. Desperate times call for desperate measures. I send up a silent prayer that Betty really will stay out of trouble.

I pull up to the diner with butterflies fluttering around in my stomach. To say I really need this to work out is the understatement of the year. I grab my portfolio and head inside. I arrived a few minutes before our scheduled meeting time in hopes that I could secure a table and set up what I needed to for my presentation. A waitress walks up to me as I am entering. "Good morning, just one dining this morning?"

"No, there will be two. I am meeting someone today."

Before the waitress can answer I hear someone calling my name. The female voice is coming from the bank of booths along the far wall. A tall woman with dark curly hair greets me. She looks familiar but I cannot place her. She gets out of the booth and makes her way toward me, "Hi, are you Chloe? I am Lara."

"Oh, hi, yes, so nice to meet you. I am sorry if you have been waiting long. I meant to be early to set up my presentation for you." I am already flustered.

Lara loops her arm through mine and leads me to the booth as if we are old friends. "Oh, you are early. I am just a smidge earlier than you. Now, don't judge me, but I have five-year-old twins at home. They missed the deadline to start kindergarten by 4 days. So, needless to say, they are more than ready to go to school, and I am more than ready to have them go to school. So, when I can escape, or I mean need to leave the house for interactions that involve other adults, I tend to be early."

"I can only imagine. I only have one at home, and sometimes that feels overwhelming, but being outnumbered daily would be a whole new challenge. Give me one quick second, and I can set up the presentation, and I will be ready to go.

"There is no rush. Have you been here before? Come look at the menu, and we can get to know each other."

Worried that somehow I already disappointed her and lost the job, I started to ramble, "I am fine. If you want to order, I can show you my presentation while you eat. I know a mother's time is limited, so I don't want to waste your time. If you just look at my work, I think you will find something that you like…" Lara reaches across the table and takes ahold of my hands, instantly stopping my ramble.

"Chloe, I am sorry if there was some misunderstanding."

She pauses and I feel utter defeat, which must show in my face. "Oh, of course. I am sorry to have wasted your time."

"No, wait, I am not explaining myself very well. You have the job, and it is yours if you still want it. There is no need for all this formal presentation mumbo-jumbo. You're hired. Now, can we order? I am starving and I for sure see dessert in our future."

"Wait! What? I know it is probably to tell your future employer that you are confused, but I am not sure what else to say."

"I am confused about what are you confused about?" Lara asks as she is now perusing the menu with ease.

"How are you going to hire me without asking for references or looking at my past projects? I could be a serial killer, and you just hired me." I am not quite sure why I am trying to talk her out of hiring me or why I just referred to myself as a serial killer. Stella can't be rubbing off on me that much that soon, can she?

The serial killer comment grabs her attention, and Lara looks up at me. "Wait, are you a serial killer?"

"What? No!"

Lara busts up laughing, "Oh, Chloe, you are fun. This is going to be so much fun!" Then she proceeds to go back to looking over the menu.

I have never had such a bizarre job interview before. I feel odd just sitting here staring at her, so I grab a menu and start looking over it, too. The waitress comes to the table and, takes our order, then turns to leave us. "Okay, now that we have cleared up, you are not a serial killer, by the way, my brother will be so proud I asked that question during the interview. Let's get into the meat and potatoes of the project, shall we."

I reach into my bag, grabbing a notebook to make notes. "Alright, what do I need to know about this project?"

"This is a family cabin. My grandparents used to go all the time, however they spend most of their time in Florida now, lucky ducks. They escaped the frozen wasteland. My parents rarely go there anymore. They find the outdoors to be beneath them, which works out great for me and my family. Like I said I have twin five-year-olds that are constantly busy, so escaping up to the cabin has been nice for us. My brother also uses the property sometimes. Although he is turning into an eternal bachelor, he will still use the property with his friends or by himself as a breather from town."

"How big is the cabin?"

"Cabin might be a misleading word. It is a 8,000 square feet. There is a three-car garage on each side of the cabin, allowing parking for multiple cars."

"Okay, yeah not sure cabin is the right word to describe this certain structure." The sheer size of the project blows me away.

"It has good bones, it is just super outdated. It is hard to describe the décor choices that my grandfather chose when he had the place built. Imagine the Brawny paper towel man asked Elmer Fudd for help decorating a serial killer's layer." Lara takes a drink from her Diet Pepsi like she did not just put me on visual overload with that description.

The waitress brings the food out, and Lara reaches for the ketchup and smothers her fries, then dives right into her food, "You're a mom, so you will understand the concept of eating a meal in peace is rare once you have kids. Eating, being asked to do something, or having your food snatched right off your plate, oh man, those were the days." Lara looks up to find me sitting, gobsmacked.

I clear my throat, "Sorry, the way you describe your cabin is visually intriguing. I have never been so interested in a project in my life. Is that why you asked if I was a serial killer, afraid I might relate to the cabin and not want to change anything?"

Lara busts out laughing, "I knew you were going to be fun the minute I saw you. No, that is not why I asked you. I was just hoping if I set the bar so low, you won't run away screaming when you see it in person."

At this point, my shock has morphed into sheer excitement at all the possibilities. "What is the budget for the project?" I always hate asking this question; this is usually where all the fun is dashed, and I have to be even more creative to make something work.

"No, budget. There is a lot of work that needs to be done. I am fully aware that we need to invest a large sum to bring it out of non-serial killer vibes."

"This cannot really be my life right now? What is the catch? A large open property that I can reimagine, and there is no budget."

Lara wipes her mouth, "Now that you bring up that small detail of a 'catch,' you might not like the next part that I am hoping you can accommodate."

And there it is; I try to hide my disappointment. I am hoping this is not a deal breaker, and I can still make this work. "Hit me, I am fairly flexible."

"I was hoping that you could start the project immediately."

Seriously, that is her concern, "That will be no problem. I am starting a new business here in Minnesota, so my schedule has not been filled out yet." Relieved that her catch was not a big deal.

"Oh, that is great news, one more thing…" She pauses, and I hate how long she pauses. "The cabin is not really in Little Falls."

"Where is it?"

"About two hours north of here."

"Not a deal breaker either. I just need to be creative with timing and order. I just need to consider my daughter."

Lara looks visibly relieved and lets out a breath that she apparently was holding. "I have no problem if you bring her up to the cabin with you whenever you want. That leads me to my last question: when can you get started?"

"When can I get keys to the property?"

Lara digs through her purse and produces a key ring with a bunch of keys on it. I can text you the garage code. I suggest going up on Friday and spending the weekend. You can get a feel for the space and how much red plaid you will need to burn to make the cabin not look like Elmer Fudd's fun house."

That sounds perfect! The best part is that Lara appears to be cool with Phoebe being with me. "Yes, that sounds perfect! I will send over the contract and bid for the project after I see the cabin and what might need to be done. Does that work for you?"

"Yay! I could hug you right now. I have a good feeling about you, Chloe! We are going to have so much fun working together."

"I know you said that it is mainly your family and your brother that stays at the cabin, are you expecting anyone else to be on site this weekend?"

"Nope, you will have it all to yourself. I can't wait to hear your ideas and talk design with you."

Now that the business side of this meeting seems to be resolved, I finally feel like I can breathe again. This project has the potential to jump-start my business. The cherry on top of this job is that Lara is so fun. I already feel like we have been friends for a lifetime, and we just met this morning. It is also nice to have another mom to talk kid stuff with. Lara has been filling me in on her twins, Zoey and Zeke, and I can't wait to meet them, they sound like a handful with all the mischief they get into. After we finish our meals and make plans to meet up after I visit the property this weekend, we say our goodbyes.

"I will email you directions to the cabin and instructions on where to park and everything you will need to know once you get there," Lara says as she throws her arms around me. She releases me from the hug but still has her hands on my arms. "I hate to tell you this, but I am afraid you are stuck with me. Even after the job is done, you are stuck with me. I will talk to you later, girl."

And just like that, she turns and hurries off to her car. Even the freezing wind that is slicing through me currently can't sour the high I am riding right now.

Chapter 10
Ralph

After the impromptu guy's night that I begrudgingly hosted at my house this weekend, only because they brought food, I realized I needed to check my attitude. I have always been the quiet, stern one of the group but even I can see I have been a giant jerk to everyone lately, and I need to work on that.

When I returned to work, I made a conscious effort to be less growly when approached by my staff, which took considerable effort on my part. Some of my officers are young, and the things that come out of their mouths are pure stupidity. One had the nerve to ask if I wanted to participate with them in a viral dance that has been taking the internet by storm. In all fairness, even if I were not working on being a giant grump at work, I still would have scowled at the request. What about me screams viral dance sensation in the making.

I brought a peace offering to Estelle. I knew that she would forgive any transgression if I brought her favorite coffee order and a breakfast scone to work. Which I was not wrong. Her face lit up when she saw me walking toward her desk carrying the loot.

"Sorry about last week, Estelle."

"Nothing to be sorry about, boss. Now hand over the goods. You have a busy morning ahead of you. I printed off your meetings for the day. I will be in there in a moment and we can go over the schedule."

And just like that, it is back to business as usual with Estelle. I really should address what she said about my dad and everything she brought up last week. I take the coward's way out, grunt my acknowledgment, and make my past her desk into my office. I might be willing to work on my grump levels, but unpacking family trauma, umm, no, thank you. I will gladly accept the pass.

I plop down in my chair and let out a deep breath. I scan over my schedule, annoyed by the number of meetings I will have to endure today. When I was a young boy and would daydream about becoming a police chief, never once did I think about attending so many meetings. My phone starts to ring. I pull it out of my pocket and notice my sister is calling. I send it to voicemail, instantly feeling bad. She has tried to call and text the past week and I haven't made time to get back to her.

Before I can feel too bad about sending her to voicemail, my phone dings with a text message. I open it to find my sister is now texting me. She is unusually relentless in her pursuit to check in with me. I need to remind her that I am the older brother and she does not need to check in on me. I click open my messages.

Lara: Please call me back! It is an emergency!!

Panic sets in. My mind goes straight to the worst-case scenario. Something happened to my grandparents or something to the twins that rained havoc on my sister's life. I call her before going down too many rabbit holes. She picks up after the first ring.

"It is about time, big brother." She sounds annoyed at me, which feels better than scared or upset by an emergency.

"What happened? Is everyone alright?" I bark out, I am blaming the fear of something being wrong for my current tone.

"Of course, everyone is alright. It is a little early in the day for you to be this cranky already."

"Seriously, Lara? What is the emergency."

"Well, maybe that specific word was not the best word to use in my text. Oops, my bad."

I chant in my head over and over again that 'I will not kill my sister.' I take a deep breath, trying to find my cool and lower my blood pressure that just shot through the roof, "What would you say would be the right word to use instead of emergency? Just to clarify Gramps and Nana are okay? What about Zoey and Zeke? They're alright?"

"Yes, yes, calm down, Chief. The old people are happy and warmer than we are currently. I spoke with Nana last week, and they had a spa retreat planned." Lara lets out a laugh, "Can you imagine Gramps in a spa being doted on? I would pay good money to see that."

She is not wrong. It is hard to picture my grandfather in a spa. I take after my grandfather the most. He was always across with a gruff exterior but there is no better man out there. "As much as I have enjoyed this near heart attack, is there a purpose to all the calls and text messages?"

"Big brother, you understand that ignoring multiple attempts from someone trying to contact you can be seen as rude, right?"

"Lara, I am swamped at work. Any chance you can cut to the chase and tell me what you want? You can save the lesson on manners for another time."

"Wow, okay, so extra grumpy today. I thought you would be in a good mood with the possibility of love on the horizon."

"What are you talking…" I stop before finishing. I know exactly what she is referring to. That stupid poster that is plastered all over town.

"There is no shame in needing a little help in the love department. I already convinced Jack to take me to the fundraiser so I can have a front-row seat to you finding the love of your life."

I need to get this conversation over with as soon as possible, so arguing about the freaking auction will get me nowhere. "I need you to focus, Lara. What did you need when you called me this morning."

"Ugh, you're no fun, you know that right?"

"I get that a lot."

"Oh, fine, be that way. When I spoke with Gramps and Nana last week, the cabin might have come up in the conversation."

"What about the cabin?" I do not like where this is going already.

"Well, it is time, Ralphie. Gramps gave his approval that I could hire someone to remodel the entire cabin. Give it a fresh look, you might say."

She knows I hate when she calls me 'Ralphie,' but I am not going to let that derail me from what she is trying to gloss over. "Lara, we have been over this. The cabin is perfect, and there is no point in throwing money at renovating it. It is already perfect."

"Right, perfectly outdated. What is your problem with a refresh? Any time I have brought this up, you shoot me down."

"Is that why you went behind my back and asked Gramps?"

"Ralphie, you are literally growling at me over a simple small project. I bet you don't even realize half the changes made."

"So are we talking about changing bed linen and a new couch or something else?"

"Okay, yeah, definitely something else on top of what you mentioned. The entire cabin is outdated and screams Elmer Fudd."

"NO way! Gramps designed the cabin. It is a classic. It would never go out of style." I am not sure I could even say what is in style and what is not. All I do know is I love the cabin the way it is and hate change. "Plus, you are so busy with the twins. How do you intend to get this done?" It is a hail mary bringing the twins into this. Those two will either rule the world one day or lead prison gangs. The jury is still out.

"That is why I said I hired someone for the job."

"No, you said he approved to hire someone not that you already did hire someone." There is a headache forming behind my eyes. Thank you, Lara, for that.

"You really are a stickler for details. So in my defense, I have been trying to get ahold of you, and you were not responding back. I set up and interviewed already this week. And save your breath, and I already hired her. The best part is she can start right away, and I am fairly certain we are on our way to being best friends."

Cripes, my sister, is insane. "Lara, you can't just hire someone like that."

"Sure, I can. And I did hire her."

"What about background checks? You should have called me to help you with this. And it is seriously unprofessional to be best friends with someone you are hiring to complete a job for you."

"I am not an idiot, big brother. I asked her if she was a serial killer, she said no. Good enough for me."

"Cripes, you are killing me? How are we related?"

"Not sure. All I know is I have all the fun genes, and you have none. Okay, this has been fun to catch up, but it just dawned on me I haven't heard the twins in the past five minutes, I need to go check for the next disaster. Love you, Ralphie. And don't pout too much about the cabin. You are going to love it." Before I can get my rebuttal in she disconnects the call.

I just sit there staring at my phone. My sister is a whirlwind of chaos to my constant order. We really are complete opposites. Maybe I am worrying about nothing, I bet the designer walks in and sees that the cabin is already near perfect and suggests little changes be made.

Estelle walks into my office with a notepad and pen in hand. "What is that look on your face? What have you been thinking so hard?"

I look up to see an amused look on Estelle's face. "Just got off the phone with Lara. She is up to no good again."

"Oh, that child is fun, and you know it. What is Lara scheming about now?"

"That is a great way to put it. Scheming! She has been bugging me about wanting to renovate the cabin for months. She was not impressed with my lack of response to her, so she went straight to Gramps. Needless to say, she got what she wanted. That man could never tell her no."

"Hate to break it to you, but he never tells you no either." No matter how true that statement might be, it is different with me. I never ask for stupid things like a cabin remodel on a perfectly good cabin.

"What is the big deal with remodeling the cabin? It's all original from when your grandfather had it built, correct?"

"Correct, it is classic. Never goes out of style."

Estelle barks out a huge laugh before slapping her hand over her mouth. "Sorry, boss. I am sure it is classic." Then, under her breath, she mumbles, "a classic hot mess."

I just glare at her. I really want to say something but think better of it. I already had to bring in an apology breakfast once this week.

"Boss, can I give you a little advice?"

"Can I stop you?"

"Probably not. Let Lara worry about the cabin. You have a lot on your plate, and more is constantly being added. I know you hate change, but maybe something good will come out of the remodel. A fresh coat of paint and a few changes here and there are not going to change the memories that you have made there."

Dang it, why did she have to go and be logical about it? She makes some valid points, but it doesn't stop me from worrying about all the changes that could be made.

"Clearly, by the look on your face, you are not going to take my advice. How about this: before the remodel starts, you should go up this weekend and spend some time. You have been working so hard the past few months. The time off will do wonders for your mood as an added bonus for all of us who work for you," she mumbles the last part.

"You might be onto something, Estelle. Do you think you could rearrange my schedule so I can leave on Friday morning? I will be gone all weekend." The thought of an entire weekend of peace and quiet sounds too good to be true.

"Boss, I am hurt that you even have to ask me that. Where is your faith in my abilities? I can re-work your schedule with no problem at all." Estelle acts all put out by the thought that she is not capable of doing the simple task of reworking my schedule. She proceeds to sit in the chair across from my desk and begins to rattle off tasks that need my attention.

I sit back in my chair as Estelle proceeds to go over my schedule for the day. I should be paying attention to her but the thought of an uninterrupted weekend has a hold on me.

Chapter 11
Chloe

As with most things in my life, nothing has gone the way I planned it to go. I spent all last night packing for our weekend away. A simple weekend away is not so simple when I have to also pack for a toddler, whose packing list is twice as long as me. For being so small her needs are great. I also had to pack up a work bag, seeing this is technically a work trip. I pack up all my design books, camera, and laptop. I am hoping I can get a lot of work done between Phoebe's naps and after I put her to bed at night.

I thought I had plenty of time and was taking my sweet time getting up this morning. The complication came when Betty so nicely brought up that there was a storm system moving into the area. I am not sure I will ever get used to having to check weather systems before leaving the house. So now I am sitting at the table, worried that Mother Nature is plotting to kill me. Is that dramatic? Sure, but very likely accurate?

"If you leave soon, you will miss the storm. It is not supposed to roll until this afternoon." Betty is trying to calm my nerves.

"Are you sure? We both know that my winter driving is subpar at best."

"Child, trust me. You have a window of clear roads. There is nothing to worry about." She is so calm as she dips her donut in her morning coffee. The coffee is more like sugar with a splash of coffee. I am starting to wonder how often this woman has her blood sugars tested.

"Okay, I will do it. Do you mind watching Phoebe while I finish loading the car?" I stand and clear the breakfast dishes from the table and move them to the sink. Phoebe is happily playing with toys that are scattered across her high chair tray.

"You never need to ask. This child is a straight angel. It will always be a yes."

I hurry and bundle myself. All our bags are by the front door so loading the car goes quicker than I expected. The freezing temperatures are a great motivator to not "dilly-dally," as Betty would put it. I should be more concerned by all the geriatric lingo that I have been incorporating into my daily vocab but that seems like a problem for future Chloe.

I return inside, grab Phoebe, and bundle her up. "Okay, I will call you when we get to the cabin. Don't expect us to be home until Sunday evening. Are you sure you don't need anything before you leave?"

"No, I will be fine. It is going to be too quiet with you two gone. I was thinking of having some friends over, you know, a quiet gathering."

I lean in and give Betty a hug, "Don't do anything I wouldn't do. Try and stay out of trouble."

"No offense, child, but you are fairly vanilla in the big scheme of life. Your list of things you do is probably shorter than mine. I will take that under advisement about trying to be good, though. Now get out of here and drive safe." Betty is practically shoving us out the door. There is a tiny voice in the back corner of my mind saying I should ask more questions about her weekend plans. Ultimately, I push the nagging voice aside because the worry of running into bad roads wins out.

We have been driving for a little more than an hour. I would be hard-pressed to admit this out loud to anyone, but the drive has been so beautiful. It would be hard to explain my thoughts on how I call it a frozen wasteland one moment and beautiful the next. The landscape is so different here in comparison to Arizona, where everything is brown year-round.

The roads are clear, and the sun is shining with clear blue skies. Maybe the weather guy got it wrong. There is not one storm cloud in sight. Phoebe babbled for the first part of the drive but drifted off to sleep a few minutes ago. I turn the radio on low to enjoy the remainder of the drive.

My GPS alerts me that my turn is coming up. I slow down and turn off the main road. I start to drive down a long gravel road noticing that it would not be big enough for more than one car at a time. I am starting to get worried that I took a wrong turn. There is nothing out here but trees. I am about to give up and head back toward the main road when the trees part, and I drive up on what Lara so ineptly describes as a cabin. I put my car in park and marvel at the structure before me. This is in no way a cabin. The building before me could easily be described as a mountain resort, and this place is huge.

I reach over to grab my work bag. I start to dig through it, searching for the instructions on how to get into the resort. Lara instructed me to drive to the left of the front door, and I could park my car in those garage bays. I shake my head that there is more than one option to park my car. I pull around the left side and find three garage doors. I jumped out and put in the code that Lara had given me. I hurry and, jump back into my car and pull into the garage. As soon as the car is pulled in, I get back out and close the door to keep the heat from escaping.

Lara had told me that she could remotely adjust the temperature on her phone through an app. She had planned to crank the heat that morning in anticipation of our arrival. It is the only upgrade that has ever been done to the place. I have never been as grateful for modern touches as I am right now. I glance in the back and see Phoebe is still sound asleep. I hurry and bring all our bags, as well as all the essential baby gear needed for the weekend inside, and drop them by the door.

Phoebe starts to stir as I finish with the last bag. I lean into the back seat and start to unbuckle her from her car seat harness. "Did you have a good nap, my sweet girl?"

Phoebe is generally a happy baby but especially after a nap, she is all smiles and giggles. "Mama, mama, mama…". Why does my daughter calling me 'mama' melt my heart every time?

"Okay, should we go explore the cabin that looks bigger than the first apartment complex Mama ever lived in?"

All I get is more giggles and smiles to my question. The entryway is cluttered with all the stuff, but I need to explore before I know where to bring all our stuff. Lara was not specific on what room we should stay in. As I walk further down the hallway, it opens up in what can only be described as the great room. I probably look like an idiot as I am standing there with my mouth open.

My eyes fly around the room. One side of the room is the kitchen.
There is a giant island that I am guessing is bigger and longer than the
bed I sleep in. Lara was right about the place having good bones. My
mind is already going in a million different directions of possible
updates for the space.

On the opposite side of the room is a giant stone fireplace that
covers the distance from the floor to the ceiling. The fireplace belongs
in a resort check-in area, not a family cabin. It is an impressive feature
in the room. I started to think of how it would look if it was decorated
for the holidays. My thoughts are interrupted when Phoebe starts to
moo. She is getting more and more loud in her moo calls.

She is now adamantly pointing while moo-ing. I look in the
direction that she is pointing to find the biggest moose I have ever seen
mounted on the wall. The monstrosity startles me, and I jump back
like it was going to come at us. Grateful no one was there to witness
my momentary lapse in sanity. "Sweet girl, what do you think are the
chances that can be the first thing to go bye-bye?" She just continues
to moo. I have no idea what sound a moose makes so I chose not to
correct her right now.

As we continue on with our tour, we come across multiple
bedrooms and bathrooms. There is one room that I am assuming is
being used for the twins. There are bunk beds on the far wall and totes
filled with kid-oriented items. Every time I thought I'd reached the
end and seen everything there was to see, another hallway would
appear, leading to even more exploration. I can't help but laugh out
loud at the thought of this family calling this place a cabin—how could
anyone consider it that?

Feeling a little overwhelmed by all the choices in where we will be sleeping, I finally pick the first one I come across that has a bathroom attached. I start with the daunting task of bringing all our stuff into the room. I start with the playpen and set it up first. Phoebe is more than happy to be set down in the playpen with lots of toys to occupy her as I make trips back in forth to gather the rest of our stuff.

What felt like a million trips later I had all the items we brought in our room.

I am really excited at this point that I was smart enough to pack groceries from home, so I didn't need to venture into town when I got here. I hurriedly put all the food away before heading back to grab Phoebe. As I walk the hallways, I am mentally making lists of any and all areas that would benefit from a refresh. I hope that Lara meant what she said about the unlimited budget. The possibilities are endless with the space that they gave me to work with.

The growling that comes from my stomach is loud enough that it catches Phoebe's attention, and she starts to growl. I feel like I have said this about every new stage she enters, but I love the animal stage, where she can relate anything to a new animal sound. I reach her over the side of the playpen and pick her up.

"What do you say we find some lunch, sweet girl?" I halfway expect her to answer me when I ask her questions. Instead, she just smiles up at me as if I am the most important person in the world. We make our way back to the kitchen. With the many trips back in forth, I am finally starting to get my bearing and not feel so overwhelmed by the space.

I decided not to pack the highchair, and I am regretting that choice right now. Phoebe is sitting in my lap, and Miss Little Independent, who has to feed herself, has more food covering us than she was able to get into her mouth.

I grabbed a notebook in hopes of jotting notes to organize my thoughts. The pressure I am putting on myself to make this a success is unreal. I put the pen down and take a deep breath. I look down at my daughter, who is perfectly content and happy. I need to take a page out of my daughter's playbook and learn to enjoy life more. I look up, and through the giant window above the kitchen window, I can see snowflakes gently falling to the earth.

"Look, Phoebe. It is snowing." I stand and brush the food onto the floor, resolved to the fact that I will clean it up later. We walk over to the window to take in the winter wonderland unfolding outside. The look on her face is a mixture of being confused and in awe. I decided right then and there that my daughter needed to learn to build a snowman. Not that growing up in Arizona has made me an expert in this area, but I still really want to make some memories together. I hurry to clean up the lunch mess. Then, it is time to embark on the task of layering to brave the weather, which feels like an eternity later, and we are finally ready to head outside. The look on my daughter's face makes all the effort worth it to see her smile.

Hours later, we are returning inside as frozen popsicles. I will be the first to admit my snowman-making skills are less than stellar, but we still had fun. There is a trail that winds down to a giant lake that has iced over for the winter. I lost track of time and didn't realize how much time had gone by since we first went outside. I strip our wet winter gear off on the tile entryway. I hurry back to our room and start the water for Phoebe. I could tell that the cold temperatures zapped her energy, and I had limited time before we entered the land of meltdowns. She looked as if, given the chance, she would fall asleep in the bath sitting up. I grab her out and snuggle her in an oversized towel. I barely have her diaper on and zipping her fleece pajamas up before she falls asleep sprawled out on my bed. I clear all the toys out of her playpen and place Phoebe in the playpen. She is out cold, but I still place her favorite yellow duck by her in case she wakes up.

I head back into the bathroom in hopes that there is still hot water left so I can warm up, myself. The sight of my reflection stops me cold in my tracks. I am horrified at the person staring back at me. Hot mess would be a kind definition of my current state. The drowned rat look is complete when I notice some of Phoebe's lunch stuck in my hair. It would be a good thing I have sworn off men at this point in my life. I am not winning any beauty contests in the near future.

I hurry and jump in the shower with the thought that I will quickly wash and condition my hair, but the hot water is doing a real number on my sore muscles and chilled bones. So I end up standing there longer, letting the water run over me. I notice a container of men's body wash in the corner of the shower. I know Lara told me that no room was off limits, but I still don't want to be intruding in there space. I am now wondering if I hijacked Lara and her husband's room when they came up to stay. I decide that I am wasting valuable time standing here when I should be working while Phoebe sleeps.

I reach for the towel and wrap myself up tightly. I grab another towel to wrap up my hair. I really do love my hair most days but sometimes it would be nice to know what it would be like to have hair that was easier to maintain. I open the bathroom door, and a puff of steam follows me. I look over and see that Phoebe has not moved a muscle since I laid her down.

I move to my suitcase to grab some clean clothes when the lights flicker on and off. I really do not want to deal with a power outage right now. Worried that the weather is going to be a problem after all, I go to check the weather app Betty insisted I install if I was going to call Minnesota home. I didn't have the heart to tell her that the jury is still out on whether Minnesota is home or not. I look everywhere and can't find my phone. I realize I must have left it in the kitchen after I had cleaned up lunch. I give one more glance and my sleeping baby and go in search of my phone.

Chapter 12
Ralph

Nothing about this day has gone the way it was supposed to. The plan was for me to have nothing on my schedule, leave first thing this morning for the cabin.

That was wishful thinking on my part. Estelle was successful in clearing my schedule, but that didn't stop the Mayor from requesting my presence at an emergency meeting in his office. He wanted to discuss the fundraiser and what efforts I had made to make it even more successful than the Fireman's Ball.

It should have been a short meeting. How long does it take to inform him I have done nothing to boost support for the event, but he was not having it. He turned what should have been a ten-minute into a two-hour meeting. He called the Sheriff and asked him to come to his office for the impromptu meeting.

The Sherriff has about fifth teen years on me and is happily married to a great woman. All that said, he gets a pass on this torturous event. He still found enjoyment in me squirming in my chair every time the mayor brought up ideas to increase female involvement. "What is the big deal, Ralph? A young, pretty girl bids on you, and you get a night out on the town. It seems like a win-win to me." He can barely control the laugh that was threatening to escape.

"Easy for you to say. You are not the one that will have to stand up on stage like a piece of meat and have some crazy woman bid on you to live out some misguided fantasy she has." I huff out an annoyed breath as I cross my arms over my chest.

"Listen, Boswell, if you had a girlfriend, you would be excluded from the event, but seeing you are single, you have a responsibility to be a good example to other younger officers who are also single." The mayor actually believes this bull he is shoveling. I want to argue with him about what my actual responsibility is, but the desire to get on the road is stronger than arguing in circles with this man.

The meeting finally concluded, and I jumped in my truck, not wanting another delay to prevent me from leaving town. As my truck was warming up, I pulled up the weather app and realized my window to get to the cabin was narrowing with the huge storm that was expected to hit this afternoon. As I was looking at the satellite maps on the projected path the storm was supposed to take, my phone buzzed with a text notification from Bubba. I tap the messages, knowing it is better just to answer him.

Bubba: Hey, anyone want to hang out tonight?

Henry: I could be available if for the right price.

Max: Are we allowed to bring a plus one?

Bubba: Max, you are killing me. You cannot refer to your fiancé, who, by the way, is our friend too, as a plus one.

Max: I actually thought it was a creative way to say I am in if the girls are in.

Harrison: I hate to have this in writing, but I agree with Max. I haven't seen Ginger very much lately, and she is available to hang out tonight.

Henry: You boys are truly pathetic. You are both a cautionary tale about what happens to a man when he falls on his face in love with a girl. Not going to lie; not pretty.

Max: Yeah, yeah, don't care. Take my man card. Can the girls come or not?

Bubba: I don't care who shows up. I was just craving some wings and thought the Moose would be fun tonight.

Noah: Hey, chief why so quiet? What say you?

As I read their rapid-fire texts that are flying back in forth, I start to wonder how are any of these guys considered responsible, productive members of the community with they spend so much time arguing over text messages. I decided to answer them so I could get my weekend plans back on track.

Me: Sorry, count me out this weekend. I have a rare weekend off and I am going up to the cabin for some relaxation.

Noah: Why is this the first time we are hearing about this?

Harrison: Seriously, dude, you know I love that cabin.

Henry: I think my invite to go with you this weekend got lost somewhere in the text thread.

Bubba: Should we pack and come with you?

Me: Umm, that is a hard pass for me. My overbearing little sister hired someone to renovate the cabin, and I am going to have one last weekend before it is turned into some preppy hipster place.

Max: Interesting…you are going to your family cabin this weekend. To stay. The entire weekend?

Me: You are really painting the complete concept for the group, Max. I don't have time to continue this never-ending banter or wonder why you are being weird. Bad weather is moving in, and I need to get going before it is too late. Have fun this weekend, and stay out of trouble. I have a new rookie training this weekend and I don't want you causing trouble for him.

Bubba: Yes, Dad, we will be on our best behavior.

Henry: Drive safe.

Harrison: So we can bring our girls tonight, right?

I click out of my messages, knowing that they could go on forever with random jabs at each other. I am finally heading out of town toward the highway. I have done this drive so many times in my lifetime that it feels ingrained in my DNA. I click through the stations until I land on a country station. The constant supply of music and the familiar drive helps to clear my mind. All the stress from the morning meeting with the mayor is melting away as well. This is exactly what I needed. This escape will help me get out of my funk and recharge my battery.

I make a quick stop at the local market for some provisions in case the bad weather does hit with the force they are projecting. I then make my way to the cabin. When I make it to the end of the gravel drive and the trees clear, I am greeted with my favorite view. Some of my favorite childhood memories have been made at this place.

I immediately notice that there are lights on inside. A loud groan escapes me. The thought that my sister had the same idea I did, and brought her family up to enjoy the cabin this weekend almost causes me to turn around and head home. Don't get me wrong, I love my sister, and her husband is a great guy who qualifies for sainthood for taking on my sister. I would even say I love her twins, but any hope of a quiet, restful weekend is quickly slipping away.

I turn right and pull into the garage. I decide I will at least go inside and say hello before I decide if I should head back to Little Falls. The storm that has picked up in intensity might be the reason I have to stay.

When I head inside, the cabin is eerily quiet. Too quiet for my sister and the twins to be here. I head into the kitchen and find that I have lost my ability to speak and think rationally; all manners are thrown out the window while I stand there. That isn't true, and I think a growl does escape.

In the kitchen, standing at the island in only a towel wrapped around her and a towel wrapped around her hair, the girl who has been playing on repeat in my brain – Chloe.

She whips around, obviously startled by the growling caveman who snuck up on her. She lets out a high-pitched scream and chucks something at my head. Before I can move out of the path of the flying object it strikes me almost square between the eyes. If pain wasn't radiating through my skull, I would have been impressed with her accuracy in her throwing arm. She continues to scream as she scurries backward with her hands up.

"Princess, stop! It is me, Ralph." I throw my hands up, trying to calm her down.

"Officer McHottie? Is that you? Why are you here? Are you following me? This is breaking and entering. I can call the police. Or maybe this is stalking? Either way, you need to leave." She was rambling so fast that I almost missed that she called me Officer Mc Hottie. As much as I want to call her out on that, we might have more pressing issues to address.

"Listen, Princess," My hands are still raised hoping she will calm down. "I am not one who broke in. This is my family cabin. So if you call the police, they might be a little confused what laws have been broken,"

"This is not your cabin! This is the Smith family cabin. They hired me to help redesign and update the space for them." I can see that she is starting to calm down, believing I mean no harm to her, but she still looks confused.

"Princess, this cabin is the Boswell family cabin. My sister married into the Smith family. I am assuming it was Lara who hired you?" I am trying to keep my voice calm and even tone, which is quite a feat seeing I am five seconds from freaking out myself. What are the chances that the one woman I vowed to stay away from and cannot stop thinking about is standing in front of me half-naked?

Oh, crap, she is half-naked. I instantly throw my hands up to cover my eyes. I want to say it was a manly gesture of a gentleman, but I am certain it came off as a small child afraid to get into trouble.

"I am such an idiot. I never even considered Smith as her married name. What a freaking rookie move."

"Honest mistake could have happened to anyone," it comes out muffled behind my hands.

"Ralph, what in the world are you doing? Why are you covering your eyes?"

I have my eyes clenched tight as I remove one hand and gesture toward her body. Even with my eyes closed, I can hear the exact moment she realizes that she is standing in my kitchen, only wearing a towel. A dramatic gasp and feet are scurrying down the hallway.

I continue to stand like a fool, covering his eyes unsure what the right thing to do next. I slowly lower my hands to my sides. I crack my eyes, and I am right. She is no longer standing in the kitchen.

I start to pace with nervous energy, not sure what to expect when she comes back out here. I am about to give up hope that she will ever come out of hiding when she emerges. I am not sure what she is wearing now is any better than the towel. She is grasping her hands together nervously. She has not moved any closer than the door frame that leads into the family room. She looks almost more tempting in her black leggings that hug all her curves perfectly, with an oversized sweater that falls off her shoulder.

"I am sorry…"

"Sorry to…". We both speak at the same time which helps to break the tension in the room. I let out a chuckle.

"I am so sorry for walking around dressed like that. I didn't realize anyone else was coming up this weekend. Lara told me that I would have the place to myself to work on some design options for her." Chloe's voice is soft timid, and I hate it. Where did my powerhouse of a woman go?

"Well, as long as we are apologizing, I am sorry that I scared you. I didn't think to share my weekend plans with my sister." There is a moment of silence as we just stare at each other. I am fine continuing to stand here all night if this is going to be my view. Chloe cracks first, though.

"Ok then, give me a few minutes to pack up all my stuff, and I will head back to Little Falls. I don't want to interrupt your weekend plans."

"That is not happening, Princess."

"And why not?" She is close to whining about her frustration at my matter-of-fact attitude.

I want to be a real caveman jerk and tell her because I said so, but think better of it. "Princess, have you looked outside recently?"

"Of course, I have looked outside. It is just a little snow, not a big deal." A little fire is returning to my girl as she places her hand on her hip and moves toward the window. She turns her face away to look outside. I can see the moment she realizes that leaving is not an option. "The snow is really coming down. The changed fast." She seems defeated by the realization that there is no escape from the awkwardness that this weekend just turned into.

I am trying to rack my brain for something to say to put her at ease. I am drawing a blank. This is not my area. I am not the one in the group that goes into a new situation with jokes or reassurance. I am the stern, grumpy old guy. For the first time in my life, I wish I had some of those other skills to help soothe Chloe.

Out of nowhere, we are interrupted by a shrill cry from the back hallway in the direction of my room.

"What is that," I recognize the slight panic in my voice.

"Seriously? I thought you were the Chief of Police. What kind of investigator skills do you have when you can't recognize the sound of a baby?"

"A baby? Where did the baby come from?" No slight sound of panic now; it is full-blown.

"Ralph, I do not have time to explain to you where babies come from right now. My daughter just woke up in a new place and sounds scared, so me helping her trumps your questions right now." As she is putting me in my place, she is quickly moving toward the sound of crying before disappearing down the hall.

I am back to pacing. A baby? What in the world? Did I know that my dream girl had a baby? Where is the father? I stop pacing at the moment, instant dread hitting me, the feeling like a bucket of ice water was dumped on me.

All I can think about is whether or not I kissed a married woman on New Year's Eve. What did I do? I have spent my entire life since learning the devastating truth that my dad was an adulterous dirt bag that I never wanted to be him. I made decisions in my life that I felt would be the opposite of what my father would choose. I never wanted to have anything in common with that man.

Except that night, the night I kissed her without any thought of consequences. That is exactly something he would do. I am not sure how long I pace back in forth, spiraling out in my thoughts before Chloe reemerges, but this time, there is the most perfect tiny mini version of Chloe on her hip. The little girl has red hair that has the same wild curl her mother has, only the child's hair is considerably shorter than Chloe's. Tucked under her arm is a yellow stuffed duck that looks well-loved.

Manners dictate that I should probably say something, but what? I am sorry that I kissed you. I had no idea that you were a married woman, or sorry if I ever made you uncomfortable. The child breaks through the silence first before I can apologize for my behavior.

"Grrr. Grrrr," Chloe's tiny mini-me puts her pudgy hand up and curls her fingers like she is making a clawing movement, I think. "Mama, Grr Grr."

Chloe bursts out loud with a laugh that her daughter finds amusing and starts to giggle along with her. I, on the other hand, am lost and have no idea to translate baby talk.

Chloe adjusts the little girl in her arms so she can look at her better, "Yes, sweetie, I agree with you. Grr."

Now Chloe is making a growling sound. I am totally lost at this point. Chloe takes pity on me and explains. "Sorry, Ralph. You will have to forgive Phoebe. She is currently in her animal phase. She associates everything with animal sounds that she is learning."

"Not sure I need a child calling me out for being a grumpy bear, too." I am not annoyed at all, though. Not sure anyone could be mad at Phoebe when she smiles up at you like she is currently smiling at me.

Chloe moves closer to where I am standing. "I think you are giving my darling girl too much credit. We have been obsessed with this princess movie lately that has been playing on repeat, Phoebe can't get enough of it. It stars a princess with wild red hair like us. There are also bears in the movie. I think your beard is reminding her of the bears."

I move closer to them until I am standing right in front of them. I am notably taller than Chloe, making it so I tower over her and Phoebe. Phoebe does not seem bothered by it at all. She starts to growl at me more in between her giggles. Whoever the man is that gets to call these two his, is a lucky man.

I bend down so I am at eye level with Phoebe. "It's nice to meet you, little lady."

Phoebe lunges for me, and I grab onto her with ease. Chloe seems surprised that her daughter so willingly came to me. I hear Chloe mumble under her breath something about being a traitor.

Phoebe is securely in my arms when she reaches for my beard and runs those pudgy hands over my beard. Then growls again. I have never seen myself having children or even really wanting them. I love being the fun uncle to the twins. I even love sneaking a snuggle or two from Noah's kid, Lola. Holding Phoebe as she growls at me with her over-the-top serious expression, I can't help but wonder if I was wrong to close that door so adamantly.

"Ralph, what are we going to do?"

Still staring at Phoebe, I reply to her mother, "Do about what?"

"As much as it pains me, you might be right. I don't think I can drive in this weather. I don't think it would be safe."

"Hold on, let me pull out my phone."

"Why do you need your phone?" Chloe asks, confused about how my phone will be the solution we need.

"I want to record you saying I am right. I doubt you will be willing to admit to that down the road." I say it straight-faced.

Chloe hesitates for a moment before she playfully attempts to shove me. She is a little thing and has no chance of budging me. "You jerk, did you just make a joke? I didn't know you had it in you." Chloe smiles up at me, and I like it way more than I should.

Phoebe continues to be fascinated with my beard as I turn my attention to Chloe. "I know this is not ideal, but we are limited on options. This storm is not showing any signs of letting up. The closest motel is not close enough to brave on these roads." Chloe starts to worry her bottom lip at the thought of being trapped here with me. "Listen, the cabin is big enough for the three of us for one night. I will stay out of your way, and you won't even know I am here. I don't want to make you uncomfortable; I just want to make sure you and Phoebe stay safe." The words I told her were true. I just want them safe. I hate that I want to be the one who is tasked with protecting them, and at the end of the day, that is not right.

"Ralph, can I ask you something?" Chloe looks back up at me.

"Sure," I am hesitant, not knowing which direction she is headed toward.

"Does your family really call this place a cabin?" She uses air quotes when she says cabin.

"Princess, what are you saying about my humble abode? I would be hard-pressed to find a different word to describe this cozy cabin." I look around, trying to see what she sees.

A laugh escaped, and then another, and before I knew what was happening, she was full-on belly laughing. At one point, she is bent over bracing her hands on her knees, trying to catch her breath. Through her laughs, she gasps out words like "cozy" more laughing and "hard pressed" insert more laughing. Even Phoebe is amused by her mother's laughing and she joins in with tiny baby girl screeches and giggles.

As the laughing starts to die down and the girls start to compose themselves, I find an opening to speak, "You wound me, Princess. How would you describe this place?" Not at all offended or wounded.

The complete opposite in fact, enjoying every moment of the interaction.

Without skipping a beat, "How about a mountain resort, a rustic palace fit for a king, or I even considered it could be a movie set. Granted, the movie would have to be going for an outdated, old-person vibe to make it work. Your sister was onto something when she described the design as an Elmer Fudd original with serial killer aspects highlighted throughout."

Before I can think of a reply to her insane thoughts on one of my favorite places on earth, Phoebe tugs hard on my beard, grabbing my immediate attention. "Ouch, little lady. Don't you know you should be nice to the big, bad bear," I growl while tickling her belly. Phoebe is distracted and clinging to her duck for dear life as she is laughing.

"Eekk, sorry about that. She is probably hungry. Do you mind if I make her some food? I will be quick, and then we will make ourselves scared the rest of the evening so you can have some peace and quiet." Chloe is reaching to take Phoebe out of my arms.

That is what I wanted when I made plans to come up here this weekend, wasn't it? The whole weekend to be alone and recharge and reset. But the thought of them hiding out and not hearing Phoebe giggle or hear the ridiculous things that come out of Chloes' mouth is not working for me. I jerk Phoebe back out of the grasp of Chloe, causing Phoebe to burst into another fit of giggles, probably thinking we are playing a new game. Chloe looks confused at my refusal to hand over her baby over, quite frankly, I am not sure what I am doing either at this point. "Or I have a better idea."

Chloe folds her arms over her chest and pops her hip out, "I am listening."

"How about we all make dinner together? There is no need for you to hide out in your room all night." I can see that Chloe is torn about which option to choose. It occurs to me that maybe she is worried about what her husband will think about her spending time alone in a cabin with a man who is not her husband. I want to reassure her that my intentions are nothing but honorable, but she speaks first.

"If you are sure, you don't mind us crashing your quiet evening?"

"I don't mind at all." Relieved that she is not worried about spending time alone with me, we move toward the kitchen. "What can I help with to get this little one fed." I tickle Phoebe's belly lightly, but the results are the same: the giggles start all over again.

"Do you mind holding Phoebe and I will get dinner ready? I brought my homemade chicken pot pie with us. While it warms up, I had planned to make a salad to go with it. Does that work for you?"

"Seeing I was going to open a can of chili for dinner, your option definitely sounds like the better choice. I don't mind holding on to this little troublemaker. It will be a hardship holding her, though, but I will try to endure somehow." I pull the stool out from the island and sit down. I sit Phoebe down on the island while keeping a death grip on her so she doesn't fall.

Chloe has a weird look plastered on her face. I start to worry that I am holding Phoebe wrong. Chloe then shakes her head and moves toward the fridge to grab the items she needs. "Have you always been this good with kids? I bet your niece and nephew love their uncle Ralph."

"I know you will be shocked by this confession, but most kids are scared of me. I don't know why I am so approachable today." I look up and give her the biggest, cheesiest, over-the-top smile.

Chloe shakes her head at my antics and continues to work on the salad. She grabs a container that has a baby on it and rounds the island toward us. She pops open the container and pours out some type of puff cereal onto the counter. Phoebe doesn't waste any time grabbing a handful of them and thrusting her fist in her mouth.

"That should keep her occupied until dinner is ready."

I am so distracted watching Chloe turn and walk back around the island that I miss Phoebe grabbing another fist full of puffs. Except this time, Phoebe takes my momentary distraction as an opportunity to shove her pudgy fist in my mouth. The amount of baby slime that was already covering her hand mixed with the remnants of the puffs left behind from her bite is now covering my lips, and sadly, some of the goo mixture made it into my mouth.

Phoebe looks so pleased with herself for sharing her beloved snack she is all smiles as she starts to babble. I can pick out certain words. She has 'mama' down pat. She also likes saying 'GRRR' randomly. "Thank you, little lady, for sharing with me." I have no idea what I am supposed to say to her or how to respond to this tiny human appropriately. I take the back of my hand and try to wipe off as much goo as possible when I notice Chloe watching the interactions with wide eyes.

"What? Did I say something wrong to her?"

"Nope," she pops the 'p' with extra emphasis before turning back around to dish the food up.

Chapter 13
Chloe

How is this my life right now? How is it possible that out of all the guys in the world, Ralph is the brother of my very important first client? I need this job to help build my business. I want to die a thousand deaths every time I replay him walking into the kitchen and getting my phone thrown at his head. Or me, not even realizing I am standing there yelling at him naked, wrapped in a towel. Yep, how is this my life?

The most surprising part is how he is with Phoebe. I have to make a conscious effort not to let my ovaries explode when I watch them interact with each other. Phoebe tends to be a little more reserved or shy around new people, but that is not the case with Ralph. It was love at first sight for her. I can't really blame her. I am starting to think that there is so much. More to my favorite Officer McHottie than first meets the eye.

I happened to turn around right as Phoebe shoved her goober-covered hand into the direction of Ralph's mouth. The look of horror the crosses Ralph's face threatens to break me into laughter again, but I recover in time to watch how he patiently wipes her hand and talks sweetly to her about sharing. If my ovaries hadn't exploded earlier, they would have with this interaction. He notices me watching them.

He looks nervous when he asks, "What? Did I say something wrong to her?"

"Nope," is all I can manage before turning around. This man was already a huge temptation for me, but if you add in the way he is with my daughter, there is no chance I will survive him. I hurry to plate the warmed leftovers as a distraction from the inner turmoil that I am battling.

I pick up the plates and turn back toward the island. I put the plates down on the island, a safe distance from Phoebe's grasp. I grab her duck and throw it out of the way. Phoebe does not love that move and lets out an overly dramatic wail to voice her discontent. She loves that stupid duck and would be completely content if it never left her grasp. I am used to her protests about the duck removal process, but Ralph is not prepared for the tear that slides down Phoebe's face.

"Have you lost your mind, woman? Give her that the duck back." Ralph looks like he could lose it at any moment over Phoebe's distress.

"Did you really just call me 'woman'?" I am more amused by this interaction than annoyed.

Ralph doubles down on his previous statement, "Yes, I did. Now, answer me, why are you being so mean to my tiny girl?" It is hard to take him seriously when he sounds like he is genuinely outraged with me on behalf of Phoebe.

I can't help the smirk that crawls across my face, "Well, your tiny girl is a giant mess maker. She is going to want her duck for bedtime, and I don't have time to wash it. So, she will have to go without it for a few minutes so she can eat her dinner." Why I feel the need to explain myself to this man is beyond me, but I do secretly love how he is acting as Phoebe's personal guard dog right now.

I try to reach around his big, hulking arms to grab Phoebe, and Ralph starts to protest. I shut him down, "If you want to enjoy your food while it is still warm, let me take her. I will feed Phoebe so you

can enjoy your dinner." Ralph reluctantly releases his hold on Phoebe.
I sit on the stool next to him and place Phoebe on my lap.

Ralph begrudgingly takes a bite of the pot pie, "Princess, this is
amazing. You have mad skills in the kitchen."

I help Phoebe take a bite of one of the carrots. She is so focused
on her food that the drama over the duck is long forgotten for her. I
blush at the compliment Ralph just gave. My ex never liked my
cooking; he always suggested we go out to dinner or door dash take
out. "That is kind of you, but it is nothing special, just chicken pot
pie."

"You're wrong. It is special, and there is no 'just' about it." Ralph
says before digging back into his food. Part of me wishes that he was
not talking about the food right now and that he could be referring to
something else entirely. I look down to see that Phoebe has her fist
tightly clenched around the sleeve of Ralph's shirt. I am not sure he
notices that my daughter is staking her claim on him. If he is aware,
he doesn't seem to be bothered by the intrusion into his personal
space.

For any outsider looking in on the scene of us sitting down to
dinner together would assume that we are a happy little family. That is
a dangerous thought to entertain. I start to feel antsy and need a
reminder of why I came up here this weekend. "So, are you excited
about the remodel?"

Ralph grunts something unintelligible in response.

"We are back to grunts? Is growling next?"

He takes a deep breath and releases it before answering, "No, I am
not excited about the remodel. I love this place. It is perfect, just the

way it is. No offense to your design skills. I really can't imagine what you could do to this place to improve on the classic look it already has going for it."

There is something about his earnest response that makes me want to not poke fun at him, thinking this place has no room for improvement. "If you are not on board with the remodel, then why did Lara hire me?"

"Lara went and used her trump card to get her way."

I don't even have to ask for an explanation, as he continued. "Lara called our grandfather. He is the one who originally built and designed every aspect of this cabin. Nothing has been changed since it was first built."

I couldn't help myself, "You don't say it is all original. I would have never guessed."

Ralph chuckles at my less-than than less-than-genuine shock I tried to convey to him. "Okay, Princess the sarcasm is heard loud and clear. Anyways, Lara called Gramps and asked him if she could move forward with the remodel. He has never been able to tell her no, and clearly, with you sitting here, he still cannot tell her no."

I really don't owe Ralph anything. I mean, I barely know the man, so I don't want to look too closely at the motivation for why the following words come out of my mouth, "Ralph, if you are not okay with me doing the remodel, I can call Lara and turn down the job."

Ralph turns to me, still close enough so Phoebe has a grab on him, "Correct me if I am wrong, but are you not trying to start your own business? Wouldn't a job this size really help you be more successful in acquiring more clients?"

He is too close. I want to move away and put some distance between us. I look away and offer another spoonful of food to Phoebe, who willingly accepts it. I can feel his eyes trained on me. I might not know this man well, but for some reason I feel like he has patience and can wait me out until I respond. "Yes, Ralph, this account was huge for me, but you are clearly not on board, and I don't want to cause any problems between you and your sister. There will be other jobs."

"Princess," he pauses, "Can you please look at me?" I reluctantly look over at him. "This is why I usually stick to grunts. You can't say the wrong thing if the other person doesn't understand what you are saying." This brings a smile to my face, which encourages him to continue. "The truth is I hate change, I always have. My hesitation with the remodel has nothing to do with your abilities to recreate the space and everything to do with being an old man stuck in his ways."

I quirk my brow at the last part. He said, "Old man, huh?" He must be in his early thirties.

"You have met my group of friends, I am accused of always being the old man of the group. Maybe there is some truth to their teasing."

"I have met your friends, and I can't speak to whether you are an old man of the group or not, but I can tell how much they all love and respect you. You are lucky to have such amazing friends in your life."

"So we agree that you are not calling my sister to quit, and I will go back to grunting my responses?"

He is teasing me, and I like it more than I should. "I will agree with you about not quitting but not the grunting. I am starting to like knowing what you are thinking."

This is the moment when both adults in the room are distracted and not focused on the toddler, who makes her presence known. I thought the plate still half full of food was far enough out of her reach, spoiler alert I was wrong. We are alerted to how wrong I was when she grabs a fistful of food and flings it in Ralph's direction. The food makes a direct hit, splattering across his face.

How much more can this man take being thrown at him, literally, before his patience runs out? My mouth is opening to start apologizing when he cuts me off with a loud, manly laugh. He grabs a towel off the island and wipes his face. He leans closer to Phoebe, "You are the best sharer. Thank you for sharing your dinner with me, little one." In response Phoebe starts to growl at him with her hand moving in a clawing motion again.

How is this man real? He is like a real-life unicorn hiding among other single men. I am dying to ask how it is possible he is still single. The auction flyer that is plastered all over town pops into my head and I realize that his relationship could be changing soon. I know I have no right to feel disappointed by this being a possibility, but there is something about Ralph; he is special. The best part of that realization is that he has no idea that he is a dream boyfriend material.

"Why are you frowning?" I look over to see a concerned look covering Ralph's face.

"What? I am not frowning. Sorry, lost in thought." I say, taking the towel to wipe Phoebe's hands clean.

"I know what is bothering you." Relentless would be a good way to describe this man, and I highly doubt he can read my mind, well least, I hope he can't.

"Are you worried about your husband? I can call and introduce myself to him."

I stand too fast, and the stool slides back across the tile. "My what?" It feels like the wind has been knocked out of me. Why would he say that?

Chapter 14
Ralph

I have always prided myself on being a good judge of character and being able to read someone. Right now, I am second-guessing that ability. Chloe is standing with Phoebe in her arms, looking around for a possible escape. Chloe's beautiful sun-kissed skin goes pale. When I noticed her sitting there frowning, I assumed that she was getting worried about what her husband might think about her being here alone with me.

"Chloe, please sit down. You look like you might fall over. When I saw you lost in thought, I assumed that you were worried that your husband would be upset with you being here alone with me." Nothing I am saying is getting through to her. She is slowly backing back toward the hallway that leads to bedrooms.

When she reaches the entrance to the hallway, she stops. In almost a whisper, "My husband divorced me when he found out I was pregnant. He signed over parental rights before Phoebe was born. There is no one but you who is worried about us." That is all she says before lowering her head and heading further down the hallway.

I am on information overload. I sit on the island surrounded by the chaos that is Phoebe's dinner splattered everywhere. How could anyone walk away from Chloe or Phoebe? The tightness I felt in my chest when I thought I had so carelessly kissed a married woman is now long gone, but it is replaced with sadness that Chloe has been doing so much all on her own. I wish I was able to lighten her load in some way. Instead of making life easier for her, I upset her, and I have no idea how bad the hurt I carelessly caused her.

Unable to sit there any longer without a purpose I start to clean up the mess we made during dinner. I put leftovers away in the fridge. I load the dishwasher and wipe down the counters. I am constantly looking over my shoulder, hoping my girls will emerge, giving me a chance to apologize for the big foot that I inserted in my mouth.

The kitchen is sparkling when I finally finish. I still see Chloe's face running through my mind as I sit on the couch and lean my head back. I am staring up at the ceiling, trying to find a solution to this mess. I momentarily think about texting the guys for advice. Then, remember that they are all hanging out together at the Moose tonight and the chances of getting anything helpful to my situation would not be likely. I would bet that Harrison and Max got their way, and the ladies are also there. Even though I am in desperate need of advice, I am not thrilled to be the topic of group gossip.

Frustration bubbles up when I can't find a clear path to fixing what I broke between us. I rise from the couch, feeling like this is my only choice, as I make my way down the hallway. There is only one bedroom that has the door shut. Of course, she picked that room to stay in out of all the rooms in the cabin. She picks my room to stay in. There is light spilling out under the crack in the door. I stand at the door, like a proper creeper, trying to see if I can hear anything on the other side. I finally raise my hand and tap on the door. There is no answer. "Please, Princess, I need you to answer the door so I can fix this." More silence. I slide down to the floor and sit with my back to the door. "You have to give me the chance to fix this, please."

The silence is broken when there is a strange scurrying sound. I am trying to figure out what caused that sound when I hear Chloe, in a muffled voice, call Phoebe a traitor. Then tiny, pudgy hands poke through the bottom of the door frame. I swear I can hear Phoebe growling. How pathetic does it make me that a baby is acting as my wingman or, in this case, wing-baby?

"Chloe, I am going to come in, okay?" I wait a moment, giving her an opportunity to tell me no, but all I can hear is Phoebe growling. I quickly stand and slowly crack the door open. Knowing Phoebe is right on the other side, I don't want to pinch her fingers. "Phoebe, sweet girl, I need you to move. I am coming in."

I hear the scurrying sound again and realize it is the sound of Phoebe crawling away. I open the door far enough that I can see inside the room. I see Phoebe sitting a few feet away from the door. Her whole face lights up when she sees me. She gets into the crawling position and zooms over to me. I am actually quite impressed with the speed at which she was able to get to me. When she reaches me, she throws her arms up toward me and starts to growl. How am I supposed to resist those big eyes staring up at me? I am not even going to try, and I instantly bend down and scoop her up into my arms.

I quickly scan the room and find Chloe sitting on the floor with her back against the door facing the wall. I make my way over to her and lower myself to sit next to her. Phoebe proceeds to crawl between the two of us. She gets down and retrieves a toy that had been discarded nearby, then comes back to offer it to one of us. We sit like this for a few minutes. I finally find the nerve to look at Chloe and right away regret that decision.

Chloe's eyes are ringed in red and puffy. She has obviously been crying. She is interacting with Phoebe but ignoring my very existence.

"I bet you are wishing I had stuck with grunting responses instead of voicing my thoughts?" I don't know what else to say, and that is the first thing that popped into my head.

Chloe looks up at me and offers a soft smile. I feel like this is progress. I send up a silent prayer that my big mouth doesn't ruin it. I try to apologize. "Chloe, can you please forgive me." I am nowhere near done with explaining myself, but she cuts me off.

"There is nothing to forgive, Ralph." She quietly says as she hands a baby doll to Phoebe who is completely oblivious to anything that does not revolve around her toys right now.

"You ran off and hid away in my room, and not to mention the tears suggest that I do have something to apologize for. Please let me try and explain." She gives me a slight nod, and I keep going, "I had no idea that you were a mother before tonight when I first heard Phoebe crying in the other room. When you went back to get her, I freaked myself out that there might be other things that I don't know about you. I made the jump that you were married because of a lot of dumb reasons. None of that really matters right now. Bottom line, I started to freak out that I kissed a married woman that first night we hung out."

I take a deep breath and continue my purge, "No one knows this about me. None of my friends, I am not even sure Lara knows," I pause, trying to find the words that I have never been able to find before.

Chloe reaches over and places her hand on my forearm, "Ralph, you don't owe me anything, least of all your secrets."

She was giving me a pass, I knew it and she knew it. As much as I want to take the pass and shut the door on this particular secret, I want to tell her more. "I want to tell you." She silently nods, giving me the courage to continue. "Growing up, I looked up to my dad. He was a pillar in the community, an important lawyer in town, everyone loved him. When I was around twelve years old, I caught my dad cheating on my mom, and it devastated me. My dad expected me to keep his secrets, and for some reason, I am not quite sure why, but I did keep them for him. There have been so many women over the years. I am pretty sure my mom knows but says nothing about it."

Chloe is running her hand softly up and down my arm. It is unreal the amount of comfort the small gesture is giving me. "I could never bring myself to tell my friends. It is the only thing I have ever really kept from them. So fast forward to me kissing you, then finding out that you were a mother, I jumped to the conclusion that you had to be married. My worst fear came true, and I became the man I swore I would never become."

"That is a huge burden for a young boy to carry on his shoulders all on his own. But, Ralph, the very fact that you are worried about that kiss or that I might be married is the exact proof that you are nothing like your father."

Her words feel like they are healing something inside me that has been broken for so long. "I am just sorry that I let my issues spoil the evening. Dinner tonight was the most fun I have had in a long time."

"Well, that is just sad if that is true. My daughter tried starting a food fight," Chloe leans into me, bumping me with her shoulder and offering me a sweet smile.

"You should know that I don't think it is possible for Phoebe to do any wrong," I sat there straight-faced, however, Chloe thinks I was joking, but I was dead serious. "Phoebe is perfect in every way. I am just sorry I hurt your feelings. I know we barely know each other, but I would never intentionally hurt you. I hope you know that."

Chloe takes a deep breath, then turns slightly into me, "You didn't hurt my feelings, Ralph. I probably owe you a secret of my own after you bravely shared yours." she pauses and watches Phoebe playing before continuing, "I was embarrassed, that you found out about my ex."

"I don't understand. What do you have to be embarrassed about?"

"In the beginning, things were really good between my ex and me. My ex had been married before, but I didn't see that as a red flag at the time. He told me that the marriage ended when she had asked for a divorce. We didn't date long before he popped the question. I was young and dumb. I bought into all the fairytale crap that a happily ever after could be real.

We didn't even make it to our first anniversary before I started noticing changes in him. I thought I was imagining the distance that was growing between us. Then I found out I was pregnant. He pulled away even more after that. He never would go to doctor appointments with me, and we stopped going on dates; everything just stopped. I was home alone all the time. The final straw was him missing a doctor's appointment, where we got to find out the gender of the baby. So when he got home late that night, I confronted him."

I hate this story. I hate how alone and sad Chloe looks sitting by me. After watching my dad do the same things to my mom, I had a sinking feeling I knew where her story was going. I take a page out of her comfort playbook and reach out to grab her hand. Our fingers interlock naturally. Chloe lets out a small gasp but doesn't pull away.

"There was a small part of me that still held onto hope that I was wrong, and he could easily explain away his actions. When I confronted him, he came clean with little to no fight in him. He packed his bags and moved in with his new girlfriend that night, who also happened to be his ex-wife. He told me that he never stopped loving her, and they wanted a second chance." Chloe wipes a tear off her cheek that had escaped.

"Princess, I wish I had some magical words that I could give you that would take the pain away."

"Like I said before, I am over the pain. It is more embarrassing. I can't believe I was so gullible and naïve to believe the lines he constantly fed me. The divorce was over pretty fast. The only demand he made was that he should be allowed to sign his parental rights away so he could walk away free in clear from us. He told me that he never really wanted children, and he couldn't see how the baby I was carrying at the time could fit into the life that he was building with his new girlfriend or his old ex. I get confused on how to refer to her."

Stella and Emma are always bragging in front of me that they could bury a body and no one would ever find out about it. There is a split second I consider calling them. Phoebe drags her duck over to us and crawls into Chloe's arms. Phoebe snuggles right into her mama and starts sucking her thumb. "It's embarrassing to not be enough for the person you made vows with. I was never enough for my ex. I was a stand-in until his real love came back around. The part I will never understand, though, is how he could walk away so easily from his child. I am not even sure he ever found out that I had a girl.”

“Phoebe is a happy kid with no lack of love in her life. You are a wonderful mother. Phoebe will grow up knowing her mother is enough and how lucky she is.” I lean over and kiss Chloe on the top of the head.

“Thank you for your kind words, Ralph. I am sorry I ran. Talking about my ex is never easy for me.” She pauses to look down at Phoebe making some sound in her sleep. “And thank you for coming to find me and not letting me hide. I really do feel better.”

“I should let you get Phoebe in bed. You both have had a big day. Sweet dreams, Princess.” I feel like I am the one needing to run and hide. How could any man resist Chloe, let alone walk away from her? I need to leave the room before I do something stupid.

“Night,” Chloe quietly says back to me as I stand to leave her room.

I head out to my truck to grab my bag, realizing I never brought it in when I arrived this afternoon. I have never met or dated a woman who has ever threatened to test my resolve not to marry. That is until now. If any woman could break me and make me want a marriage and family life, it would be Chloe.

Chapter 15
Chloe

I stretch as I wake up the next morning. Last night was a roller coaster of emotions. I was drained when my head hit the pillow last night. I hate talking about my past. When people learn about the messy details of my marriage and divorce, I am usually greeted with varying looks of pity. I desperately did not want Ralph to look at me that way. After I spilled my guts to him, not sparing any of the gory details, he never looked at me any different than before.

Phoebe starts calling for Mama, alerting me that my lounging around daydreaming of a handsome officer of the law has come to an end. I sit up and peer over the end of the bed to see my daughter standing up, leaning against the side of the playpen with one of her arms draped over the side. She has her other arm draped securely around her duck. Her face lights up when I smile at her. "Okay, sweetie, Mama is up. Let's get your diaper changed, then. Should we go find you some breakfast?"

Phoebe responds with an intense, girly growl. "I get it, girl. I am excited to see Ralph, too."

Phoebe is changed and playing on the floor with some of her books that I brought. I hurry and change for the day. As we are walking down the hallway toward the kitchen my nose is assaulted by the smell of bacon and coffee. When we enter the kitchen, I am greeted with a beautiful sight that takes my breath away.

Ralph has his back to us and is humming a familiar tune, oblivious to us standing there watching him. He has his baseball cap turned backward, and I never realized that the backward baseball cap is turning into my kryptonite. I love how his brown curls stick out the sides. He is dressed casually in jeans and a T-shirt. I am assuming he is wearing an apron with the straps that are tied around his neck. I could spend all day staring at the sight before me. My daughter, on the other hand, is not interested in being parted from her new favorite person any longer.

Phoebe is not as content, stares at Ralph's backside and starts screeching her happiness over the sight of Ralph. I wish it was that easy for adults to express themselves. You like something you see and scream out with joy, it seems simple enough. Ralph turns around with a spatula in one hand. He greets us with the biggest smile covering his face. I was wrong; as much as I enjoyed the view from behind, the view from the front threatened to leave me in a pile of goo right here in the middle of the kitchen.

Ralph turns to move the pan off to the side and turns back to us. "Morning, ladies! How did you sleep?" Ralph is acting overly cheerful and smiling more than I have ever seen him smile before. It is kind of freaking me out. Where is officer grumpy pants at?

I am still rendered stupid by the beautiful sight walking toward me. You know that you have no game when your toddler has to help you out. Phoebe is fidgeting in my arms, wanting to get to Ralph. As soon as Ralph is close enough, Phoebe lunges for him. She then moves her hands to his beard and growls at him.

"Good morning, my tiny princess. Are you ready for breakfast?"

Why does this man seem perfect? Better yet, why did I find him after swearing off men forever? "Umm, you made breakfast?" I can't remember the last time someone made me breakfast, or any meal for that matter.

Ralph turns his blinding smile on me, "Yes, I did. I am a little worried I messed up. I have never made a tiny person's food before. I wasn't sure if she had allergies or if she had all her teeth. I might have consulted Google this morning about what to feed a toddler, and that overwhelmed me more. Do you only feed her organic?" Ralph is talking so fast; it kind of makes me want to laugh, but I don't want to hurt his feelings after how thoughtful he has been.

I reach and place my hand on his upper arm. The gesture was meant to bring comfort to him, but I lose track of any previous thoughts at the feel of his freaking giant bicep that my hand is currently curled around. Is it too much to ask for this man to just have one flaw? He starts to chuckle, drawing my attention from his arm back to his eyes. My reaction to his muscles amuses him.

I clear my throat, "Sorry, umm, yes, breakfast would be great. Phoebe is a great eater with no allergies. I try to buy organic when I can and avoid a lot of sugar, but for the most part, she eats anything."

"I made pancakes, bacon, and eggs." I halfway expected him to hand Phoebe back to me, but he headed back to the stove. "I also just made a fresh pot of coffee. Why don't you help yourself? The food is ready. Phoebe and I will bring it to the table." Yep, I woke up in an alternative universe, or maybe I am dreaming. Who cares? It has been so long since someone took care of me. Even if it's not real, I am going to revel in this feeling.

It took Ralph a few trips to bring the food over to the table. I offered to help or hold Phoebe, but he wasn't having it. On their trips back in forth, I would overhear Ralph and Phoebe having a conversation. Ralph is talking to Phoebe like she is fully understanding every word. Every once in a while Phoebe would contribute with some well-placed babble or random words she does know.

When all the food is finally out on the table, Ralph pulls the chair next to me out and slides into the chair. I reach for Phoebe so Ralph can eat while the food is still warm. Ralph and Phoebe both pull back at the same time. A laugh bubbles up out of me at their similar horrified expressions at the thought of being separated. "I see how it is, you little traitor," I reach out to tickle Phoebe's tummy. "Seriously though, Ralph, you should have her over so you can enjoy your breakfast hot."

"When was the last time you enjoyed a hot meal, that you didn't have to re-warm after Phoebe had finished eating." I sit there stunned into silence. When you are a single parent, you get used to putting your child's needs before your own. "That is what I thought. You eat and Phoebe will make this work with her sitting in my lap."

I want to ask him if anyone ever tells him no, but eating a meal while it is still hot wins out over sassing him. I start to dish up a plate for Phoebe and one for myself. I cut Phoebe's food up and put it before her. My sweet daughter shows no signs of manners as she starts to shove a fist full of eggs into her mouth. I also dig in and am a little surprised to find that Ralph is a pretty good cook. "This is delicious. Thank you for cooking us breakfast. As soon as we finish eating, I will get us packed up, and we will be out of your hair. Hopefully, you can still salvage some of your quiet weekend."

"About that, now don't freak out. Promise you won't freak out."

"Ralph, no girl ever, has ever loved when a sentence starts that way. What is going on?"

"The storm last night was bigger than originally anticipated. They are also saying that there is another storm front that switched directions and is expected to hit the area as early as this afternoon." Ralph looks nervous as he is delivering the awful weather report.

"Okay, what are you saying? So, I have a small window to get out of town?"

"Not exactly. I called a buddy who does Highway Patrol. He told me that there have been some road closures."

I just sit there, unsure how to respond. Ralph must think I am about to freak out because he jumps into trying to 'calm me' mode. "This is not a big deal, Chloe, I promise. They close roads around here often. The important part is that we have a warm place to wait out the storms. I am sorry if this was not what you had planned."

"It is you that I am worried about. We are intruding on your weekend off."

"Yes, you and Phoebe are such a hardship for me." He is overly dramatic when he says it, bringing a smile to my face.

"You better be careful, or I will share your secret with all your friends. I bet they would all love to know that you really aren't that grumpy. It is just an act."

"First of all, no one will believe you, and secondly, you wouldn't dare." I love this side of Ralph. He seems more carefree since our talk last night, almost playful. This could be dangerous for me.

"Now we can get on with the important issues that need to be tackled."

"Ralph, it is not even eight am. I do not have a full cup of coffee in me, and you are saying there are more important issues than being stranded in the middle of a frozen wasteland," I pause for my own dramatic effect. "Not sure I am up for any new problems until after breakfast."

He chuckles, which I am growing to love way too much. He grows serious and then asks, "Princess, what is the first thing we are going to tackle on today's schedule?"

Now I am laughing. "Not sure that scheduling issues rise to 'important issue.' I am not sure what your plans are for the day, but I have to get some work done. There is this pesky issue that I was hired to do a job, and I should probably have something to present to your sister next week."

"Yeah, that sounds kind of awful. Are you sure Phoebe and I can't talk you into blowing work off and playing with us?"

"When have you ever blown work off to play."

"First time for everything."

"I really do need to get some measurements and start making some mockup designs."

"Fine, be that way. I warn you though, when you hear Phoebe and I having fun, we are going to remind you that you didn't want to blow off work."

"You and Phoebe, uhh. You don't have to watch her. I can get my work done and keep Phoebe out of your hair."

Ralph isn't having any of it, "Listen, let me hang out with the kid. Maybe with fewer distractions, you can get through work faster, and we can enjoy the rest of the weekend."

Feeling like this is a losing battle, I cave to him, "Answer me this, you're not used to taking no for an answer, are you?"

This annoying smirk creeps across his face, and he knows he won. "No, I am not familiar with the concept of being told no." His good mood is still kind of creeping me out but how could I deprive my daughter of this? Phoebe has never taken to anyone this fast, and she clearly already adores Ralph.

"You seem pretty cocky now, but you will be begging for my help when she is five minutes past nap time and your tiny princess, as you call her, becomes a tiny demon."

We finish breakfast, and I try to clean up, but Ralph ushers me out of the kitchen, telling me to go to work and that he has everything under control. I head back into my room grabbing my work back. I start with making a list of all the rooms and what I think could be done to update the space. While I am working I can hear Ralph and Phoebe laughing in the other room. I am tempted to join them. I have to remind myself over and over that I need this job, and the success of my business depends on getting this account right. I am grateful that the wifi doesn't seem affected by any of the storms. I spend the next few hours pricing materials out.

I decided that even though I was not given a budget, I would still design conservatively. The bedrooms have minor changes like paint, bedding, and some new light fixtures. The main area I wanted to concentrate on was the great room and kitchen. The more resources I find online, the more my excitement grows. Although Lara hired me, I find myself looking at my designs and wondering how Ralph would feel about certain changes I am suggesting.

I lose all sense of time. I am sitting in the middle of the room with paper scattered all around. My laptop is open, and my sketchbook is flipped open with colored pencils also scattered around. It might look like a mess to someone else, but to me, it is a beautiful, organized chaos.

"You're working too hard, Princess." Startled, I look up to find Ralph standing in the doorway with Phoebe laying her head on his shoulder. I look down at the clock on my laptop, realizing I have been tucked away in here for hours.

"Oh my gosh, Ralph, I am so sorry. Phoebe must be hungry. It is way past her lunchtime. Not to mention past her nap time."

"Don't worry, Phoebe and I shared a bowl of mac and cheese. We read books and played with some toys. We discussed the merits of me purchasing a new snowmobile that I can attach her car seat to."

My eyes get wide and feel close to bugging out of my head, "You can not…" that is all I manage to get out before he starts to laugh.

"Half kidding. We did discuss the snowmobile, and she gave some great points for me to consider, but I know she is too young right now, to go for rides." When I don't immediately respond he continues on. "Everything has been going so smoothly until about ten minutes ago. I think she is trying to tell me something and I am not getting it. Can you help us?"

"What is she saying?"

She just keeps saying 'DUH'. At first I thought she was calling me out on being clueless about kids, but I don't know how." As if on cue, Phoebe raises her head and says, "Duh."

"See, she just keeps saying that. What does it mean? What am I missing?" I would laugh, except Ralph looks devastated that he doesn't know what Phoebe wants.

I rise up and move over to the playpen, bending over to retrieve the 'DUH.' I stand and turn around with Phoebe's yellow duck. Phoebe pops her head up and puts her hand out, excited to be reunited with her favorite duck.

"So, 'DUH' is the duck? I am not sure I would have ever gotten that on my own." Ralph looks bummed that he was not the one to figure out what Phoebe needed.

Phoebe reaches for me. I give her a snuggle and whisper to her that I love her. I place her in her playpen and cover her with her favorite yellow blanket. Phoebe must have played hard with Ralph all morning. She rolls over and cuddles her duck. I swear she is snoring before a minute passes.

I walk back over to Ralph, who is still standing by the door. Even though Phoebe could sleep through a marching band, I still whisper to Ralph, "Phoebe has been obsessed with anything duck themed or related. She loves all things yellow. I should have told you about her duck obsession."

Ralph just nods his head as he watches Phoebe sleep. "Thank you for taking care of her this morning. I was able to get so much work done. You are a true lifesaver."

"Phoebe is a great kid. I was happy to do it."

An awkward silence falls between us. I finally can't take it anymore, "I will probably keep working while she naps." He still stands there. "I guess that means you have the afternoon to yourself." Hint, hint.

"Right, okay. Have fun working, and I will catch up with you later." Ralph abruptly turns and leaves the room. I am fairly certain, no matter how much time I put into trying to figure that man out. I will still come out confused.

I peek at my sleeping daughter one more time before I resume my spot on the floor, diving back into work.

Chapter 16
Ralph

Me: I am bored.

I have never texted anything more truthful than that before. I have been sitting in the great room, staring at the wall for longer than I care to admit. I tried watching tv for a while, but nothing really kept my attention. I couldn't stop thinking about Chloe and Phoebe. There is no way that Phoebe can still be sleeping, or maybe she is. I really have no clue about kids. I spent a good twenty minutes staring at the hallway leading to their room, trying to Jedi-mind trick them into coming out to hang with me. Spoiler alert: that didn't work either.

Then I opened my favorite app on my phone and found some trouble to get into – Amazon. It is a well-known fact that I am a huge supporter of it. The guys constantly give me a hard time about how much and what I buy from Amazon. The funny part is they have no clue how much I really do buy. Funny how all their jokes dry up when they are the beneficiaries of my good finds.

I was not planning on buying anything, just killing time. That was before I went down the rabbit hole of anything and everything yellow duck-related. I started adding things to my shopping cart. My sole purpose was to show Chloe what I had found. My good intentions went out the window when I had over forty-seven duck-related items in my cart, and then I pushed the buy button. All the items will be at my house within the next two to five days. I found so many things that would make for the perfect duck-inspired bedroom for my tiny princess.

Buyer's remorse has never been an issue for me, and money is not an issue, thanks to the trust fund my grandfather set up for me. Moments after buying my entire cart I worry if Chloe will think I am insane. Maybe she doesn't want Phoebe to have a duck-themed room. Cripes, the woman, is an interior designer; she probably does not need my help designing a room for her daughter.

That is how I ended up opening the guy's text thread and randomly sending a text to them.

Henry: Are you feeling okay, Ralph?

Max: Seriously? Do you have a fever?

Bubba: That is what you get for ditching us and not inviting us to the cabin with you this weekend.

Noah: Hi, bored, nice to meet you.

Harrison: Noah, umm. Was that a cheesy dad joke or a cheesy principal joke?

Max: Does it matter? Cheese, at the end of the day, is still cheese.

Noah: I will have you know. I have been told that I am very funny. Emma laughed.

Bubba: She has too.

Henry: We need to get back on topic, men. Ralph has a fever and is dying alone in the forest.

Me: I might be regretting starting this.

Bubba: No, you're not. We are a delight.

Max: In all seriousness, what's going on? You love your alone time at the cabin.

Me: Not really alone.

Bubba: You dog! Who did you bring with you? Did anyone else know the Chief was dating someone?

Henry: I am hurt over the revelation that you are dating. No, actually, I am annoyed that I am the remaining single guy in the group. Thanks for leaving me on an island by myself.

Bubba: Henry, seriously. The last single guy? You suck!

Noah: Focus men. This is not the time to chase squirrels.

Harrison: Ralph, maybe some more context would be helpful.

Me: It's not what you idiots think.

Max: You know it hurts every time you call us idiots.

Me: You're fine, Max. Want me to call Jane to go over and give you a hug?

Max: The joke is on you, sucker. She is already at my place, willing to give me hugs while you continue to bully me.

I laugh out loud. Are my lifelong friends idiots? Yes, but they are my idiots.

Henry: Need more information on the girl you are snowed in with for the weekend. Rough life, by the way.

Me: It is a funny story.

Noah: I doubt that. You are not really known for being the funny one.

Me: Do you guys want to know or not?

Bubba: His grump levels are returning.

Harrison: We promise to be good, spill!

Me: Chloe and her daughter Phoebe are snowed in with me.

The guys are shooting off emojis left and right. Question marks are rapidly flying out in multiple messages.

Me: Calm down, and stop spamming me with your stupid emojis.

Henry: I think it is safe to say the grump levels are back in normal range.

Me: Haha

Me: Lara hired Chloe to renovate the cabin. Chloe was coming up this weekend to get started on the job. I didn't tell my sister I was planning on coming up. The weather didn't help and we are both stuck here now.

I feel like I can hear literal crickets waiting for someone to respond. This never happens. Normally, there is an overload of texts flying back in forth.

Me: No one has anything to say?

Bubba: Oh, you don't say. Chloe is there. That is weird.

Me: No, what is weird, is how you and everyone else responding.

Henry: How is it going?

Me: Fine. Phoebe is pretty awesome.

Noah: I am confused. You think a toddler is awesome?

Me: What are you confused about? Have you met Phoebe? She is perfect in every way.

Noah: Yes, I have met her. She is Lola's best friend. They have had a few playdates. You generally avoid small humans.

Me: Is that a wise idea?

Noah: Umm, I need more context to your question.

Me: Phoebe is an angel, and I don't want her to be corrupted by Lola's demon tendencies.

Max: I agree that Lola has acted demon-like in the past, but only toward me. Otherwise, I have only heard that she is sweet.

Noah: She is your niece, Max. Your glowing review is overwhelming.

Noah: Ralph, not sure it is up to you to screen Phoebe's playdates. You don't even like tiny humans.

Bubba: Does anyone else feel like our text convos have taken a weird turn the past few months?

Henry: I, for one, am more interested in finding out if I am the lone wolf of the group or if Ralph is still riding the single bus with me.

Me: Still single. Planning on dying that way.

The sound of a tiny girly growl breaks my focus on my phone. I look up to see Chloe walking toward me with Phoebe in her arms. Chloe puts Phoebe down on the floor, and she zooms her way toward me. She is all smiles looking at me with bright eyes when she reaches me. She pulls herself up and is holding onto my pant legs. I scoop her up and place her on my lap.

"I tried to keep her distracted after she woke up, but she was not having it. She wanted you, and nothing else would do."

I really want to text Noah right now and brag that there is at least one tiny human who likes me. "You guys should have come out earlier. I am man enough to admit that I am dying of boredom out here all by myself."

Chloe looks relieved by what I said. "I am done working for the day. Could Phoebe and I interest you in hanging out with us?" Chloe asks hesitantly as if she thought I would turn her down on spending time with her.

We spent the rest of the afternoon together. We braved the cold and explored the outside winter wonderland the storm had left. I have always loved being at the cabin and being outdoors, exploring around the area. But seeing it through the eyes of Chloe and Phoebe and how excited they were by the little things was like I was experiencing it for the first time too.

When we finally came back inside, we spent the rest of the afternoon just being together. Chloe and I found our rhythm being together. We could talk about anything. I loved that I could get her all riled up, and her sassy side came out. I equally loved when she would talk about her thoughts on the redesign of the cabin. I am still in the camp of thinking the cabin is perfect as is, but listening to Chloe's passion for her designs, I was momentarily swayed. Phoebe was a constant source of entertainment. I helped her try to walk, but the moment I let her hand go, she would plop down and zoom away on all fours, giggling while she went.

We had dinner together again. As a bachelor, I got used to eating alone and never really thought much of it, until now. Sharing mealtimes with Chloe and Phoebe has opened my eyes to one more thing that I have been missing out on. After dinner, Chloe took Phoebe to give her a bath and get her ready for bed.

I had just finished cleaning up the dinner mess when Chloe came into the room carrying Phoebe on her hip. Phoebe was proudly wearing her fuzzy yellow pyjamas. "I think we have a problem." Chloe was worrying her bottom lip between her teeth.

"And that would be?"

"Phoebe is wide awake. I thought for sure that she would be zonked and ready for bed." As if on cue, Phoebe starts making lively gestures and babbling excitedly.

I can't help but laugh and her excitement for life. "I am sure this has happened before when you were home. What would you do then to help her calm down?" I really am clueless when it comes to kids.

"Sometimes it helps to wind down in front of a movie," Chloe suggests.

"Sounds like a great idea. I say we set up blankets in the family room, and we can watch a movie in there. What movie would she want to watch." Phoebe growls and has her hand up, making the clawing motion again.

"Of course, I will watch with you, tiny Princess."

Chloe smiles up at me, "It is a given that she will want you to watch the movie with us but I think she is asking to watch the princess movie I was telling you about, the one that has the bears in it."

"How about I grab the blankets, and you two get comfortable on the couch while I get everything set up."

I grab an armful of blankets out of the linen closet and head back into the family room. I find Chloe and Phoebe snuggled up on the couch together. I pull up the movie on my streaming service. Chloe then proceeded to lecture me when I bought it instead of renting it. Don't care. I want to make sure we have it available if this is Phoebe's favourite movie.

As we all settle in, it is not lost on me how out of character this entire weekend has been for me. I am not the guy who volunteers to babysit or craves spending time with someone who has the potential to break my walls down. I spend the first few minutes of the movie distracted with thoughts of what this weekend means in the big picture if it means anything at all.

My focus is only brought back to the movie when Phoebe crawls into my lap. She hides her face in the crook of my neck, and I swear a tiny whimper escapes her. "Chloe, what is she doing? Does this mean she doesn't want this movie? Is she tired now? I could use some direction on what to do."

"Oh, crap! I got distracted and forgot to fast-forward this part. Phoebe hates this part that is coming up."

I look up at the screen to find a bear that is somewhat horrifying ripping across the scene. Chloe grabs the remote and fumbles with it to fast-forward until the bear is gone. "I know I am grumpy, but that thing is what Phoebe thinks I remind her of?" I am borderline panicked, "Should I shave my beard? I would, for her. I don't want her afraid of me." I am rubbing circles on her back. There is a young girl with wild red hair on the TV now, and this grabs Phoebe's attention. She turns in my arms and plops down on my lap, looking as if she was not just traumatized.

Chloe lets a giggle out next to me. She tries to cover her mouth, but another one escapes. She is clearly amused with something.

"And what is so funny, Princess?" It comes out more of a growl than a question.

"You are! You are hilarious. How is it you have everyone believing you are a grumpy tough guy when you cave to a toddler at the first sign of distress." She pauses to laugh at me some more. At this point, Phoebe is amused with her mama and joins in to giggle along with Chloe. "Do you realize you just offered to shave your beard off for a little girl who already thinks you walk on water? You are ridiculous. Now that I think about it, you are more like a gooey cinnamon roll than a grumpy bear."

"Can you believe your mama is being so mean to me, Phoebe? I think we should teach her a lesson." I turn my gaze to Chloe, who has abruptly stopped laughing and is staring at me in disbelief.

"You wouldn't dare…"

"Princess, you have no idea. You are in so much trouble." I put Phoebe down on the couch between us. "Phoebe, should we get your mama?" Phoebe is bouncing up and down with excitement. Before Chloe can get away, I lunge for her, pinning her to the couch easily with one hand. The other hand is being used to tickle her mercilessly. Phoebe is screeching with joy as she claps her hands.

Chloe is gasping for air, "You have to…" more loud laughing mingled with gasping. "Stop, you have to stop." I am nothing if not a gentleman, and I stop the attack. I turn to look at Phoebe, "Phoebe you want to come get your mama?" She doesn't have to be asked twice she crawls toward her mama. Watching her try to tickle Chloe is one I hope I never forget. Chloe plays along and makes dramatic sounds that make Phoebe think she is really getting her mom.

"Okay, Princess, did you learn your lesson?" It does not escape my attention that I am still pining Chloe on the couch, and our faces are almost touching as I ask her that.

"If I say yes, you have to promise me something…" she trails off as she stares at me with a weird look on her face. "Promise you won't shave your beard."

Ah, my girl likes my beard. This is dangerous, this conversation and having thoughts that she is my girl. "On one condition, you have to admit I am tough and not a gooey cinnamon roll."

"Yeah, no deal. You are so gooey." And just like that, her sass starts the wrestling tickle match all over. After the tickle war, we all settled into the couch. Phoebe was the first to snuggle up with me. Chloe followed her daughter's lead and snuggled into my side. She made some excuse that it was cold in the room. I want to call bull on her excuse to be close, but I also don't want her to move away either. It is not long before Phoebe lays her head on my chest and drifts off to sleep.

The final credits start to fill the screen. Phoebe is sprawled across my chest, dead to the world. I racked my brain to come up with an idea to prolong the night and have come up with nothing that doesn't sound stupid. Chloe is the first to break the silence.

"Ralph, can I ask you a question?"

"Anything, Princess."

"We are friends, right?"

I cock my head to the side to get a better look at her, "I hope we are, why?"

"I think we should play a game to get to know each other better."

I'm not sure where this is going. Just excited that she does not want the night to end either. "What type of game?"

Chapter 17
Chloe

I have been trying to think of a plausible reason for the evening to not come to an end. How is it that the only thing I can come up with is; do you want to play a game? I am so pathetic. I need to say something, but what do I say that allows me to walk away at the end of the night with some of my dignity still intact? I realize I must be taking too long to respond to him because he repeats himself.

"What game were you thinking, Princess?"

"Ya know, it is probably a dumb idea. I should get Phoebe in bed."

"No." that is all he says? I think a grunt would be just as helpful right now.

"No? Just No, What?" I sass back at him.

"No, it is not a dumb idea. What game were you thinking about?"

Relieved that maybe we were on the same page, and he was not thrilled for the evening to end either. "How about a version of twenty questions? We trade off asking each other questions. You have to answer, no matter what. We both get a pass on one question. What do you think?

"I won't go easy on you," Ralph says with a chuckle.

"Don't you worry about me. I am pretty sure I can handle whatever a cinnamon roll can dish out."

"Woman, you are lucky this baby girl is sleeping so peacefully, or you would be in trouble."

"Yeah, yeah, big talk. You can go first." I sit up and fold my legs under me. I want to stay close but I also want to stay close to him.

"Easy, the night we all hung out at the Moose, you mentioned that you had a nickname for me. What is it?" Ralph has an annoyingly big smile plastered across his face. Okay, so this is how it is going to go.

I groan, and I hide my face behind my hands, "Seriously, that is the first question. It is too early to use my pass."

"So just answer it then. Fess up. What is the nickname you gave me."

I throw my hands up in the air more out of embarrassment than anything, "Fine, not like your head can get any bigger. I might refer to you as Officer McHottie. I hope you are happy now."

"Yes, actually, I am." Ralph starts to chuckle, and the rumbling in his chest causes Phoebe to stir. Ralph freezes. "Don't make me laugh. I don't want to disturb her."

"Want me to go lay her down? That can't be very comfortable for you."

The horrified look on his face is priceless, "Don't you dare try to move her. Now, let's see what burning question you have for me. Ask away."

"Why do you call me Princess? It is not like I fit the typical mould for a princess, so what gives?"

"That is an easy one. You ooze quiet strength and natural confidence that most girls try to pretend they have these days. You are hands down one of the most beautiful women I have ever laid my eyes on. You took my breath away on New Year's Eve. You broke the freakin wall, Chloe. Never let anyone tell you differently."

"Umm," I don't know what to say. He took some of my biggest insecurities and obliterated them. "Thank you, Ralph. I am not sure anyone has ever seen me the way you see me."

He shrugs slightly to avoid disturbing Phoebe. "My turn. Do you see yourself ever getting married again?"

"Nope, been there and done that."

"You said earlier that you don't believe in happily-ever-afters anymore. So why show the princess movie to Phoebe, then?"

"Fairly certain that was two back-to-back questions, which is against the rules, but because I loved your first answer to my question so much, I will let it slide. Even though I don't believe in a happy ending for myself, I really hope Phoebe gets one. The moment I saw her for the first time in the hospital, I wanted nothing else in this life but for her to be happy. I know there are some out there lucky enough to find them like your friends, for example. Emma, Jane, and Ginger seem to have found their happily ever after. Just not in the cards for me, it seems. I used to be overcome with sadness at the idea of never finding the one I could share my life with."

"What about you? Why are you not married? You cook, you are funny, you have a good job, and we already went over the fact that you are ridiculously hot."

"Princess, you have to stop; my ego can't take much more of the compliments. My head is already too big." He is deflecting the question with his humour, but I stay quiet, not willing to give him an out to my question. "Fine, I am still single for lots of reasons, I guess. The main one is my dad. The way he treated his marriage really messed me up with what love should look like. I have never wanted to put myself in a position to hurt someone or be the one who is hurt."

"We make quite the anti-love pair, you and me. A solid base for a friendship, if you ask me." I turn to sit with my back against the couch and my feet propped on the giant ottoman in front of the couch. Nothing in this house is small. I lean against Ralph and lay my head on his shoulder.

This is how we stay for the next few hours. We volley questions back and forth. Neither one of us chose to use our pass on any question asked. Some of the questions are silly, and some of them are hard and take more courage to answer. He told me about his grandfather and how much he meant to him. I tell him about my fears about not being enough for Phoebe. Ralph shared his favourite memories of being at the cabin. I tell him about always wanting to be an interior designer. There seems to be no topic that is off-limits with us.

My eyes start to feel heavy, but I refuse to be the one to end this night. "Princess, you are exhausted we should get you and Phoebe tucked into your beds." His voice is rough. I am not sure if it is from all the talking or if he has grown tired as well.

"Please, just a few more minutes. I am so warm and comfortable right here. I am not that sleepy yet." That is the last thing I remember saying to him before my world went dark from sleep.

Chapter 18
Ralph

My watch is going off in the distance, and I have the urge to throw it against the wall. I have never minded Monday mornings; to me, it is just another day, no use in complaining about it. That was before this morning. The difference is that yesterday morning, I was waking up at the cabin with Chloe plastered to one side of me, and Phoebe was still sleeping on my chest. We had fallen asleep while we were talking. I should have insisted on them going to get in their beds, but the selfish part of me loved every moment I held them.

I woke up when Phoebe was playing with my beard, growling at me. I opened my eyes to see her sweet smile shining back at me. Slowly, Chloe started to move and stretch. Any worry I had that it would be awkward quickly passed. We picked up right where we left off with a twenty-question game. Chloe changed Phoebe while I made french toast. I got an alert on my phone that the roads home had been cleared and were open again. I was disappointed that we didn't have an excuse to have more nights of staying in the cabin.

Chloe didn't seem to be in a rush to get on the road either. We spent the day hanging out. We cleaned up the cabin, and I helped Chloe pack her car. It all seemed so domestic and routine. I didn't want to stop and think about how it will feel when we go our separate ways tonight.

I followed Chloe back to Little Falls. Once we got to town, I should have turned toward my house, but I followed her to her aunt's house. She didn't seem surprised when I pulled in behind her. I told her to take Phoebe inside, where it would be warm for her. I unloaded her car. I might have been telling myself that this is what a friend would do because it was easier than examining why leaving them there and driving away was wrong.

That is how I find myself grumpy again, wanting to throw my alarm through the wall. I really wanted to text her last night just to make sure they got settled and unpacked. I resisted the urge. I decide to man up and get my day started. I mindlessly go through my morning routine. I barely remember making it to work this morning. I am on autopilot as I head to my office. I am pulling the chair from behind my desk when Estelle grabs my attention, pulling me out of my zombie funk. "Why do I feel like that? You are just as grumpy now as when you left Friday. I thought the weekend away would help," she starts to wave her hand up and down, gesturing at me, "whatever is going on here."

"Good morning to you too, Estelle. I am not grumpy, just focused, extremely focused, that's all."

"I'm not buying anything you are trying to sell me right now, but I don't have time to argue with you. And quite frankly, you don't have time either, and your schedule is jam-packed."

I didn't resurface from the mounds of paperwork and random meetings until midafternoon. My saving grace was the sheer amount of work that needed to be done, which didn't allow time to daydream about a certain sassy redhead.

I hear my phone vibrating on the desk. It is currently buried under all the paperwork I spent all morning completing. I have to move a few piles before I locate my phone. My lock screen shows I have an unread text from Princess. Before we left the cabin, I convinced Chloe to exchange numbers with me in case she needed help on the way home.

I unlocked my phone and opened the app a little too energetically. If the guys were here, I would never hear the end of it.

Princess: Hi.

Before I can respond, more messages start coming in rapidly, one after another.

Princess: This is okay, right, texting you?

Princess: You did say we could be friends, right?

Princess: Friends text friends, right?

Princess: You are probably busy.

Princess: What am I saying? Of course, you're busy. You are the Chief of Police.

Princess: I just realized I am spamming you. Don't mind me; just over here dying at my afternoon text fest—party of one.

I decided to put her out of her misery.

Me: Hi Princess.

Princess: Sorry to bother you at work.

Me: I think I prefer Officer McHottie over the boring old Chief of Police.

Princess: The regrets keep coming. Any chance at your advanced old man age you will forget I said that this weekend?

Me: Not a chance.

Princess: Okay, well, I just wanted to send you a text to inform you....

Princess: Did you like my dramatic pause?

Me: Tell me what, woman.

Princess: You broke my baby?

It is literally my job to remain calm in high-stress situations, but as soon as I read Chloe's last text, I am seconds away from losing it. I am going through a mental check list of things that I need to do to get help to Chloe as fast as possible. I need more information, though.

Me: What is going on?!

Princess: Why do I feel like if we were face to face right now, that would be a mix of a growl and shouting?

Princess: Calm down, and I will explain. Before this weekend, Phoebe was a well-mannered, sweet and loving child. Then this weekend happened. Now, she growls at everyone she sees. She also is going throughout the house looking in every room. I think she is looking for you.

Princess: See broken.

I swing from feeling the worst panic of my life that Phoebe is hurt to relief that she is fine. Then I swing toward wanting to kill her mother for putting me through all that.

Me: Princess, I might revoke your friend privileges if you ever scare me like that again. I was terrified that my tiny princess was really hurt.

Princess: I am sorry. I didn't think my delivery went through all the way.

Me: It is fine; you probably shaved a few years off my life with your dramatics, but no big deal.

Princess: Oh, no! At your age, you can't afford to shave any years off.

Me: Ha ha. Someone has jokes today. Anyways, do you think Phoebe is really looking for me?

Princess: Yes. She will go from room to room. She looks around then does her girly growl, like you are hiding from her.

Me: I should come over, right? What does the parenting book say? Will this cause abandonment issues if she can't find me?

Princess: You are ridiculous, you know that, right? My toddler will have to survive without her gooey cinnamon bear being at her beck and call.

"What is that on your face?" I was so distracted with texting Chloe I didn't hear her enter my office.

I start wiping at my face haphazardly, wondering if some of my lunch was on my face. "Do you knock?"

"Rarely, why do you have something to hide, boss? And seriously, what was that on your face?"

"What are you talking about? There is nothing on my face." Annoyed by the interruption.

"I thought I saw a smile on your face when I came in. Whoever you were texting with must-have magic powers to get you to smile." Estelle folds her arms, seeming overly pleased with herself.

I immediately put my hand down, knowing that there was no food stuck in my beard. I do not want to acknowledge that the woman that I was texting does indeed have magical powers that I like more than I should.

"What can I do for you, Estelle?"

"Afternoon patrol was hit hard with multiple fender benders this afternoon and are requesting some assistance covering their routes while they finish up reports."

And just like that, my afternoon distraction is over, and I am back to reality. "Yeah, can you radio them and let them know I will be joining them out in the field."

Chapter 19
Chloe

This week has been weird. There are moments where it has dragged by at a snail's pace. Then I have moments where I wonder where the day went and how busy it was. I emailed all my drawings, spreadsheets, and the proposal for the budget to Lara first thing on Monday. A few hours later, she called me and was over the moon with all my ideas. She gave me the go-ahead to start ordering what we needed. Some of the work will need to be contracted out, but I have already started the process of finding people to fill those positions.

My life is finally starting to feel like it is moving in the right direction. Who am I kidding? I am just excited it is moving in any direction again. There is a nagging in the slower parts of the ache inside me that if I were being honest with myself, I would miss Ralph. This weekend was amazing in so many ways, and I am having a hard time remembering that he is just a friend who happens to adore my daughter.

Phoebe, on the other hand, is in full mourning without her Ralph. I was not exaggerating when I texted him this week to tell him he broke my baby. Even Betty commented on her spirits being down. It occurred to me that maybe a playdate would cheer her up. I am grateful I am alone, working on my laptop, when the idea of Phoebe having a playdate with Ralph immediately popped into my head. The snort laugh that came out of me was not attractive, but the idea of Ralph, a manly man type of guy, having a play date with my toddler had me cracking up.

I decided her other bestie would be a less complicated choice to try and set up a playdate with. I texted Emma, hoping we could get them together.

Me: Hey Emma! I wondered if we could get the girls together for another bestie playdate. Phoebe is recovering from her first broken heart and could use her bestie.

Emma replies almost instantly.

Emma: Yay! Great minds think alike. Lola has also been missing her bestie too. I had planned to reach out to you today anyways. But what is this about Phoebe having a broken heart??

Me: Long story. I will fill you in when we get together.

Emma: What about tonight? You and Phoebe can come over tonight.

Me: Perfect!

Emma: Do you mind if the girls come over too?

Me: Of course not. It will be fun to catch up with everyone.

Emma: Funny you should say, everyone….

Me: Emma?

Emma: Ahh, fine, EVERYONE is planning on coming over tonight. The guys will be here, too. I have been trying to think of a way to sell it to you all morning so you would want to come.

Me: Not a problem.

Emma: Not a problem, as in you changed your mind about coming over, or not a problem like you don't care the boys will be there?

Me: I don't mind that they will be there.

Emma: Are you sure? I will tell the boys tonight turned into a girl's night and kick them out. But you should know that multiple grown men will cry like big babies over being kicked out. Tears have no power over me, though, so I am happy to do it.

Me: LOL. There is no need to break out the tissues. It will be fun to hang out with everyone.

Emma: Yes, girl! Let's plan on around 5. There will be so much food, so come hungry.

I put my phone down, excited to see everyone tonight. I wanted to clarify with Emma that everyone had to include Ralph coming over, too. "My sweet girl, what has put a smile on your face? You look happy for the first time since moving here." Betty had wandered into the kitchen.

"You know what, Betty, I am happy. It finally feels like I am in the right place at the right time."

Betty tops off her coffee and joins me at the table. "That does my heart good to hear, child. I have been worried about you. I am glad you are finding your footing here."

"I can never repay you for all you have done for Phoebe and me." I get oddly choked up thinking about how one simple phone call a few months ago has so profoundly changed my life.

Betty gets a weird twinkle in her eyes, which I have learned to be afraid of. This woman has not let her age slow her down when it comes to getting in trouble. "Betty, why are you looking at me like that? You are starting to freak me out."

"Well, I found a way for you to repay me." The words come out sweetly, but I am terrified of asking her to continue.

"Okay, how?"

"First, tell me this. Do you feel like you are settled here in Little Falls? You seem to have made some new friends, right? Your business seems to be taking off with this big job you have been working on. Everything is good, right?"

They are innocent questions, but nothing about Betty is innocent. I am scared to reply, in fear of how she will spin it. "Yes, all true, Betty. What are you getting at, though?"

"Suspicious, you learn fast. I was just thinking that the only part of your life that needs tweaking is your dating life." I go to open my mouth to shut this line of conversation down, but Betty keeps talking. "Now hear me out, child; I know that loser you were married to did a real number on your heart. And for that, I am sorry, but you can't be afraid of getting hurt again to stop you from trying in the love department."

She makes some good points for a woman who has never been married. None of which I want to hear, "Betty, I appreciate your concern for me, but I promise I am fine. I am in no way looking for a man now or in the foreseeable future. My not wanting to date has nothing to do with my ex. I am happy with how my life looks right now."

"Listen, at my age, I don't have time to be sneaky. Back in the day, I would have an entire secret operation to find you a man underway, but now I am old and more direct." She takes a sip of her coffee like it is no big deal what she just said. "I have already set you up on multiple dating sites. I have been interviewing candidates all week."

"I am almost afraid to ask you to explain what you mean by any of what just came out of your mouth."

"No need for you to be scared. That is why I am meeting them first in public places."

"What?! Betty, are you meeting strangers to interview for my possible future boyfriend position? How are you meeting them?"

"Oh, sweet girl, the internet is a beautiful thing. You can find anything on the internet if you look hard enough."

How can I go from being choked up with gratitude for this woman to wanting to choke her for all she is doing? "Betty, first of all, that is not safe. You can't meet random men by yourself."

"I am not alone. We meet at the diner, and my friend Estelle comes along for the interviews. She has a keen eye and has been extremely helpful in the process."

"I am speechless, and I have no words."

"Good, just listen. We have compiled a list of top contenders. I can set one up for tonight, and we can start moving forward with phase 2 of my plan to find you a man. I moved poker night to Sunday night, so that frees me up to watch Phoebe for you." She is sitting across from me, looking pretty proud of herself.

"Betty, I hope you picked guys that you liked because you will be going on the dates with them, not me." I stand and start to gather the mess that is covering the table.

"You're not even going to give them a chance? Some have real potential."

"Nope, not giving them a chance. Plus, I have plans tonight, anyway. I am taking Phoebe to hang out with Lola again."

"Fine, be that way. It will have to be another night, then."

As I head toward my room, it occurs to me that Betty will not give up easily. Bless that crazy old woman for wanting to help. I would have loved to be at the dinner watching the young guys arrive thinking they were having a first date, but find out that Betty and her friend were there to interview to fill a future boyfriend position for a stranger. I couldn't make this up if I tried. At least moving to Minnesota has proven to be entertaining.

Chapter 20
Chloe

When we arrived at Emma's, I thought we were a little early, but the number of cars parked outside their house says otherwise. I hate that I scan the area and find myself disappointed that I can't see Ralph's truck anywhere. I try to tell myself that I am disappointed for Phoebe, not because I was looking forward to seeing him.

We make our way to the front door. I don't want to say I am getting used to the blast of freezing wind knives that slice through me anytime I leave the house, but some days seem more tolerable than others.

I barely knock before a very pregnant Emma swings the door open. It has only been a week since I was here last, but Emma's baby bump seems to have exploded at that time. "You made it. Hurry, come inside before you freeze."

We enter, and Emma quickly closes the door. "Be real with me, please, Emma. When doe spring come?"

Emma's expression shifts from one of a happy host to one who has bad news. "Better to not focus on that. It will only depress you. Let me take your coat."

I juggle Phoebe from one arm to the other, trying to take my coat off. Once I was free of my coat, I started to take off all the layers that Phoebe was sporting. Once free, we follow Emma toward the noise and find where everyone has gathered. I scan the room and realize Ralph is the only one missing. I have no time to be disappointed as the other girls hurry over to everyone and start to say hello.

Noah is holding Lola and standing with Henry, talking. When Lola sees Phoebe, she gets so excited that she tries to throw herself out of Noah's arms. Noah puts Lola down, and she waddles over to me. Lola grabs onto my pant leg. "Bee, I want Bee."

Emma comes up beside me and looks down at her daughter. "Lola has been relentless since their last play date. I kind of love that she can't say her full name and calls her 'Bee.'"

Phoebe is now wanting to be put down so she can be with her friend. Emma grabs Lola's hand and leads her to an area she has already set up with toys for the girls. I plop Phoebe down next to Lola, and the girls start chatting away in babble that only they understand.

"Can I get you something to drink?" Emma asks as we stand there watching the cuteness overload.

"Yeah, I wouldn't mind some water." We headed back to where everyone else had gathered. I love that I can still able to watch the girls and say hi to everyone else.

I am still having a hard time wrapping my head around the way that all these people are so willing to accept me into their inner circles, no questions asked. It feels like we have all been friends for longer than the few weeks it has actually been.

"Chloe, I hear congrats are in order. You landed your first big job here." Stella announces, grabbing everyone's attention.

"Yes, I am so excited. The project should take a few weeks, but I am so excited about its potential."

"That cabin has needed an overhaul for so long, glad someone is finally brave enough to get the job done." Henry comes up beside me.

"Not sure it has anything to do with bravery and more to do with I like paying my bills. And please tell me that you all don't refer to the place as a cabin, too?"

"Chloe is right; the place is bigger than any cabin I have seen before." Jane sweetly agrees with me.

"Mountain resort is what I titled this project." That got some laughs from everyone. "Lara has already given me the green light to move forward on all the changes I proposed."

"I bet Ralph is freaking out." Stella elbows Bubba in the gut, "What, the dude hates change and loves the cabin more than anything in this world." Bubba is rubbing his stomach as if Stella, who is a fraction of his size, could actually cause real pain to him.

I am about to respond to Bubba when the doorbell rings out. I hate that I get excited thinking that Ralph just arrived. Noah offers to answer the door. When he returns, it is with six large pizza boxes, not with Ralph. The arrival of pizza distracts everyone from any talk of the cabin again.

Everyone grabs a plate of food, and we make our way into the family room, where the little girls are still happily playing together. The guys are a fun addition to the group dynamic tonight. I am so invested in the story that Henry is telling me I missed the knock at the door. Noah went to answer the door, but Ralph suddenly appeared with an Amazon box tucked under his arm before Noah could get to the door.

"The door was open; I hope you don't mind that I let myself in." Even though Ralph was talking to Noah, he was scanning the room.

"Of course not, man, you are always welcome. You better grab some pizza before Bubba eats it all."

"Hey, I heard that. I know you think you are being funny, but I am not ashamed; I am still a growing boy. It takes a lot to fuel this body." Bubba says as he pats his belly. Stella, who is sitting next to him, smiles and looks away. This makes me think that she likes Bubba more than she lets on.

Everyone starts to make comments and tease Bubba about still growing when there is a high-pitched tiny scream that stops all talking. I think it is safe to say that Phoebe realized Ralph was here. She drops her toys and takes off as fast as she can, trying to get to Ralph. Ralph is no better, and he heads straight for her. In one swooping motion, he puts the box down and grabs Phoebe, pulling her up into his arms. Phoebe immediately puts her hands on his beard. She lets out a pathetic little growl. She looks like the reunion is more than her little emotions can handle. I want to laugh at the dramatic scene unfolding before me. Ralph proceeds to whisper comforting words to Phoebe.

It then hits me that the room is still dead silent. I look around and find everyone stunned into their silence. The confusion that is plastered over all their expressions cracks me up, "Phoebe thinks Ralph is a bear. She growls every time she sees him or wants him. Kind of adorable, right?" Still nothing out of anyone. "Why are you all being weird?"

Noah is the first to speak, "Is Ralph holding a small child?"

"Shouldn't we be more concerned that the small child is adopting his growling as a form of communication?" Henry adds.

"This is not helping my baby-hungry-ness," Jane says with a dreamy look replacing her confused one.

"Oh, crap, that is all I need to hear." Ralph puts the baby down and walks, Max is borderline freaking out by his fiancés comment.

Ralph doesn't even break eye contact with Phoebe when he replies, "Not a chance am I putting my tiny Princess down."

I feel like I should explain, "So, funny story. When I went up to the cabin this past weekend to start the project, Ralph also showed up. Neither one of us knew the other was going to be there. The snowstorm closed roads, and we were stranded up there all weekend. Phoebe became a little attached to Ralph." The silence continues.

Emma was the first to help me out. "Interesting, it sounds like an interesting weekend." I take that back that was not helpful as it was overly suspicious.

Ralph does not seem bothered by the responses from his friends. He actually looks really happy to be holding my daughter.

"What's in the box, dude? What is the latest great find on Amazon." It sounds like Bubba is trying to tease Ralph but is also genuinely curious about what is in the box.

"Ahh, I almost forgot." He lowers himself to the ground, and Phoebe naturally takes her seat on his lap, like this is her spot. Ralph grabs the box and opens the flap. He looks over his shoulder at me when he says, "Don't be mad." That is all he said before dumping the box out on the floor. A shower of yellow rubber duckies rains down on the floor. The ducks are all dressed in different outfits. The silence is broken at this moment when Phoebe screams "duh" over and over again. She would pick one up and hold it up to Lola or Ralph. Lola was totally invested in the duck happiness overload and moved closer to Phoebe and Ralph. At one point, Phoebe turns to show me a duck, "Mama, duh, duh!"

Can toddlers stroke out from excitement? What a way to go, death by happiness over ducks. "I see, sweetheart. Did you tell Ralph thank you?" Even though she is just starting to learn words, I still want to teach her to be grateful. Phoebe turns and throws herself onto Ralph, giving him a hug. Ralph visibly melts before my eyes. Yeah, gooey to the gore, this man is great.

Bubba is the first to speak up, "Ok, a box of yellow ducks is cool and all, man, but not going to lie, a little disappointed in this Amazon haul."

Ralph just shrugs and grunts in response. Looking like he really doesn't care that Bubba is not impressed.

Everyone joins in with teasing Ralph. I don't see what the big deal is; maybe him holding Phoebe on the ground feels normal to me after the weekend we spent together. Eventually, everyone moves on with other conversations, and the attention shifts away from Ralph. I remember that Ralph had yet to grab any food. I get up and make my way into the kitchen. I fix him a plate. I guessed which pizza he would like, went with the safe bet, and grabbed the one with the most meat.

I make my way back toward him. He looks up when he notices me walking toward him. He instantly smiles at me. I lower myself down next to him. "You should put Phoebe down so you can eat."

"Not a chance am I putting her down. I am man enough to admit I was missing this little girl all week." He takes the plate I am offering him, and with impressive skill, he is able to balance eating while Phoebe crawls all over him. He bumps into me with his shoulder and leans in close to me, "She is not the only one I missed this week."

"Oh yeah, did you miss all your friends this week or just your newest friend?" I need to keep reminding myself that we are friends- nothing more than nothing less.

He shrugs my question off without answering it. "You are not mad about the ducks, are you?"

"No, of course not. They are adorable, and look how happy Phoebe and Lola are. I had no clue there were this many types of rubber duckies. I am a little impressed, actually."

Ralph physically relaxes when I tell him I like the duckies. "How was your week?"

"It was good. Your sister passed off on all the design suggestions I made. She had one additional change that I didn't include in my initial proposal because I was worried about that." I paused, not wanting to let him know how much I worried about how he would take the changes I made.

"What were you worried about? I can take it I am a big boy."

"Well, I was worried it would be too much change for you. I know you are not crazy about the project happening at all, and I want to be respectful of your memories of the place." I look toward the girls and pretend to be invested in the yellow ducks, and what they are babbling about to avoid the confession I just voiced out loud.

"Princess, what is the change my sister wanted to add?"

I take the approach of delivering the news like ripping off a band-aide, and I say it really fast, "She wants me to get rid of Big Bertha."

"What, no way! She has gone too far this time!" I don't think
Ralph meant to get loud and growly with me in his response. His
growling and stern looks have little effect on me. I know he is all bark
and no bite. He draws everyone's attention back to us again. Way to
go, big mouth.

Noah speaks up before I can answer him, "Bro, what is your
problem?" He seems more confused than upset with Ralph.

Phoebe does her best to bring some humour back to the room. She
stops playing with the ducks and climbs Ralph like a jungle gym.
When she is closer to eye contact with him, she gives her best girly
growl. This time, she has her pudgy hand out in front of his face,
making the clawing motion as she growls.

I heard Jane whisper to Max from the couch, "Oh, cheese and
crackers, why do I want a baby bear now, too?" The other girls are
snickering and giggling at the color draining from Max's face.

"Yeah, man, not cool being grumpy with our new friend. You are
going to chase her off with the growling and weird duck thing you
have going on tonight." I think Henry was trying to be funny, but
Ralph turned a pretty intense glare toward him.

I reach out, placing my hand on his forearm. I should care that
my every move is being watched, but my desire to reassure Ralph is
stronger than hiding away. "That is why I told her no. I think I can tie
Big Bertha into the room design that makes sense and looks good. So
everyone will end up happy."

Something I said piques Harrison's interest, "What, you can't get
rid of Big Bertha. That is her home." I want to point out that we are
talking about a giant moose head that is mounted on the wall, not a

living, breathing animal. I think better of it, though. If I am reading the room right, rational thought might be too much for some in this group to ask for right now.

"I agree. Big Bertha is not going anywhere."

Bubba breathes a sigh of relief, "That is a relief. Let me preface this next question: I know nothing about kids, but is it normal that Ralph turned the cute kid into a cute growling bear? I didn't realize his grumpy growls were contagious. Should the rest of us be worried."

Everyone starts to laugh. Ralph looks like he is about to let a string of growls free on Bubba in response, but I stop him. I lean in and whisper so only he can hear, "I kind of love that Phoebe has you, and if growling comes in her friendship package, even better." I pull back in time to see him flash a smile at me that does funny things to my stomach, similar to the way I felt when he kissed me. I pull back even further, needing some space.

Lola did me a solid and offered another distraction. She is clearly done sharing her bestie with Ralph. She picks up a duck and chucks it at Ralph's head, hitting him square between the eyes. There is an audible gasp from the adults in the room as soon as the duck strikes Ralph. His frown returns, even though this was a tame one in comparison to others I have seen him give before. He and Lola proceed to have a staring match. Lola crosses her arms over her chest and continues to stare.

Now it is Max whispering to Jane, "See, I told you; you can't trust tiny humans."

Phoebe is still in Ralph's arms, and she bobbles back and forth between Ralph and Lola. The whole scene is ridiculous. I can't contain it anymore; I start to laugh. I slap my hand over my mouth, but the fight to hold them feels like a losing battle. Phoebe quickly snuggles Ralph, then wiggles her way down until she is back in his lap. She picks up a duck and hands it to Lola. Just like that, Lola is happy and playing with her bestie again. Ralph sends a scowl in my direction for laughing, which only causes me to laugh harder.

Chapter 21
Ralph

After Friday night, Chloe and I fell into a regular routine of texting each other randomly. It usually was just a check-in with each other. My favorite messages were the pics she would send of Phoebe or selfies of the two of them making silly faces. All is normal within the bounds of friendship. At least, that is what I keep telling myself.

I feel like I can be myself with her, and that is enough. We even Facetimed once when Phoebe was sad and needed her GRRRR to make her feel better. The big fat tears that she had rolling down her face when the Facetime call connected were almost the end of me. Chloe had to keep reassuring me that it is normal for toddlers to be sad every once in a while. She listed off a long list of perfectly good reasons that a sane person would accept as to why a toddler might be sad, but I apparently do not fall into the same category. She spent the majority of that call trying to cheer me up instead of me cheering Phoebe up.

I have been sitting here for the past two minutes, staring at the flashing light on my phone. I know who is on hold, and I can't seem to muster up the energy a conversation with the mayor will require of me today. I know he wants to go over the last-minute details for the fundraiser. So, instead of being an adult and talking to him, I am sitting here, hoping a text will come through to distract me.

"Boss, do not make me get up to come to remind you what falls under your job description. Pick up that phone and talk to that annoying man before he hangs up and calls back." Estelle is hollering from her desk, but she is loud enough the whole station can hear every word.

With no possible reprieve in my future, I pick up my phone and hit the line that is flashing.

"This is Chief Boswell," I am hoping by playing dumb, I can avoid the lecture by leaving him on hold.

"Boswell, we have been over this. You can't just leave me on hold and hope I will go away. We have a lot to go over, and you wasting time is only delaying the inevitable." He huffs out his dismay at my behavior as if I was a child acting out.

"Sorry about that, sir. I had a few things I am juggling and it took me time to get to the call." If you consider me going back in forth between the pictures that Chloe sent me, then it would be an accurate description of the last two minutes.

"Fine, fine. Where are we at with the fundraiser?"

This man is obsessed with beating the fire department, all because Harrison's boss can't stop bragging about how much they earned. I am so tempted to pull a lump sum out of my trust and donate it anonymously to shut the mayor up.

"Everything is ready to go. We have been getting positive feedback from the advertisement. The caterer emailed me a finalized menu. The Sheriff's office is coordinating with the volunteers to set up the community center. All the bachelors are excited for their five minutes in the spotlight." I pause, knowing this is a hail mary but I have to try, "Which leads me to a question I have for you."

"Go ahead and ask your question, Boswell. So help me if it has anything to do with you not participating in the auction."

"Well, now that you mention it, sir, we had more sign up for the auction than expected. You don't need me."

"I disagree; every bachelor we auction off will drive up the money raised." He pauses the continues with, "Plus, I have it on very good authority that you are the one everyone wants to bid on."

"Good authority, you have got to be kidding me. Does this authority attend the weekly quilting bee circle and make you dinner every night." Everyone knows that his wife is a big-town gossip.

"Don't you trust my sources? The bottom line is that every dollar counts. Maybe think about shaving, too. You are taking 'no shave November' a little far, seeing we are in February now." And with that parting jab, he hangs up on me. Just once, I would love to be the one to hang up on him.

Totally defeat. I lay my head down on the desk. I really do not want to be auctioned off; this is so humiliating. Maybe I can get one of the girls to bid on me so I can avoid the awkward date. My only options would be Stella or Emma; no way Max and Harrison would be okay with their girls bidding on me, even if it was pretend. The idea starts to pick up speed, and I am about to text the girls when I hear a squealing giggle. I sit up so fast, I know that giggle. I am moving around my desk and head out of my office to find Phoebe.

I get to my door, and I see Chloe standing at Estelle's desk. Phoebe in her usual spot on her hip. Estelle is reaching out, pretending like she is going to get her, which sends Phoebe into another fit of giggles.

"What is going on out here," I say as grumpily as possible in an effort to tease them.

Chloe whips around and is not fooled by my grumpy tone. She just smiles and shakes her head. Phoebe is growling and lunging for me.

I reach for Phoebe at the same time Estelle unleashes on me. "Ralph Boswell, you know better than to use that tone with any woman, let alone one holding the most perfect baby ever. You better apologize for this instance, or not only will I be quitting but I will also let your grandfather know about this behavior."

It is taking everything I have in me not to laugh. And then Phoebe faces Estelle and with a straight face, does her girly growl with the accompanying clawing hand motion. That is all Chloe and I can take, and we both lose it laughing.

Poor Estelle looks so confused. Chloe puts her out of her misery. "Ralph was just teasing us. He is nothing but a gooey, warm cinnamon roll. No need to quit or call his grandfather. I promise it was all in good fun."

I turn my scowl on Princess now. I kind of like that she doesn't see me as a grumpy ogre but still has to show my face around here without my staff offering me cinnamon rolls.

"This has never happened before?" Poor Estelle looks confused.

"What has never happened before?" I ask, trying to figure out what she is missing.

"You are smiling and having fun. You seem I don't know how to say it, not grumpy?" Estelle's lips quirk up for a split second before composing herself again. "You must be the reason for the Chief's good mood as of late. Keep up the good work; if it continues, maybe I can get you on the payroll." She just laughs, so pleased with herself,

"Chloe, we need to do lunch, and you can tell me your secret to taming the beast." She is still laughing as I usher my girls into my office and close my door with more force than needed.

"Oh, she is fun. I can't wait to have lunch with her. I bet she has some good dirt on you."

"You are not going to lunch with her."

"That is cute that you think you can stop me."

"Is there a reason you are full of more sass than normal?"

"Is there a reason you are filled with more grump than normal?" She stands with one hand on her hip, staring me down. Why do I like her standing up to me and not letting me get away with my crap?

"Sorry, Princess. Before you got here, I was on the phone call that put me in a sour mood."

"What was the call about."

"The mayor called and wanted to talk about the meat market auction he is forcing me to participate in." I pull my chair out and, plop down and place Phoebe down on my desktop and look around for any kid-friendly thing I can give her to play with and come up empty.

"Meat market auction? Are you referring to the fundraiser that has made your face the poster boy for eligible bachelors? You have plastered it all over town. Seriously, I can't go anywhere without you staring me down from one of those posters."

"I am glad you are. You can find some enjoyment in my pain."

"What can I say? What are friends for?" Chloe has moved around my desk and is standing by my chair. There is a certain ease when Chloe and I hang out that comes naturally. Even though she is giving me a hard time, her being here feels natural, as if we have done this millions of times before.

"I am desperate. I was even thinking this morning that I could get one of the girls to bid on me to save me the torment of a blind date."

I can see Chloe trying to hide her amusement, "I haven't known your friends very long, but the way Harrison and Max act regarding their girls, you have no chance of them being okay with them bidding on another man, which leaves Emma and Stella. I think Noah wouldn't mind sacrificing his wife in the name of friendship, but would it be weird to have a married woman bidding on you? Leaving Stella, she might go for it."

I hate that she is making logical arguments about Emma, Jane, and Ginger and why they would be absolutely no help. When she brought up Stella, her tone changed a little, my oversized ego was wishing I heard a twinge of jealousy, but I was probably overthinking it.

I look away from Chloe before I do something stupid, like pulling her into my lap, and plead with her to bid on me. That is clearly not a good idea, so I focus my attention back on Phoebe. She now has her hands full with a rubber duck in each hand. "And where did you find the ducks?"

"Oh, that reminds me, your box of ducks is making my life harder. It is one of the reasons I stopped by this morning."

"You mean Phoebe's ducks. How can something that brings that smile to her face make your life hard?"

"Because, Ralph, she wants to bring them with her everywhere she goes. After she had a meltdown this morning about the ducks, the best compromise we could come to that would allow us to leave the house is she could bring whatever fits in her pocket. I could only get one duck in each pocket."

I smile at Phoebe, pleased that she loves her ducks. "Does my girl need a way to carry more ducks?" Phoebe kicks her legs, thrusts her duck-clad fists into the air, and proudly chants, "DUH, DUH, DUH."

I am itching to pull my phone out right now and start searching for some carrying case that would allow Phoebe to bring more of her ducks with her.

"No, Ralph, I don't know what you are thinking, but no. You already spoil her as it is." She pauses as she assesses me, "You have a weird twinkle in your eyes. It is freaking me out."

"I have no idea what you are referring to, Princess. Let's talk about why you didn't call me this morning when she was having a meltdown. I could have helped." I ask all annoyed, for reasons that are escaping right now.

"Right, like you were so helpful the last time she was upset, and we called over Facetime. I spent more time calming you down than it would have taken to calm her down without the call."

Although that might be true, I like being part of their day and being involved in the small things. I spend a lot of time focusing on Phoebe for lots of reasons, but the biggest reason is that it is easier than admitting that her mother has wormed her way past my defenses, and I have no idea how to deal with that.

"Agree to disagree, Princess. What was the other reason you stopped by this morning," Not that I am complaining.

"Oh right, I almost forgot," she reaches into her purse and pulls out some folded paper. "When we were at the cabin, you mentioned that Phoebe and I were staying in your room."

"Yeah, so?"

"First of all, I am sorry we stole your room. Lara said to pick any room that we wanted, that they were all available."

"Princess, I don't mind that you and Phoebe were in my room. I might be biased, but I always thought that I had the best room in the house, so naturally, I am glad you guys were in there. Why are you bringing it up now?"

Chloe looks nervous and is starting to fidget, "I know this redesign has been hard for you. And you hate change. Last night, when I was going over rooms and listing out items that need to be ordered," She takes a few breaths before continuing, "I wondered if you wanted to see what I had planned for your room. You can veto anything that you hate."

This woman will be the death of me. She knows this has been hard for me, and she is still trying to find ways to make it easier. "You know what, I trust you. I don't want to know anything else that you have planned, and I want to be surprised by the final reveal."

"Are you sure?"

"Definitely. I have complete faith in your abilities." This answer got me rewarded with a bright smile from Chloe. I feel bad that she has been so worried about how I will react. I mentally kick myself for causing extra stress for her. We visit a few more minutes before Estelle pops her head in to remind me that my schedule does not permit any more slacking. I know she is teasing me, but I wish I had a few more moments with my girls. We say our goodbyes, and they leave, but not before Chloe stops at Estelle's desk, and the women exchange numbers. I shake my head, knowing that no good will come of that duo getting together.

Before I jump on the next call that is on my schedule, I pull out my phone opening up my Amazon app. It takes me no time at all to find the world's best backpack for Phoebe. The yellow duck backpack can unzip and has the potential to carry way more than two ducks. I hit the buy now button, knowing that Phoebe has to have this. Now, I need to find a way to give it to Phoebe without her mother finding out.

Chapter 22
Ralph

It is the night of the auction. Would I prefer to be anywhere but here? Yes. Have I found a plausible excuse to get out of this that does not result in losing my job, not yet. I was so desperate I was willing to risk my life; I ate a hot dog from the gas station in the hopes of a good food poisoning. The only thing the hot dog that tasted like an old shoe gave me was a bad case of indigestion. I made the mistake of telling the guys about my feeble attempt, only to be met with old man jokes about getting indigestion.

I am starting to rethink the guys being in the best friend category. I also brought up the idea of one of the girls bidding on me to save me from being bought by someone crazier than the girls present at the auction. Their responses were almost tailor-made to what Chloe had said they would be. Max and Harrison said it was never going to happen. I even tried to explain that I wouldn't actually go on the date, and I was even willing to put the money up for the bid. All I needed was one of the girls to be the one shouting the bid. Harrison was more chill in his "no thank you" to my idea. Max on the other hand, acted as if I wanted to kidnap Jane and runaway with her. I seriously wonder if the three years he lived in California didn't fry what little brain cells he had left.

With Jane and Ginger being in the firm no column to help me, that left Emma and Stella. Noah looked like he felt bad for my predicament, but a married, very pregnant Emma was not my best option for a scapegoat. That leaves me with Stella, my last hope. When I approached her about my plan of needing a fake bidder, she acted nervous. She turned me down and told me that she already had a date that night, and she wasn't going to be able to make it to the fundraiser anyway. I wanted to call bull on her story and call her out for acting weird. I ended up letting it slide and not calling her out.

With no plausible exit plan for tonight, I arrived at the community center in a black suit and a proper scowl fixed on my face. "If you have any hope of raising money tonight, you might want to look less murderous." Harrison comes up behind me, slapping me on the back.

"What are you doing here?"

"Calm down with the warm welcome, Ralph. I might never want to leave your side when you are whispering such sweet growls at me."

"You're an idiot."

"I know, but I am your idiot." Harrison has a giant smile on his face. "I came early to help out. I know you are having a hard time tonight, so I thought a friendly, extremely handsome face would help elevate the space."

"So when you say help, does that mean you won't freak out if Ginger fake bids on me?" There is no hope in my question. I know what he is going to say before he says it.

"Not a chance. You know how long it took me to get her to be my girl. Not letting her go, even for a fake reason or not." Harrison hesitates before going on, "I, however, did draw the short straw and was sent as the group representative tonight to address the elephant in the room."

"There is no chance I want to hear this, is there?"

"Probably not, but I am duty-bound by the oath I took as your friend. To continue on with my mission. Your attitude sucks. This is a fundraiser, man. My chief told me that the money raised here tonight will go to help victims of domestic violence and victims of violent crimes."

I do not like where this lecture is going because he is not wrong. I am being a big baby about it. No matter how many reasons I have that I feel are just, the money being raised will help so many.

"Dude, are you even listening? I practiced my speech for you and everything."

"Yes, Harrison, I am listening. I get it; the money will help others, and I am being a giant baby."

"I had way more of a speech prepared but I feel like I delivered the first part so well that you might not need the entire speech." Harrison has the nerve to puff up his chest with pride as if he accomplished some big feat.

"As much as it pains me to admit this, you are right. I will try to scowl less, but I make no promises."

"That's the attitude I was hoping for," his response is dripping with sarcasm. He was probably hoping that I would just stop scowling. "Let me ask you this: there was one obvious choice of a person you could have asked to fake bid on you tonight, and you didn't."

Playing dumb is my only option right now, "I did ask Stella, but she was busy tonight."

"Not who I was talking about, nice try. Why didn't you ask Chloe? She seems great and appears to be immune to your personality."

I have to give him some answer, but what can I say that doesn't reveal too much. "It wouldn't be right. She is a friend, that's all."

"Yeah, you're definitely onto something. It would not be right to ask your friend who is single and appears to have a good time when you guys are together. Over asking your friends who are dating, engaged, or, my favorite option, married and pregnant. Yeah I can see how the choice was clear to pass on Chloe."

My scowl says enough, and no words are needed. Harrison speaks first, "Okay buddy good chat, good luck tonight. I might go see if they need help anywhere other than here." Then he scurries off. I am a jerk. I should go after him and apologize. He came to support me and nothing he said was not true. The Chloe subject is frustrating to me. I have always known what I wanted, and she is complicating things.

I don't have the luxury of spending any more time thinking about Chloe right now. The Mayor and Sheriff walk up to me, both appear to be looked pleased about the set up. People are starting to filter in. Whether I like it or not tonight is happening, might as well try to enjoy myself.

Harrison's words replay in my mind about where the money is going every time I shake the hand of a possible donor. As people are getting seated for dinner, the mayor takes the stage to announce the start of the bachelor auction. By this time all my friends have shown up and are seated. They all went in together and bought an entire table which seats ten, so they could sit together. There are two spots open, with Stella and Chloe missing tonight. I assume the girls invited her and she chose not to come.

"Ladies and Gentlemen, can I get your attention? We are going to get started with tonight's festivities. Can I get all our bachelors to meet behind the stage to get ready?"

I inwardly groan; the moment has arrived, no getting out of this now. The mayor continues to talk as we all make our way behind the current they set up by the stage. I hate to admit that the mayor does a good job getting the audience excited not only about the bachelor auction but the other items in the silent auction that are placed around the room.

I am the only one who looks like I am going before a firing squad while all the other guys are having the time of their lives. They are eating up the attention. I watch through an opening in the curtains as they go out one by one. They are flexing and acting like complete fools as they strut down the runway. Then it comes to my turn. I try to give myself a pep talk, but then the mayor calls my name, and I have no option but to go out there.

I part the curtain and walk out, and the cat calls coming from the audience cause a great desire in me to scowl in their direction, but I resist. How did the others walk down the runway that had been set up? They had so many spotlights shining on the stage I was blinded. The audience is nothing but a sea of blackness, and I can't make out anyone's face.

"Okay, ladies, we saved the best for last tonight. Our Chief of Police is Little Falls's most eligible bachelor. What would you pay for a date with the illusive Chief Boswell?"

Cheers erupt from the crowd. I know I told myself that I would shelf the scowl tonight but the mayor deserves the one that I am currently giving him.

"Let's start the bidding at…" The mayor starts the bidding.

Chapter 23
Chloe

I woke up this morning thinking it would be a quiet day at home with Phoebe. I was hopeful I could get some work down while Phoebe napped. I end up being too distracted to get any quality work done, and I can't help but worry about Ralph. I know it is silly to worry about him, but he really doesn't want to go tonight.

I was texting with the girls last night and they were telling me how Ralph was trying to get one of them to bid on him so no one else could win the date. I already knew Ralph wanted to get one of them on board to save him after I stopped by his office earlier this week. The reactions from the guys to Ralph's request had tears rolling down my face as the girls described how they all responded.

The afternoon passes by with a large number of rubber ducks being played with, which only made me think of Ralph more. I tried to work with Phoebe on her walking as we played with the ducks. She has it down and is great with the first few steps. The problem is when she sees something she wants or gets excited, she knows it is faster to plop down and zoom herself over to the desired object by crawling.

When dinner finally rolls around, I place Phoebe in her highchair and spread a handful of Cheerios onto the tray so she can snack while I cook dinner. All thoughts of my quiet day continuing into a quiet evening fall apart as soon as Betty enters the kitchen and sits down at the kitchen table.

"What big plans do you ladies have for tonight?" Betty asks nonchalantly.

I have been living here for a few months now, and my gut is telling me the old woman is up to something, "As soon as I lay Phoebe down for the night, I might start a book that I have been wanting to read. Why what trouble do you have planned for yourself."

"Child, you wound me!" She places her hand on her chest, but it is all an act. I just stand there staring at her, not willing to be the first to cave. I know she is up to something, but I am not sure what.

Betty is the first to cave, "Fine, do you remember the interviews I have been holding on your behalf with men I met off the internet?"

"Betty I have to tell you, not loving where this is going already."

"Chloe, trust me I have all the work all you have to do is smile, and maybe flirt a little. Do you want any pointers on how to get your flirt on?" Betty looks over to the clock on the wall and frowns at the time. "We don't have much time, but I can show you a few techniques that have never steered me wrong when flirting."

The cautious unease that I felt when Betty started talking is quickly moving toward full-blown panic. "What are you talking about? We don't have much time for what?"

"For Steve"

"Betty, how about you pretend I am completely clueless, and you use complete sentences to explain what you think is happening tonight and how it will be affecting me."

"The interviews that I was doing for you. I told you about them. Well, Steve is the first to make it to the next stage in the process. He should be here in the next 30 minutes."

"What?! You're joking, right? I don't want to date Steve. You need to call him and stop him from coming over. There will be no dating Steve, do you understand."

"What is the harm? You already said you don't have any plans. He was free to; I love it when things come together so nicely. In all fairness his availability is wide open currently. He has a very important job he was telling me about that has something to do with electronics or games. He tests out new games that are on the market. He is so dedicated to his work that he moved back in with his parents and made their basement his workspace. So, refreshing to find a young person with such a good work ethic."

"Are you kidding me? No, it does not sound like a work ethic to me at all. It sounds like Steve is unemployed, lives with his parents in their basement, and spends any free time he can on video games. So you are telling me the only guy to make it through to the next stage in the interviews is an unemployed gamer boy who lives with his parents?"

"Well, when you put it like that, sure, Steve has some areas to worker harder in, but regardless, I really think you will like him when he arrives."

I can't even get my next rant out when the doorbell rings. You have got to be kidding me. How is this my life? I just stand there, staring in the direction of the front door. Betty gets up and goes to answer it. "This should be fun, my dear. Maybe while I go get Steve, you should wipe your face clean. You have some food or something on it."

I don't even care. I am so mad right now. I know Betty loves me and thinks that finding me a man right now is helpful, but it is, in fact, the complete opposite of helpful. I should probably care that I am standing in the kitchen looking like a bridge troll. I am wearing leggings and an oversized shirt. If I was being honest, I didn't comb my hair today, I just threw it up on top of my head in a messy bun. Ralph pops into my head. I want to call him to rescue me from Betty and her good intentions. Then I remembered he couldn't rescue me, he couldn't even rescue himself tonight from a similar fate.

It is not lost on me that Ralph and I suddenly find ourselves doomed to the same fate. Going on dates with people we did not want to. I hear Betty's voice coming down the hall. I turn around and stir the macaroni that doesn't need stirring, I just need a few more seconds before coming face to face with Steve.

With my back to them, I hear Betty say, "This is quite a surprise. If I had known you were going to stop by, I would have asked Steve to bring a friend."

My confusion about what Betty said had me slightly glancing over my shoulder. I am flooded with relief when I see Stella standing there. I am not sure how much Betty has told her, but she is clearly amused by what she just walked in on.

"Hey, Stella. What are you doing here? I thought you had a date tonight?"

Stella walks over closer to me as Betty takes a seat at the table again. "My date stood me up. Bubba texted me and told me that there were two open seats available at their table tonight. I came by to see if you wanted to come with me to check out the fundraiser?"

My options are to stay home and be forced to spend my evening with Steve. Or go watch some lucky woman claim my friend as her date. Yeah, I really hate both options. Stella interrupts my thoughts when she whispers so only I can hear, "Betty told me about Steve; this should be a no-brainer. Go get ready really quick, and I will get Phoebe."

She is right. I would rather spend time with my friends tonight than Steve the gamer-boy. I turn to face Betty, "Betty, I was wondering if you could cancel Steve and watch Phoebe for a little while tonight. Stella needs help at the fundraiser that is happening tonight. Do you mind if I go help her?"

"Are you sure you want to give up the chance to meet Steve? Not sure when he will have another break in his schedule to come to meet you."

"Yeah, definitely a hard decision, but I would feel bad not helping Stella after all she has done for me since moving here." I am hoping that Stella will play along with my little white lie about her needing help. When Betty looks to Stella for confirmation, Stella shrugs, "Chloe is the best, I know it wouldn't be the same without her tonight."

"Ok, girls, you go work hard. The mayor's wife has not shut up about this fundraiser at our weekly quilting bee. You would think she had something to do with the planning. If Chloe helps I can rub it in her face the next time we get together."

I'm not sure that should be the takeaway, but who cares? I am avoiding gamer-boy. "Are you sure you don't mind watching Phoebe? She should be ready for bed soon."

"How many times need I tell you that I adore this sweet child? I never mind watching her."

Stella interrupts, "Chloe I am glad you can come but you might want to change and or comb your hair."

"What are you saying, Stella? My bridge troll look would not fit in?" I dramatically spin and strike a pose, causing the two women and the baby in the room to laugh at my silly antics. "Fine, I will go change and be ready in five minutes."

Chapter 24
Chloe

As Stella and I walk into the community center, my nerves start to take over. Am I glad to have avoided the Steve situation tonight? Of course, I am. The flip side is now I have to watch as Ralph is auctioned off to another woman. It is also ridiculous that I have any feelings on the matter at all. Ralph and I are friends. I should be more supportive, but I can't seem to muster the excitement of watching this all go down.

We enter a giant room that is set up with tables and decorations. There is a giant stage that is taking up the front of the room, with a longer, narrower stage that extends for a makeshift runway, I am guessing. I can't take my eyes off the stage, hating that I probably chose wrong for tonight. Stella is busy scanning the room and is missing out on my internal meltdown.

"Ah, I see everyone," she grabs my hand, and we wind in and out between the tables. As we make our way over to everyone, it is hard to miss the tables that only have women sitting at them. Those are, by far, the loudest tables in the room. The nerves that I was feeling when I first arrived are starting to sour into wanting to puke. I cannot do this, but how can I explain my leaving to Stella?

Before I have the chance to come up with a believable excuse, we arrive at our table. The girls jump up and come around to greet me. "Chloe, I am so glad you came; the food is so yummy. My friend is in charge of all the catering, you won't be disappointed." Janes says as she pulls me into a hug. She is definitely the hugger of the group. It never fails that every time we see each other I will be getting a hug from her.

"Jane, let the girl breath; she needs to pick out something on the menu." Emma is simultaneously pulling Jane back from me while handing me a folded pamphlet.

I take the pamphlet from Emma, "Seriously they have this many dinner options? I have never been to a fundraiser that has offered a menu before."

Ginger pipes up from her spot at the table, "It is not that type of menu, Chloe." She couldn't even get it all out before she started to giggle. Harrison, who is sitting beside her does not look happy with his girlfriend's comment.

I opened the folded paper, curious to see what was on the menu that would cause Ginger to giggle and Harrison to scowl. The inside is covered with pictures of guys and a short blurb about them. Being a redhead means I fail at hiding my emotions, and they are always on full display whether I want them to be or not. My skin gives me away every time, whether I am turning bright red from embarrassment or going ghost white from being upset. This is exactly what happened when I saw a picture of Ralph staring back at me. It was as if I could feel the color draining from my face.

"I don't think I can do this." The words barely sound louder than a whisper to me.

Stella must pick up on my impending freak-out, "Girl, no worries, that leaves more for me." She grabs the pamphlet out of my hand.

Bubba mumbles under his breath, "Geez, it is not a buffet." If I heard him, Stella had to hear him for sure.

Henry stands up and pulls a chair out for me. "Why don't you have a seat, Chloe."

I want to turn and walk out of the room, but instead, I say, "ok."

My mini freak-out is quickly forgotten as they bring out the food. There is something special about the group of people at this table. I have never seen people making fun and teasing each other so freely, to turn around then and defend each other so fiercely. Henry was in the middle of telling me about another one of his stories involving a naught animal at the zoo when the mayor took the stage to start the night's main event, the auction.

After the mayor had only been speaking for a few minutes, I could totally get why Ralph wants to pull out his hair after his meetings with the mayor, the man is a little extra. The auction turns out to be sort of fun.

It is a toss-up on what is more entertaining: the women in the audience who are taking this so seriously and letting their intentions be known or the bachelors that are strutting their way down the runway acting ridiculous are really. Some of the women even brought a few homemade signs for certain bachelors and waved them about. Everyone at our table is keeping the evening light and fun with their constant commentary and teasing.

Stella gets in on the actions and throws random bids out. I don't really think she was interested in any of the guys she was bidding on. She was just trying to have some fun. Bubba was the only one who did not look amused with Stella's bidding.

As the latest bachelor that was just auctioned off is strutting off stage feeling quite proud of himself with how much his bid ended up being, the mayor says the words that I have been dreading since arriving.

"Okay, folks, now we have had a great night and raised a lot of money for a great cause. Thank you so much for all your participation. We have one last bachelor that is dying to come out here. It is Little Falls's most eligible bachelor. Let's welcome Chief Boswell to the stage."

The curtain parts, and Ralph steps out onto the stage. The women in the audience lose their minds, and the screaming is off the charts. I have never seen Ralph so dressed up; it is a good look for him, but he still looks so uncomfortable. I have learned Ralph's expressions over the past few weeks, and I would bet money that we are seconds away from a scowl appearing on his face. I want to yell at him to run and these women are out for wedding rings, but he probably couldn't hear me even if I were brave enough to yell it.

"Okay, ladies, we saved the best for last tonight. Our Chief of Police is Little Falls's most eligible bachelor. What would you pay for a date with the illusive Chief Boswell?"

One woman screams from the other side of the room, "Three hundred dollars!"

Another woman, equally passionate about securing the date, "Five hundred dollars."

Henry leans over to me, "Chloe, are you okay? You look like you could murder someone." I don't say anything back. All I can do is stare at Ralph.

The mayor gets involved at some point and starts egging the women on and the bid is climbing slower but still higher. The more it climbs, the more anxiety rises up in me. Before I know what is happening, I am jumping out of my chair and yelling out my own bid, "Three thousand eight hundred and seventy-two dollars."

This causes silence to fall over the room. Even the mayor takes a few seconds to recover. Ralph is standing on stage with his hand held above his eyes as if he is trying to see who it was that made that bid.

"Well, well, the lady has spoken. Can anyone outbid this enthusiastic bidder? Now is your chance." More silence. "All right, sold to the woman in the black dress."

"What did I do? What did I do? You are so stupid, Chloe…" I thought that my freak out was in internal monologue but I even screwed that up. I was saying it out loud for the entire table to hear.

Stella leans over, "That was nice of you to rescue Ralph."

"Yeah, no need to stress. No harm done." Noah leans across the table, trying to help.

"I am not sure Ralph is worth that much on the current market, but I am sure you just boosted his ego after that bid. He will be even more insufferable now." Henry leans in and bumps into me with his shoulder.

"I can't believe I did that," is the only response I can muster. What is Ralph going to think? This is all Betty's and Steve's fault. Is it irrational to blame a man that I have never met for my life problems, sure but it follows the theme of the night for me. I cannot believe I just bid my entire savings on a man who wants nothing to do with me outside of friendship.

As if the mayor hasn't done enough damage in my life, he reminds everyone that those who had winning bids can see the volunteers stationed at the back of the room to make their donations before leaving.

"Umm, is this a bad time to point out that Ralph is walking this way, sporting a rather nasty-looking scowl? You think he would be excited he pulled in the highest bid tonight," Max sounds confused by Ralph's attitude. I think I understand his attitude and I am not interested in sticking around for this. I want to pay my pathetic life savings to the volunteers and get out of here before I have to talk to Ralph. I am sure if I have some time to think up a story, I can explain this to him.

I lean over to Stella and whisper, hoping she is the only one who can hear me, "Any chance you will give me your keys? I think I should head home and check on Phoebe."

Stella's head bobbles back in forth between me and Ralph. We both know what she is not saying; there is not enough time to escape. Ralph stops abruptly by my chair.

"Did you really just bid on me?" Apparently, he is back to growling when he talks to me. He seems way madder than I thought he would. I was worried he would be embarrassed that it was me who won or disappointed one of the other women didn't win, but being angry was not the response I was expecting.

"Dude, you need to chill out right now. Chloe was just trying to help you out. You clearly don't deserve her kindness, but she doesn't deserve you being a jerk either." Henry is giving Ralph a run for his money on who is more angry right now.

I reach over and place my hand on Henry's back, "It's okay, Henry. I am a big girl I can handle this."

Ralph lets out a feral caveman grunt from behind me. I have never seen him this upset before. I chose to ignore him and continue focusing on Henry. "Thanks for trying to help; I appreciate it."

I stand, aware of the grizzly that is still making grunting and growling in my direction. "If you will all excuse me, I need to get home and check on Phoebe. Thank you for such a fun night." Everyone joins in saying their goodbyes. Emma and I made a play date for the girls this week. At this point, steam could be coming out of Ralph's ears. I am still in full-on ignore mode.

I grab my purse and turn to walk past him, hoping that this is coming off more confident than how I am actually feeling. The plan is simple: pay for the date that Ralph is clearly angry about. Then, try to arrange an Uber home where I plan to put something comfortable on and not leave the house again for the unforeseeable future.

I know I am walking faster than is normal for me, but the desire to escape is quite real at this moment. The problem is Ralph seems just as determined not to let me leave, and he will win the power walk battle every time with his long legs in comparison to my short ones.

"Princess, stop; we are going to talk about this." I guess that command came out less growly this time, but I don't love he just gave me a command in that tone.

Over my shoulder, I respond back, "No, thank you. Have a good night." Ralph is now mumbling something under his breath. I am annoyed with the whole situation and decide that the perfect person to receive my annoyance should be the one causing the bulk of it.

I stop abruptly and turn to face him. Ralph doesn't miss a beat, though. He lowers his head to ensure I am the only one to hear what comes out of his mouth next, "Woman, this is all your fault." That is the only warning I get before he lowers his shoulder more proceeds to throw me over his shoulder. Never in my life has anyone just thrown me over their shoulder and walked off like it was not a big deal. It is a very big deal!!

"You put me down right now, you big oaf! I will scream. The room is full of cops, and they will help me!!" I can only imagine the scene that is unfolding when everyone in the room has a front-row seat. Ralph has tossed me over his shoulder like a sack of potatoes, and I am kicking and flailing my fists into his back.

"Princess, the cops in this room either work for me or with me." He heads out of the main room and down a darkened hallway. "Put me down, I can walk! You are going to hurt yourself carrying me."

"I tried to get you to stop and talk to me, and you refused, so now we do this my way."

I am trying really hard not to be impressed that he is not even a little out of breath as he hauls me around. That seems like some ridiculous thing to be thinking about after being essentially kidnapped. Ralph tries the first door we come to, and it opens. He steps in and, I assume, is looking for the light switch. Hard to tell, though, hanging upside down over his shoulder. My guess is accurate, as the room is suddenly filled with light.

Ralph then pulls me over his shoulder and places me back on my feet. I had a whole rant prepared to give this man when I was hit with a wave of dizziness. I stumble back and grab my head, hoping that the spinning will stop.

Ralph reaches out for me to try and steady me, "Whoa, Princess are you okay?"

I try to pull away, but who am I kidding? I need him to prevent falling, but that doesn't mean I can't give him a piece of my mind. "No, Ralph, I am not okay. You practically kidnapped me. You threw me over your shoulder, and did you notice that my little black dress is not really proper attire to be kidnapped in?? I probably just flashed half of the town." I am nowhere near done with the rant but Ralph still interrupts me as he mumbles under his breath, "Trust me, Princess, I noticed the dress."

"I am sorry if bidding on you made you mad. You just looked so uncomfortable, and I thought I was helping. You know that this is all your fault, right!? You suck at communication. We are supposed to be friends, and friends tell other friends stuff. A good example of telling your friend something would be that you were hoping that one of the other many women in your fan club that showed up tonight had won the date, I would have kept my mouth shut. But no, you never said a word, and now I spent my entire savings helping out a big oaf that…" That is all the rant I am able to get out before Ralph silences me.

He grabs me by the nape of the neck and pulls me closer to him. He crushes his lips down onto mine. Just like New Year's Eve it only takes me a few seconds of being stunned before I quickly catch up. The independent woman in me is screaming to "push him away," but every other part of me is screaming, "Don't you dare."

Kissing Ralph is nothing I have ever experienced before compared to other guys who have kissed me. He takes control of the kiss, but at the same time, I feel safe and cocooned in his arms. This kiss is just as desperate as out first one we shared, but there is something more to this one. The Ralph that I have gotten to know the past few weeks, the one he only shares with me, that is the man kissing me right now, and I love it too much. Just like our first kiss, it ends way too soon. Ralph pulls back, resting his forehead against mine. Both of us are slightly out of breath.

"You kissed me again," I whisper.

"It was the only way I could get you to shut up. I wanted to talk to you." He no longer seems mad as he is speaking in hushed tones as well. We are in this weird little bubble in a dirty supply closet that neither one of us wants to pop.

"What do you want to say?" I want to look away after asking my question but can't break the hold he still has on my neck. Ralph's scowl has no effect on me, but the look he is giving me right now has me scared for my life, there is so much vulnerability in his eyes.

"When is our date?" Of all the possible things that come out of his mouth that were not in the top hundred things I would have guessed he would say.

"What?!" I popped our quiet bubble with my shock at his question.

"When is our date, Princess? Oh and let me be clear that I am paying the money you bid for me. I will take care of it as soon as we clear up when the date is."

"What is happening? I am so confused, which, if I am being honest, is a natural state of being for me when you are involved."

He chuckles; the jerk starts to do this insanely hot man chuckle that momentarily distracts me before I can focus again. "Stop laughing at me, you big jerk. Five minutes ago, you were a growling caveman, barking orders out at me. You were so mad at me. Then you kiss me senseless and now appear to be in a good mood as you throw out some hot man chuckles. What the heck, Ralph? Way to give a girl whiplash."

Even though the jerk still looks amused, he has some smarts to stop the hot chuckling. "Sorry, Princess. I was mad after you won the bid, except I didn't know it was you who won the bid, at first anyway. I couldn't see who was bidding on me, and the lights were blinding. When you made your bid, and I heard your voice, I thought my mind was playing tricks on me because I hoped it was you who had won."

"Still doesn't explain why you were so mad when you walked up to the table?"

"I wish I could explain it, but you might not like the explanation coming from someone you see as a friend."

More leery now but still needing his truths, "Try me."

"I was upset by how much money you wasted to save me from the fate of going on a date with someone else. I was marching over to tell you were not going to pay that ridiculous amount, that I would." He pauses and takes a deep breath before continuing, "And then I saw Henry lean into you and whisper in your ear, I didn't like it."

"What? Why not? Henry is one of your best friends. Do you not like me hanging out with your friends?" I would be crushed if Ralph was not okay with the friendships that I am slowly creating with the others.

"No, that's not it."

"Then what is the problem with Henry talking to me," I stop abruptly when the thought pops into my head of why Ralph has a problem with Henry talking to me. Could he be jealous? That would be crazy, and we are just friends; why would Ralph be jealous of one of his best friends talking to me?

"I am assuming by the look on your face that you might be understanding now."

"Ralph, are you jealous of me talking with Henry?"

"Yes."

I want to shake this man. I hate when he slips into short, non-helpful answers. "You have got to be kidding me. What is there to be jealous about?"

"Princess, it is hard to explain."

"Try anyways, and you have to use more than three to five words to do it."

Ralph smirks at my demand for more words, before speaking, "I know you and I are just friends, but I feel this sense of protectiveness over you and Phoebe. I know it is not fair to act that way, but I don't like you talking to other guys. Henry has been one of my best friends since kindergarten, and you won't find a better guy out there, but I don't like it. Call me a cave man call me a jerk, I don't care. Besides, friends can be protective, right? That's a thing, right?"

Well, I have to give it to the man; he did use more than three to five words. I'm not sure if his explanation really clears any of the confusion swirling around in my head. "He is just a friend. It could never be anything more between him and me." I am not sure what

spurred me to give this reassurance to Ralph, but I couldn't help
myself.

"Before we go back out there, I need to know something."

I am not sure how much of this I can take tonight. "And what
would that be?"

"So, when is our date? I am thinking of tomorrow night. I can
ask Emma and Noah to babysit. Even though I am not crazy about the
possible negative effect Lola will have on Phoebe's behavior, I could
risk a few hours to go on our date."

I am not sure what I expected when I came tonight, when I won
the bid, or even when I was kidnapped and taken to a dirty supply
closet. Ralph seems excited about a date that was not supposed to
happen. I was just trying to help him avoid one of the women in his
fan club.

I push him away and take a step back. "What are you talking
about? We can't go on a date?"

"We are going."

"No, we are not. We are friends. We both agree love is dumb and
not for either one of us. Any of this refreshing your memory?"

"You won. We are going."

I want to scream while pulling out my hair. This man is
infuriating at best, and he is back to short caveman answers. "When
you asked the other girls to fake bid on you, did you expect them to go
through with a date?"

"No."

"Then why am I any different?"

"Because."

Now he has done it, I let out a mini scream of frustration. This only causes the stupid hot chuckle to return.

"Oh, Princess, stop with the dramatics," as he bops me on the nose. "Don't act mad; a night out on the town will be fun. I will make all the arrangements. You and Phoebe should be ready by five, and I will swing by and grab you. I will arrange babysitting and everything else." Ralph turns to leave the room like he did not just set off a bomb.

I pop my head out the door and yell after him, "You realize girls do not like to be called dramatic, right?"

He has the nerve to pull out another hot chuckle and keeps walking away from me.

Chapter 25
Ralph

"I was thinking about calling in sick today. I was certain you would be a bear to deal with after the fundraiser even though you brought in top dollar. I will be the first to admit when I am wrong. In fact, I am a little creeped out by the smile you have been wearing all day." Estelle just waltzes in like this is her office not mine.

"Please come on in, Estelle. Make yourself comfortable." My dry tone does nothing to discourage her from sitting down.

"So inquiring minds want to know what is going on with you and that girl."

"I am going to stop you right there; Chloe is my friend. Nothing more, nothing less." I didn't even believe that anymore, but I didn't feel the need to have this conversation with Estelle. It has been less than twenty-four hours since Chloe won me at the auction. The aftermath was a little messy when I became a jealous idiot, and it was not my proudest moment. I only told her half of the truth yesterday when she asked why I was so mad.

I didn't know she was coming to the fundraiser, but then finding out that she was there made me see red. Had she come to bid on someone else? Logic would dictate that she just came to have fun and felt bad for me, – that iswas All logic flew out the window when it comes to that sassy redhead, though. After the auction ended, I went in search of her, and I saw Henry talking to her. It spiraled out of control after that. I am not going to say I regret anything that happened between Chloe and me in the storage room, but it still was not my finest moment.

"Fine, be that way. I hear that you have a date tonight, so I will have to check with my sources on how it goes." Estelle gets up and moves toward the door. She turns her head when she gets to the door, "Seeing as you are leaving soon for your hot date, I will be heading out as well. Have a good night, Chief. Don't do anything I would do." She has the audacity to laugh as she walks back to her desk.

I call after, "You need a hobby, you know that, right?" Nothing but more cackling comes from her desk. Not even my gossiping secretary is going to ruin this night for me. Chloe and I will be going on a date soon.

I texted asking Emma and Noah if they would be willing to babysit Phoebe for a few hours, and they were more than willing. All that needs to be done is to run home and change, then head over to get my girls.

I arrive early, but I don't care. I am too excited to see my girls. I even brought a present for Phoebe that I am too excited to wait any longer to give to her. I hope she loves it. I searched the internet thoroughly for this gift. Hopefully, Chloe doesn't mind too much that I am spoiling Phoebe because I don't see myself stopping anytime soon.

Betty answers the door. "Well, well, Chief Boswell, were your ears burning? We were just talking about you."

Before I could respond to Betty, I heard Chloe yell, "We were not! Don't believe anything the old woman says she is losing her facilities'." Chloe comes out from the back hallway carrying Phoebe on her hip. Phoebe's face lights up the minute she sees me, and I hope that never stops. Phoebe is desperately trying to get to me. I grab her as she lunges toward me. "Hello, my tiny Princess, I have missed you." I start to tickle her belly. She gives the best giggles. When she calms down, I halfway expect her to growl at me, which is her normal greeting, but instead, Phoebe smiles as she casually says, "Hi."

My jaw drops open, shocked by the new word, "What is this? Does she have a new word? Why didn't you tell me?" I look at Chloe for answers.

Chloe smiles at her daughter, "I keep telling her not to grow up, but she won't listen to me. It seems every day, she has more and more new words. I can set you up with regular text updates on any new changes on the vocab front."

I know she is sassing me, but I don't care. "That sounds great, but maybe a Facetime call for bigger milestones." Phoebe starts to grab at the gift bag that is looped on my arm. "Mine, mine, mine" is all Phoebe can chant over and over. I look at Chloe again.

She shrugs at me, then looks at Phoebe, "Phoebe, you need to use your manners. That might not be for you."

Phoebe's girly little voice then starts to plead, "Peazz, peazz, peazz grrr."

I am on the fence between hating that I have missed so much change in the last few days and wanting to see her face when she opens her gift. "Yes, I brought you a present." I hold the bag out to her. With no hesitation, she grabs the bag, rips the tissue paper out, and peers down into the gift bag. Phoebe's eyes open comically wide when she sees what is in the bag. She looks between me and the present in the bag. She screams out with excitement.

"Oh my, what on earth is in that bag, Ralph? Phoebe looks like she is going to implode from excitement." Betty looks enchanted by Phoebe's reaction.

Before I can answer Betty, Phoebe is reaching into the bag, pulling out a yellow, fuzzy duck. She starts to squeeze the duck in her pudgy arms. It is safe to say that it is love at first sight. I notice she has some of the rubber ducks I bought her scattered on a blanket by the fireplace.

"Want me to show you something fun about your new duck?" I walk us over to the scattered toys. I squat down and place Phoebe on the ground next to me. "Can I see your duck, please?" Phoebe is hesitant but finally hands the duck to me as she continues to watch my every move. I locate the zipper on the back of the duck. It is hidden by all the fuzz. I unzip the bag, grab a handful of rubber ducks, and show her how to put them in the bag. After zipping it back up, I show her the straps that are attached and show her how to put the backpack on. "Now you can take more duckies with you when you go anywhere."

Phoebe throws herself at me, offering me the best hug I have ever received. I look up to see Chloe and Betty both watching the interaction. A little nervous, I overstepped, "I hope this is okay. I thought she would love this?"

"Ralph, I think it is safe to say she loves it. It is kind of perfect for my girl. Thank you."

I am taking this as a win, "We should probably get Phoebe over to Lola's so we can make our reservations."

"You made reservations? Isn't that kind of fancy for a fake date that I bought but you insisted on paying for."

"Princess, this is not fake, and of course, I made reservations. You deserve the best, and I intend to give it to you."

"You hear that, deary, Ralph intends to give it to you. Isn't that nice of him?" Betty is acting innocent, but what she says does not sound innocent. I look over at Chloe, who has turned bright red. Betty keeps her laughs from escaping.

Chloe hurries over to grab her coat and Phoebe's snowsuit. "Time to go, don't want to be late." I really want to laugh at how uncomfortable Chloe is, but I think better of it, not wanting to start the date off on the wrong foot.

We get Phoebe settled with Lola, and they are in heaven with each other. Noah and Emma are pushing us out the door, telling us to enjoy ourselves.

"Are you sure you don't mind watching Phoebe?" Chloe looks torn about leaving Phoebe behind when she asks Emma.

"Look how happy they are playing. If it makes you feel better, we should trade it off. We will do date night next, and you can keep the girls." Emma offers suggestions to help reassure Chloe.

Chloe looks happier with the suggestion, "Yes, I love that idea!"

"Great! Now go enjoy your date."

"Oh, it is not a…" Chloe can't finish her sentence before I cut her off, "Princess, do not finish that sentence. This is a date."

Emma turns to hide behind Noah's back to hide her giggling. I am glad that she finds it amusing that I have to keep reminding Chloe that this is a date, but I am not about to call her out on it. I need a babysitter tonight to make this date night happen.

Chapter 26
Chloe

Even though it felt weird to be driving away without my daughter in the car, a small part of me was looking forward to going to a nice restaurant and sharing a meal with another adult even when that adult keeps calling this a date and correcting me whenever I say something different.

Speaking of the annoying adult who keeps correcting me, "How was your day today, Princess."

"What are you doing? You're being weird tonight."

"No, I am not. This is me being normal." Even in the dark cab of his truck, I can see that this is not his normal.

"Okay, whatever you say. Where are we going to dinner in this small town where you need a reservation? I would have been good with the diner or going to the Thirsty Moose for dinner."

"Princess, we have been over this. Now dinner is a surprise, so sit back and enjoy the ride."

"You are being extra bossy lately."

Ralph has the nerve to shrug as if he knows it is true, and he doesn't care. Silence falls over the truck as we make our way to dinner. We are about twenty minutes outside of town when he pulls off the main road and into the parking lot of a small restaurant. There is a bright sign with the restaurant's name, and at the bottom, it says 'fine Thai cuisine.'

I turn to Ralph, momentarily speechless. I am trying to rack my brain if I ever mentioned that Thai food was my absolute favorite. "How?" is all I manage to get out.

"How did I know that Thai food is your favorite?"

I just shrug my head.

"I might have had a little help with the restaurant's recommendation, but you're excited, right?"

I throw myself across the cab of the seat and wrap my arms around his neck, trying to get as close as the truck will allow. It is not lost on me that this is the exact move Phoebe does every time she sees Ralph. Mother like daughter, I guess. "Thank you, this is so nice of you. I am supposed to be treating you to a date. I technically asked you out by bidding." Everything comes out muffled with my face pressed into him.

He hugs me back and seems content to stay this way. He finally breaks through the silence, "How about we go inside and see if the food is worthy of that hug." He gives me a quick squeeze and loosens his hold on me.

I move back from him, "Thank you for finding this place for me."

The hostess seats us toward the back in a secluded, quiet part of the restaurant. She asks if we want a booth or table while we are walking. Without any hesitation, Ralph chooses a booth. The hostess nods and directs us toward a booth that is half-circle with seating all the way around.

Ralph gestures for me to sit first. The man is a walking contradiction; when he is not a bossy caveman who is capable of kidnapping, he is a gentleman who researches my favorite food and offers you to sit first. He is not boring; I will give him that.

Ralph sits and slides around until he is sitting closer to me. The hostess hands the menus to us and lets us know that our waiter will be with us soon. I don't even know why I am looking at it; I get the same thing every time I eat Thai, Pad Thai with Shrimp. Ralph is equally decisive with his choice. He lays his menu down as our waiter walks up to take our drink order.

"Princess, do you know what you want?"

"Yeah, I am ready to order." I turn toward the waiter and place my order, "I will take the Pad Thai with shrimp. Please make it mild spice. Thank you." I hand him the menu and look toward Ralph to place his order.

"I think I will try the green curry, at maybe a medium spice." Ralph handed his menu over to the waiter. The waiter promises to be right back with our drinks before walking away.

"Did you just order something you have never tried before?" I would be impressed if he did. I get in these ruts of only getting the things I already know that I love. I want to try something new, but I always chicken out.

"Yes, but to be fair, it is all new to me. I have never had Thai food before." The way that Ralph so nonchalantly says it makes it unbelievable.

"You're kidding!! You seriously have never had Thai food before. Why would you pick this place for tonight? What if you hate it? That is a lot of pressure you are putting on my favorite food group."

"I have had Chinese before, but the guys told me that doesn't count. And I would not pick on something you liked; I want you to have fun tonight."

"This is the gooey 'cinnamon roll behavior' that I mentioned before. This is incredibly kind of you. Thank you for making this special for me."

Ralph noticeably puffs up his chest with the praise I am throwing his way. "Do you mind if I ask you a question? It is kind of personal."

"Oh, a personal question uhh? I am too curious now to back down ask your question."

"Did you come to the auction hoping to bid on someone else? I know we have talked about this before, and you did not want to date. Did something happen that changed your thoughts on dating?"

I am not sure I will ever get used to this man and all the different sides of him. "That was more than one question, Chief." I am trying to bring some humor into this situation, but it is falling flat. When he doesn't respond, I decide that even though the answer is embarrassing, there is no point in hiding it from him. "The decision to go was a last-minute one on my part. The persuading point was my aunt Betty's good intentions with what she thinks I need in my life on a personal level."

"I am not sure I understand. What good intentions does Betty have with regard to you?"

I want to crawl into the table and hide from this conversation, "Uhh, this is embarrassing, but Betty has been finding men online for me. When she deems one worthy to make it to the stage in her interview process, she and her friend meet them at the diner in town and do an in-person interview. I found out she was doing this awhile back, and it never went anywhere Until last night."

"What happened last night." Ralph has turned into a serious, growly Chief of Police right before my eyes.

"I was making dinner for Phoebe last night, and Betty came into the kitchen with news that Steve had made it through her entire crazy process and that he was coming over last night to meet me."

"What?!" Ralph looks unhinged by the last part of the story. "Phoebe was there. What if he was a psycho?"

I just keep trying to explain before the vein on Ralph's temple pops out anymore, "Nothing I said seemed to sway Betty into canceling Steve until Stella came over. Her date had been canceled, and she was hoping I would go to the fundraiser with her."

"What happened with Steve?"

"Betty called and canceled because I ended up going with Stella. Betty has it stuck in her head that I need to be dating. She has been relentless about trying to set me up on blind dates."

"So you didn't go last night hoping to bid on someone else?"

"Nope."

Ralph sits there staring at me. Finally, when he speaks, I am the one left confused. "Okay. I have a solution to your problem."

Before I can ask him what my problem is that needs a solution, our waiter brings our food out. It all smells divine, momentarily distracting me from the large mountain of a man sitting across from me, just staring at me.

"Why are you not eating?" I ask as I dive my fork into my noodles.

He makes no effort to start eating. All he says is, "My plan will work."

I pause before shoving the fork of noodles into my mouth, "Ralph, you should know you have a little bit of a crazy look in your eyes. Betty gets the same look, and it freaks me out. I don't have any problems that need any solutions. So I suggest you try your curry and be amazed by the world of Thai food." I can't wait any longer and shove the fork full of noodles into my mouth. Best decision I have made in a long time. It is better than I remember. I even groan out loud because it tastes so good.

Ralph is not letting this go easily and gears up to plead his case again, "Okay, so listen to me before you shoot me down. It might sound like an unorthodox solution to your problem, but it is a sure-fire plan with a low probability of failure."

Between bites, I cut him off, "Ralph, I am going to stop you right there. I have no idea what you are talking about. Your crazy is starting to show a little. Maybe your blood sugars are low? Phoebe gets a certain way if she is hungry. Try your curry." I dive in for another bite.

Ralph has still yet to pick up his spoon. "The problem is you want to be single, and Betty wants to set you up on dates."

I give up and put my fork down. The poor man is not going to eat until we can resolve whatever issue he thinks he has the solution for. "Yes, that is a problem, but in the big picture, not a big deal. Betty will get bored soon with me always refusing to meet the guys she picks out and move on to her next project."

"We could fake date. If you were my girlfriend, Betty would stop trying to have random guys come to the house." Ralph says it with such ease that it seems like a no-brainer solution.

"I am sorry, I think I blacked out. I thought you called me your girlfriend." I am shaking my head, confused about how we got here.

"You heard me correctly." Yet another side of Ralph, the confident side. He now seems satisfied that his solution is out in the world that he can start to eat. He grabs his spoon and stirs his curry. He is content to let me sit there; it is my turn to freak-out. I just sit there and watch him bring a spoonful of the milky green liquid up to his mouth. Immediately, he had a big smile on his face. "This is so good. Do you want to try some?"

I shake my head, trying to focus on whatever this is because staring at Officer McHottie is not going to get me anywhere. "I cannot believe I am jumping on your crazy train with you, but here we go. How does my being your girlfriend help when my goal is not to be anyone's girlfriend?"

Ralph wipes his mouth and patiently returns his napkin to his lap as if this is the most normal conversation we have ever had. "It is so simple that it is genius. With me as your fake boyfriend, Betty will stop trying to set you up on dates. I am not sure what part you are confused about?"

I bark out a loud laugh, "Seriously, you don't know what part I am confused about? Your idea sounds like a bad lifetime movie. It doesn't even rise to the level of a bad Hallmark movie."

"Princess, this will work, trust me."

I must have had a mini-stroke because that is the only explanation for the next words that come out of my mouth, "If I was to agree to this, how would it even work? No one will believe us, and I hate the idea of lying to our friends. I have been so adamant with everyone, especially Betty, that no one will believe that we go on one fake date and become boyfriend-girlfriend. Betty would be too suspicious to believe that." I take a breath, mainly to try and calm my rising anxiety over the idea of really dating Ralph. Later tonight, after he drops me off, I would probably entertain the idea of what it would be like to be Ralph's girlfriend, but right now, one of us has to keep it together.

"Are you done?"

"No, actually, what do you get out of this arrangement? I get my crazy aunt off my case, but how does this benefit you?"

"Let's start with the last question and work our way through your other concerns. You seriously need to ask what I would get out of our arrangement?" I nod my head, hoping he will answer. "Princess, you are not the only one that gets pressure to date. Even my secretary has opinions on my relationship status. This arrangement gives both of us a reprieve from opinions for a while."

"And…" I want him to keep talking. I somewhat hate myself for wondering if this could work.

If the smirk he is sporting currently is any indication, he already thinks he has won this battle. "I agree lying is not optimal, but they will never know. When the time comes that you don't need a fake boyfriend, you can dump me for real. Everyone will believe that our relationship ran its course. I am sure that I can get Betty to believe we are a legitimate couple; you just leave that part to me."

How is it possible that as I sit here going over everything, he is saying the only part that is sticking with me and making me kind of sad is the thought of breaking up, which is completely mental? Who gets sad to break up with a fake boyfriend? I think Ralph misunderstood the quiet sadness that suddenly came over me.

"Princess, nothing really changes for me and you. I am still going to annoy you and want constant updates about you and Phoebe. Maybe we hang out with all our friends. Maybe I can bring dinner over, and we can do a movie night with Phoebe. Nothing will change. We will still be friends."

I hate myself a little, and my resolve crumbles with every word he speaks. The picture he paints is what I have always wanted. My heart is at real risk of being broken if I don't keep reminding myself that this is fake and he doesn't really want me.

"Princess, what are you thinking? If you give me the thumbs up, I will prove to you that it could be believable."

I want to say yes so badly, but I have to be smart with my heart. My ex leaving me was heartbreaking at the time, but moving on was surprisingly easy. Moving on from Ralph, even if it is a fake dating situation, could ruin me. Even as a friend, he means so much to me. That is why I will never understand why I utter the words to him that I do, "Okay."

Ralph wastes no time, pulls out his phone, opens the screen, and starts typing away. When he is done, he puts his phone on the table and looks proud of himself. It didn't take long before I became aware of what he did, I could feel my phone vibrating like crazy with message alerts.

"Tell me you did not text someone that we were dating."

"I did not tell someone." He pauses long enough for me to feel relief that is quickly ripped away when he continues on, "I texted lots of someone's that we are dating. I texted the group thread. Now that it is resolved, dig into your food; this is so good."

Yeah, that is not going to happen; my appetite long forgotten. I grab my phone and open it to find numerous unread text messages waiting for me. Sure enough, Ralph added me to the group thread with all his friends. I click in and start reading them.

Ralph: Listen up, everyone. I added my girlfriend to the group thread. Try not to embarrass me or yourself.

Bubba: I am sorry, what?

Henry: Ralph, your autocorrect really screwed you this time. What did you add to the group thread?

Max: Please tell me it's true!! Are you joining the relationship train? Choo Choo, all aboard!

Harrison: Remember what Ralph said about not embarrassing yourself, Max?

Noah: IS this real?

Stella: Yes, girl, get it! Welcome to the group chat. Let me warn you: the guys are more annoying than not, so that is why we mainly stick to the girl's thread.

Jane: Congrats! I am happy for both.

Ginger: Yay, welcome to the "I have an obsessive, crazy caveman boyfriend" club. Girls, this calls for a girl's night to dish about the men.

Harrison: Sunshine, I said I was sorry.

Max: What did you do to my sister that the rest of us are getting punished for with the girls wanting ANOTHER girl's night?

Harrison: It is not my fault; the waiter at dinner tonight smiled at her.

Henry: Ralph, are you sure you want to drink the same Kool-Aid that these other idiots are guzzling?

Bubba: Harrison, I have little hope that you will learn to stop acting like a caveman anytime a male is within five miles of your girl.

Emma sends a picture of the little girls playing. Phoebe has her new yellow fuzzy duck backpack tucked under her arm and a rubber duck in her other hand.

Jane: That is so adorable.

Max: Emma, are you trying to kill me? What have I ever done to you that you would send that picture to EVERYONE??

Noah: We have our hands full over here. Let me see if I understand what is going on. Ralph finally figured out how to get the girl. And that girl is way out of his league. Harrison is still acting like an idiot with his girl. And Max is about to have a panic attack. However, I am unclear if it is from the mention of a girl's night or Jane seeing a picture of cute babies making her ovaries want to explode. Did that cover it all?

Henry: I have to say I like the recap; it's very comprehensive. I will make a motion for us to end all text threads with a recap. It is refreshing.

Ralph: I am willing to agree if you all stop blowing up my phone. My girlfriend is so distracted by your constant texts she is ignoring me.

My head flies up to see Ralph smiling at me. "Told you it would work. Now, as your boyfriend, I insist you eat your food. We should probably head back soon to grab Phoebe soon."

And just like that, I have a boyfriend, and I am more confused than ever.

Chapter 27
Ralph

The drive from the restaurant is quiet but not uncomfortable. I never started this evening to bag her into a fake relationship. When she explained Betty's plan to set her up with random guys from the internet, I knew I needed to find a way to stop that from happening. The idea popped into my head, and I should have been freaking out at the thought of having a girlfriend. It has always been like this in the past, and that is why I have steered clear of dating the same person consistently.

I know I am in trouble with Chloe, though. The only part of my plan that I find upsetting is its inevitable end. I am trying not to focus on that and enjoying being with her. I am so lost in thought that the drive to Noah's home to retrieve Phoebe flies by.

Chloe breaks the silence first when I put my car in park. "Seeing this was your plan, how is it going to work when we walk in there?" Chloe is clearly nervous as she chews on her bottom lip.

I reach over and, with the pad of my thumb, pull her lip free from her nibbling. She looks over at me, not as shocked by the touch as I was expecting. It seems like progress. "Just be yourself, Princess. Think of this as practice for when we tell Betty tonight."

"Don't remind me." She grumbles. "I swear that woman is a part bloodhound and can smell our bull a mile away."

We both exit the truck and make our way to the front door, trying not to freeze to death in the process. Emma is the one that opens the door and ushers us in. "So, there is a situation currently happening that is truly horrifying. Nothing to worry about." Emma rushes out of the last part when Chloe's face immediately shows panic. Emma continues, "The girls are fine, and they were complete angels tonight. There really are no words for what is happening in my living room. You need to see it to believe it."

We both follow her into the living room, not sure what to expect. My wildest imagination could not have prepared me for the sight I am greeted with. Noah is sitting in the middle of the room with his legs crossed. He has his eyes closed as both girls are applying, what I am assuming is Emma's makeup to Noah's entire face. Scary clowns have nothing on the way Noah looks. The little girls have outdone themselves. Even his hair has bows all throughout it. I am assuming Emma helped with that part. I lean toward Emma, "Please tell me you have pictures?"

"Of course I do! They are serious contenders to make the Christmas card this year."

I cannot help the laugh that escaped, it was loud, filling the entire room. Noah's eyes fly open at the same time the little girls turn their heads to us. Noah just glared at me as I continued to laugh at him.

The real surprise is Phoebe. I expected her to take the position and crawl to either Chloe or myself. Instead, she pulls herself up using Noah's arm. Lola takes her hand, and they waddle toward us. Chloe squats down so she is on her daughter's level. "My sweet girl, look at you go!"

The whole scene has me on cuteness overload, which is not a normal feeling for me.

Emma nudges me with her shoulder and speaks so only I can hear, "You are looking like a proud papa right now."

I just grunt my response because what can I say right now? Yes, Emma, I am a proud dad to that little girl, even though it took me an entire evening to convince her mom to be my fake girlfriend. I would do anything to have this feeling last forever.

Noah is now standing with us. "Lola has been holding her hand all night as they walked from all over the room. Phoebe has refused to take her backpack off either. We tried a few times, but she was committed to wearing it."

"Ralph brought it for her and gave it to her tonight. We might never get it away from her now." Chloe explains over her shoulder.

"Dude, what happened to your face," I ask Noah, barely able to contain my laugh again.

"You will figure this out pretty quickly that saying no to tiny girls is impossible. Lola got a pretend makeup set from my mom, but Lola did not like the pretend option, as you can see." He then shoots a fairly tame glare toward his wife as he explains the next part. "Then this one decided to be helpful and give Lola and Phoebe real makeup to apply."

Chloe is now standing by me, also trying to hide her amusement, "Noah, you are a great girl, Dad. I really think the red across your forehead might be your color." Chloe can barely get it all out before letting a giggle escape.

Emma pats her husband on the back, "You were a trooper, babe. The girls had the best time tonight."

Phoebe waddles over and pulls on my pants leg. I reach down and scoop her up in my arms. In her tiny voice, she whispers, "Hi," before laying her head on my shoulder.

"I should get my girls back home, and it looks like someone played a little too hard on her playdate."

As Chloe is packing up Phoebe's stuff and trying to maneuver her backpack off and her coat on, Noah comes up to me and pats me on the back.

"I know you need to get them home and Phoebe tucked into bed, but just wanted to let you know we are happy for you guys. We love Chloe and Phoebe. They fit in seamlessly into the group. I am happy for you."

"Thanks, man, they are great, I agree." I look over and see Emma and Chloe whispering back and forth. I would bet money they are talking about me. Chloe looks up and notices that I am watching her. She offers what feels like a genuine smile in return.

We are finally loaded in the truck and heading back to Betty's house. I can't believe how much longer everything takes with a baby in tow. I am dying to know, so I decided to just ask, "What were you and Emma talking about so seriously?"

"You, of course. What else would there be to talk about?"

"I can't tell. Is this sass, or are you being serious?"

"Can it be both?"

I shake my head at her, "Well, are you going to tell me what you two were talking about?"

"I was nervous that I wouldn't be able to pull off the story and have her believe that you wanted to date me. But she cut me a break and asked an easy question to answer, and the answer was ever truthful."

I want to ask her more about why she thinks someone like me would not want to date her, but curiosity over the question that Emma asked her wins out, "What did she ask you then?"

"She asked if I was happy. It might sound stupid to say, but I am happy. Even though we are faking this relationship, I am happy. Ralph, you are one of my favorite people, and your friendship means a lot to me. So, as you can see, I did not lie, I really am happy."

Maybe there is not as much ground to cover in trying to convince her that this is as real as I originally thought. "I am happy too, Princess. I am happy, too." I trail off, not wanting to give away any more thoughts than that.

We pull into Betty's place. We sit in the car, staring at the house as if a tactical plan for battle is needed to enter the house. "I will concede that you were right, and our friends accepted that we were dating a lot more easily than I originally thought."

"I like it when you say I am right, continue."

"Ha, don't get used to it. I have a feeling that was a one-time thing. You are right. Betty is not going to easily believe you."

"We will never know if we continue to sit here and freeze. Where is the faith in your boyfriend? I am truly hurt by the lack of faith in my abilities."

She playfully shoves my shoulder. Even though I can tell she is freaking out about how the next few minutes will go, she is still giving me sass. "You grab the diaper bag, and I will grab the kid." I can see she wants to refuse my offer of help, but she stops herself.

"Thank you, Ralph. Now let's go get this over with."

"Now that is the spirit, Princess."

We hurry inside. There are still quite a few lights on, which gives me hope that Betty is awake. We are taking our coats off when Betty walks into the room. "Well, well, what do we have here? Anything you kids want to share with the class?"

Chloe and I look at each other, unsure what she is talking about. Chloe cracks first. "Ralph found this great restaurant with my favorite food. Do you like Thai food? Maybe we can take it out from there sometime."

"Don't you Thai food me, child. Why was I not the first to hear the news that you finally made it official with the Chief here? Now, there are going to be so many broken hearts in the morning when the rest of Little Falls wakes up to realize the most eligible bachelor is off the market. I will probably keep the online boyfriend search in place in case this fizzles out. Always good to have options."

I grab Chloe by the waist and pull her into my side, trying hard not to jostle Phoebe, who has fallen asleep on my shoulder. "Let me be clear with you, Betty: there is no need for a backup plan. Chloe is mine. No more bringing home random guys to my girlfriend."

"Wait, how did you even find out?" Chloe doesn't seem phased by my over-the-top possessive declaration that she is mine or calling her my girlfriend.

"A gossip never reveals her sources, deary. And Ralph, if you mess this up with my girls, I will not hesitate to start the search for someone that is worthy of them." She quickly flips switches, "Okay, well, I had a big day and need my beauty rest. Chloe, please lock up when you go to bed. Good night, kids." The tornado that is Betty drifts down the room with ease.

I look down at Chloe, who is still firmly secure in my arms. "Seriously, how did she know?" She looks adorable, looking up at me, all confused.

"If I was a betting man, it would be either Bubba or Stella or both. Those two are the worst gossip in town. I thought by texting the friends first that there was a good chance that one of the gossips would take care of telling Betty for us, and I was right."

Chloe groans and puts her face on my chest. "Do you honestly expect me to tell you were right twice in one night?"

The distress in her voice over having to tell me I was right makes me laugh. "Can I help you get Phoebe into bed, and then can I interest you in watching a movie with your fake boyfriend?"

"Yeah, I think that can be arranged."

Chapter 28
Chloe

I have to say, waking up every day with a fake boyfriend is way better than it was when I would wake up with a deadbeat husband ever was. The rational part of my brain understands that Ralph is my fake boyfriend. That this is all pretend, all the text messages, the times he drops by to say hello, or the treats he brings for Phoebe and me. It is all pretend, the rational part screams over and over.

The other stupid organ in my body, my emotional heart, is increasingly becoming louder with thoughts that this might be real. He always grabs my hand because he wants to hold it and not because he is putting on a show for someone and watching him with Phoebe, teaching her new things. It is often just the three of us hanging out doing nothing special; those are the times I love the best. My stupid heart screams at me that Phoebe and I have found the missing piece of our family.

As if he knew I was thinking about him, he texted me his normal morning text.

Ralph: Morning Princess.

It is so Ralph. Never any fluff, just direct and to the point. I like it a lot. I have also learned that he becomes increasingly impatient and grumpier with me if I don't respond promptly. The best was when I left my phone in my room one morning. I was busy ordering some new products for the cabin and responding to work emails that piled up on me. By lunchtime, there was a loud pounding on the front door. When I opened the door, I found a hulking mountain of a man about to lose his mind. Once, he calmed down enough to realize that I was not ignoring my fake boyfriend or that I had fallen into a well. Try not to laugh when your fake boyfriend is explaining how he was worried someone had fallen down a well, and that was why you had not responded. I should have received an Oscar for my performance in the supportive fake girlfriend category that day, so now, instead of pushing his buttons, I just respond.

Me: Hi Ralph.

Ralph: What are the plans today?

Me: The contractors will be finishing up at the cabin by the end of the week. I need to be ready to go in and work my magic by next week.

Ralph: I bet it will be awesome. Everyone is excited to see it.

I send him a smiley face emoji.

Me: What about you? Any big plans for today?

Ralph: Besides my normal superhero duties, my day is looking fairly boring.

Me: Poor Ralph, so bored at work.

Ralph: Careful, your sass is shining through.

Me: Weird, how did that happen?

Ralph: I need a favor.

Me: If it involves me breaking the law, so you have something to do today, I am too busy for that.

Ralph: Ha Ha. No laws will need to be broken for this favor.

Me: You're no fun. What's the favor?

Ralph: It is actually a favor for my fake girlfriend.

Me: Color me intrigued….Go on.

Ralph: There is a work party on Thursday night. Families are welcome, so we can bring Phoebe with us. These things can be boring and not very fun, so I thought you could come if you were available.

Thursday just happens to be my birthday. I haven't told anyone here it is my birthday. Birthdays seem less fun the older you get, and I don't need a reminder that I will be turning twenty-six years old and starting over in every aspect of my life. So, I decided to keep quiet about my birthday and attend the party. The silver lining is I will get to hang out with my two favorite people that night.

Me: Wow, you are really selling it to me, fake boyfriend.

Ralph: Please, I will owe you.

Me: No need to beg. Of course, Phoebe and I will be your plus 2 for the party. What is the dress for the event?

Ralph: Clothes.

Me: Wow, now look who is sassing who?

Me: Okay, fake boyfriend, you have a city to protect, and I need to knock out my to-do list if I want to attend a boring, no fun party this week. Stay safe out there.

Ralph: Have a good day. Don't forget Phoebe wants you to send me pics and videos. Talk soon.

I can't help smiling as I climb out of bed to start my day. I am going through the checklist in my head, hoping I didn't forget anything, when I am greeted with a happy giggle coming from Phoebe's crib. "Well, good morning, my sweet girl. I know why mommy is so happy, but what has made you so happy this morning?"

Right on cue, Phoebe lifts her hands in the air and waves her ducks around. I am starting to wonder if I should be worried about how obsessed my daughter is with ducks. I lean over the side of her crib and lift her up and over the side railing of the crib. I lay her down on my bed and changed her.

After she is all cleaned up and ready for the day, we head toward the kitchen in search of some breakfast. Phoebe has really mastered walking ever since her playdate with Lola, and she rarely crawls anymore. She is currently waddling down the hall in front of me, wearing the fuzzy duck backpack that Ralph gave her. I couldn't help myself, so I snapped some pics and sent them to Ralph.

I get Phoebe her breakfast, which is all set up on her tray, and she is devouring her eggs like I haven't fed her all week. "Whoa, slow down or you will choke." She responds with a toothy grin and a fist full of eggs shoved into her mouth.

I made a list of all that needs to be done this week. I should also research finding a part-time nanny or someone available to watch Phoebe when work arises that does not allow me to bring her along. I add that to my never-ending list of stuff that needs to get done.

Chapter 29
Ralph

Me: Morning men.

Bubba: Beware, he is using kind words, he wants something.

Henry: Aren't you curious about what he wants?

Noah: Doesn't curiosity kill the cat?

Max: I am not a cat. I will ask him. I am not afraid of the reformed grump turned overly smiley guy. Ralph, what gives with the nice text?

Me: It is too early for you all. I am regretting my decision to open the guy thread. I should just start one with the girls and leave you all out.

Me: And saying 'morning' makes me nice?

Harrison: There he is…way to go, guys, poke the bear enough, and you will get the growl.

Henry: That would be a good saying on a shirt.

Noah: Talk fast, Ralph. What do you need? I need to go lecture some kids about being responsible.

Me: Fine, I do need some help. My girlfriend's birthday is on Thursday. I want to throw her a surprise party. She doesn't know about it.

Bubba: I understand that we are idiots most days, but we understand the concept of a surprise birthday.

Henry: Why do you insist on calling her girlfriend all the time instead of her name? We get it. You have a girlfriend, and some don't.

Harrison: Henry, anything you want to talk about?

Noah: Why are you not involving the girls in the plans? They will have something thrown together that would be perfect for Chloe.

Me: I don't want them to plan it. I want to be able to do this for her.

Max: Oh man, when the love bug bites, it bites hard. Am I right, guys?

Noah: I am ignoring the dumb comment, Max. Ralph, what do you need from us?

Me: I am going to email you each a list of things that I need help with. Does that work?

Harrison: I can help. I am off that day.

Henry: I am in, too.

Bubba: Count me in.

Me: Bubba, do we need to go over what a secret surprise party means? No gossiping!!

Bubba: You wound me, Ralph. But fine, I'm not telling anyone. I get it.

Noah: I am in.

Max: Me too.

I turn my phone off and start making a list of things that need to be done to make this a birthday to remember. I don't know where the lines that we drew for our fake relationship are. It doesn't feel fake to me anymore, not that it ever really did feel fake for me. I keep hoping that she will one day want something not fake with me.

I was hoping to keep the girls out of the loop, fearing they would spoil the surprise for Chloe. After making the assignments for the guys, there were a few things that only the girls could help with. So, I reluctantly start a chat thread with just the girls to ask for their help.

Me: Ladies, I need your help.

Stella: It took you long enough to ask. We have been waiting for your text.

Emma: Stella!! You are supposed to play it chill when he asks.

Me: You have got to be kidding me; Bubba already blabbed, didn't he?! That man has a serious problem.

Jane: He means well; does that count?

Ginger: Let's put a pin in the gossiping friend issue for the moment. What can we do to help you?

Me: I want to throw a surprise birthday party for my girlfriend on Thursday. There are a few things that I need help with to make it happen, though.

Stella: You know it is creepy you only call her girlfriend and never Chloe.

Me: I need new friends.

Emma: Okay, clearly Ralph is wound a little tight trying to make her birthday special. We should go easy on him, ladies.

Jane: Want me to make a specialty cake?

Me: That would be perfect!! But I also have another request for you.

Jane: Sure, anything for you and Chloe.

Me: Do you mind if we have the party at the bakery? It would be early evening, so you are normally closed. We won't be interrupting business hours.

Jane: Not a problem at all. This will be so much fun!

Me: Thank you for helping. I just really want to make her birthday special for her.

Stella: I would have never pegged you for the softie in the group, but you are giving the other guys a run for the title.

Me: Thanks, I think? Okay, I need to get back to work. I will send out detailed emails; thank you again for the help.

Chapter 30
Chloe

This day can curl up and die! I have been busting my butt all week trying to finalize orders that I placed weeks ago for the cabin. The vendor I ordered all the bedding through emailed this week to let me know that the bedding would not be ready for pick up this weekend due to a supply shortage. One of my subcontractors who was hired to paint the entire house, asked if they could have another week. A million other little things happened that just kept adding to this week's awful, and I want it to end.

I haven't seen Ralph that much either. He has had to stay late at work, covering shifts for officers who are out sick. I know he is just my friend or fake boyfriend, but I really love the evenings that we spend together. He has become an expert at Phoebe's bedtime routine. She prefers him some nights, which he loves so much. I watch from the doorway as Ralph reads Phoebe a book and rocks her to sleep. It has always been just Phoebe and me. I thought I would hate sharing these moments with anyone else, but the opposite is true. Ralph lightens my load if he gets it.

I have been running errands all afternoon, and I look like a drowned rat from all the stupid snow that has been falling all day. I couldn't avoid it, though. The errands needed to be checked off the list before heading into the weekend. Ralph is supposed to be here any minute, and even though this is not a fancy work party, I still want to look good.

Phoebe is currently distracted by toys that I laid out for her in my room. I try combing my hair, but to say it is a lost cause would not do it justice. There is no time for anything fancy at this point. I pull it into a loose braid that falls over my shoulder. It's not perfect, but at least I no longer look like a lion on crack. I grab whatever I see first that is clean and change quickly. I throw on some fresh mascara and a new layer of lip gloss. I inspect my final draft of what the last four minutes produced will have to do.

I grab the packed diaper bag and head for the door. "Phoebe, we have to go; Ralph will be here soon." That was all she needed to hear. She stands and starts to waddle out to the living room, where we find Ralph already here talking with Betty.

"Ralph! You're here; I didn't know you were waiting out here. I am sorry." I can't shake the lingering feelings of being frazzled by how the week has gone and is now coming through for Ralph to witness. Phoebe race waddles right by me to get to Ralph. He doesn't hesitate to scoop her up into his arms.

He walks toward me, "You need to breathe, Princess. I was early, so don't worry about me waiting for you. Betty was actually filling me in on her weekly poker game that has some not-so-legal issues."

I crane my head to look around Ralph so I can see Betty. The woman has the nerve to not look apologetic for anything that was said or done and just shrugs back at me. I shake my head, realizing that it is a fight for another day, not right now.

"Princess, you look beautiful tonight." He pauses and steps back to take me all in. "You look too good to be hanging out with my co-workers tonight. Let's ditch and stay in."

Those words were music to my tired, stressed-out ears. I wanted to shout yes, but Ralph does so much for me; I want to be able to do this one favor for him. "Not a chance, Chief. We are going to that party."

He tugs on the end of my braid, "If you insist, Princess." He leans even closer, "But for the record, I love it when you wear your hair down, and it is wild and free. Reminds me of you, absolutely gorgeous." He steps back again and heads toward the door to collect the coats. This man is going to kill me with his words that leave their mark long after he has walked away from me.

I shake my head and try to remind myself that a fake boyfriend is not real; this is fake! As I put my coat on, I turn to Betty. "What are your plans tonight? Unless they are not legal, then maybe we shouldn't share them right now."

Betty just giggles, not even trying to hide her amusement with the question. "Oh, you know me, just a quiet evening at home, no trouble for me. Now, you young people, go have some fun."

I hug Betty quickly and head outside with Ralph, who is carrying a bundled-up Phoebe. Ralph insists that his truck is safer than my car. When I explained to him how much it would suck to constantly be switching Phoebe's car seat back and forth, Ralph's solution was to buy another car seat for his truck. I tried to tell him it was a waste of money, but he didn't care, and that is how the town's most eligible bachelor found himself driving around town these days with the car seat in his back that belongs to his fake girlfriend's daughter.

"Do you mind if we make two quick stops?" Ralph asks as we are backing out of the driveway.

"No, of course not."

"How was your day? You seem distracted." The snow is still coming down like crazy, but Ralph has a way about him that even though he is not looking at me, he is still focused on me.

"I don't want to spoil the night with my bad attitude, so let's pretend that everything today went as planned."

"No."

That is all I get, and a no grunted at me. I want to laugh at his caveman response, but I do not think he is trying to be funny today.

"No, uhh?"

"There is no pretending with us. If you had a bad day, then I want to know about it." His sincerity is one of his less appreciated qualities that I think people look over about him.

"What do you mean there is no pretending between us? You are literally talking to your fake girlfriend?" Even the simple act of bantering back and forth made me feel lighter already. I wonder if that was his intention. He has me so distracted that I don't even notice that we are pulling into his driveway.

"Sorry, I just need to grab something I forgot. You ladies stay in the truck and stay warm." He is jumping out and trudging through the freshly fallen snow. He did not have to ask me twice to stay in a warm, dry truck; he would get no arguments from me.

Phoebe is happily talking to herself in the back. I am amazed how her babble is turning in real words more and more every day. I wish I could hold onto these days, but things seem to be constantly changing, and I do not care that I would like them not to. Ralph is back just as quickly as he said he would be, and we are off to the second stop.

"Princess, explain your day now."

"Are you only allowed a certain number of words a day before
you are cut off? That is why you speak in a shorthand caveman lingo."

Ralph smirked at my sass but stayed quiet, and I knew he still
wanted an answer to his question. It is not as simple as explaining my
day was crap; it is the fact that someone cares enough to ask. Even
before I knew my ex was cheating on me, he rarely made an effort to
ask how my day had been. Looking back, I can clearly see how it was
always about him and his needs. Not wanting to go down that spiral of
regret, I try to focus on Ralph.

"Fine, anything that could go wrong did go wrong. That has
actually been the theme all week." I huff out my frustration, feeling a
little better to have been able to just express that small truth out loud,
so I keep giving them. "You know what got me going all day, even
though nothing was going as planned?"

Ralph looks over at me, patiently waiting for me to answer my
own question. "It was the thought of hanging out with…" I pause.
Normally, I would finish that thought by saying, 'fake boyfriend.' The
part of me that wants it to be real won't allow me to say it right now.
So I go for total truth, "It was the thought of hanging out with you,
Ralph. I missed you this week because our schedules were off. I have
never had a friend like you before." I stop myself there. I have said
enough.

"Princess, you have no idea how much I have been looking
forward to being with you tonight as well. I am sorry your day has
been crap. My offer still stands to go home and order a pizza and
watch a movie."

"Not on your life. The way you spoke so highly of this party with your co-workers, I wouldn't miss it for anything in the world." I am genuinely smiling at him. None of my work issues have been solved, and no stress was magically taken away, but this time, Ralph and I feel so much better. I reach over and squeeze his arm, "Thank you, Ralph. I feel so better; thank you for listening."

"You should hold your appreciation until you hear my next request." Ralph pulls into the parking lot that attaches to Jane's bakery. Ralph looks nervous suddenly. "I need to pick up the cupcakes that we ordered for the party tonight. Normally, I would tell you to stay in the car and stay warm, but when Jane heard you and Phoebe were coming with me tonight, she insisted that I bring you inside. She needs her baby fix, whatever that is."

"A baby fix is what raises Max's anxiety every time his fiancé is around a baby." I giggle at the thought of Max turning white every time Jane asks for lots of babies at that very moment. "We are definitely coming; I would love to see Jane, even though she would love to see Phoebe more."

Ralph grabs Phoebe and starts to head around the back of the bakery. He notices that I am confused that he is going in the opposite direction of the front door.

"The bakery is closed, so Jane told me to go around and pick up the order."

I follow behind him, stepping in his footsteps. I can't believe how much snow we have already gotten, and it doesn't seem to be lifting anytime soon. We reach the back entrance to the bakery, and Ralph opens the door for me. I walk in and head toward the light of what I assume is the kitchen, which is empty.

"I don't see any packaged cupcakes. Do you think Jane forgot?" I look to Ralph for answers.

"Let's go check the front of the bakery; maybe she is out there."

I move in the direction of the large swinging doors that lead to the front of the bakery. I swing them open, and a light flashes, lighting a dark room. Then, so many people jump out and scream, "Happy Birthday." I am trying to play catch up but experiencing sensory overload. I look around the bakery, and it looks like every square in the space has been decorated.

I look around and see faces staring back at me. They all look happy, and some continue to shout, "Happy birthday." So, I have the most rational response ever to a surprise party. I burst into tears and turned, running back through the swinging doors I had just entered.

Chapter 31
Ralph

I am the first to admit that I do not have a lot of experience when it comes to women or even surprise parties, for that matter, but I can safely say that Chloe's response was not what I had expected. I am still standing here staring at friends and family that had gathered, just staring back at me. Phoebe is still in my arms, completely oblivious to the drama unfolding.

Jane is the first to walk up to me. "Want me to take Phoebe so you can go talk to Chloe?" Jane is reaching her arms out for Phoebe, but Phoebe turns and clings to my neck, unwilling to go to Jane. Jane reaches for something off a tray and presents it to Phoebe. "Pheobe, you wouldn't want a duck cookie, would you?" That got her attention. Phoebe whips her head around and practically jumps into Jane's arms at the sight of a bright yellow duck cookie. So grateful that I had the thought to ask Jane to make some duck cookies for Phoebe. With Phoebe content in the arms of Jane, I turn to go find my girl.

When I do find her tear streaked face is almost my undoing. "Princess, I am so sorry. Please don't be mad. I found out it was your birthday, and I wanted to do something nice for you." She just continues to sob quietly. Hating the space between us and not caring if she wants that space, I walk over to her and pull her into me.

I hold her until the sobs turn into whimpers. She tried to say something, but it was too muffled because her face was crammed into my chest. I reluctantly pull back so we can talk.

"How can I fix this? Want me to go grab Phoebe, and we can head back to your place?"

"No, that is not what I want."

"Then what? You name it, and I will make it happen."

"I want to rewind time and not freak out in front of everyone. I want to be the type of girl that a surprise party is something fun, not so unexpected that I lose my mind and ruin all the hard work you put into night."

"Do you not like your birthday? Some people are weird about getting older." I feel so helpless to make this better for her.

"No, it is not that. My ex never made a big deal out of my birthday, and it was just another day to him. I guess I started to believe that, too. It was just overwhelming how many people were out there willing to spend time with me on my birthday, and I guess I freaked out by all the kindness. I am sorry I ruined all the hard work."

"You didn't ruin anything. You are perfect. Now, it is still your birthday for a few hours; we have options. We can either go home and enjoy a quiet evening at home, the three of us. Or we could go out there and be bombarded by people who love and adore you. Trust me, that option is leaning toward the more annoying option because that will take time away from me adoring you, and I don't like to share."

She laughs at what I just said and probably thinks I am joking, but I am completely serious. I don't want to share her. She surprises me when she gets on her tippy toes and tries to reach me. I lean down into her, and she kisses me sweetly on the lips. I am sure that was her intention, just a quick peck on the lips, but I don't release her when she tries to move back. This kiss seems different. This is the first time she initiated a kiss with me. She is timid at first but quickly becomes more confident. She is moving her hands up to hold my face in place. I am not sure how or when it happens, but I have her pushed up against the fridge. She is pinned between me and the fridge. All thoughts of surprise parties or the room full of people just a few feet away are long forgotten. Nothing else matters but the woman in my arms.

Reality comes crashing back to us when Betty walks into the kitchen. Chloe and I are breathing hard when we pull apart enough to break the kiss. Chloe hides her face in my shirt. "Oh, I see how it is, and to think I was worried about you. Instead, I find you back here getting an early birthday present." She is still holding the door open with one hand; the noise from the other room filters into the kitchen. Betty yells over her shoulder to everyone that has filled the bakery, "They will be out momentarily; Chloe was just sucking Ralph's face off." Loud laughter erupts from our friends and family as Betty turns and walks back toward the party.

Chloe quietly mumbles, I think that woman is clinically insane."

"You will get no arguments from me, Princess." I tuck a strand of hair that had fallen free from her braid behind her ear, loving the connection I feel even with simple touches. "Okay, decision time. Are we staying or going?"

Chloe looks up at me; her cheeks are still tinted pink from the embarrassment of Betty catching us making out. "I want to stay and enjoy the party but made such a fool of myself."

"Hear this woman; there is not one person out there who is not worried about you and loves you. They are not going to care that you ran out. They only want you to return."

She is nibbling on her bottom lip as she thinks over her options, "Okay, let's do this." She puts her hand out for me to hold, and I grab hold without needing to be told twice.

We start to head for the doors leading to the party when Chloe stops abruptly. "Wait, before you came, you gave me multiple chances to back out and hang out at home. What if I had taken you up on the offer? All the hard work you have done would have been for nothing."

"Not nothing, Princess. If you had decided to stay in tonight, I just would have texted the guys and they would have taken care of everything." I pull her toward the doors, suddenly overcome with a desire to get this party over with so I can have her all to myself.

We walk through the doors, and I know she is nervous as she has a death grip on my hand. I lead her around the counter to the perfect response by the party goers. Some shout happy birthday, some wave but continue on with the conversations that they were having. I can visibly see Chloe relax when she realizes that no one cares that she freaked out.

Phoebe waddles up to us with Lola in tow. "Hi, mama." Her face is stained bright yellow.

"Seriously, Jane, did she get any cookie in her mouth?" I am not mad at all, and Jane knows it too.

"Listen, I only offer cookies and distractions; what you do with the bundles of joy afterward is your problem."

I give her a smile, grateful that she was able to help.

Chloe made her way through the room, thanking everyone that had come. Lara and her family were able to make it. Betty and her poker gang all came out. Even my assistant Estelle came. I am fairly certain that she is a bigger fan of Chloe than she is of me. Chloe looks so happy as she makes the rounds talking to everyone. I stay behind, letting her have her moment to shine.

I know the exact moment when Chloe finds out that I had her favorite Thai food catered for tonight. She shrieks from across the room with pure joy. She is looking around the room, and when her eyes land on me, she mouths, "Thank you." I just nod back.

Even though it was a rocky start, I would call the party a success. The girls inform me that it is time to cut the cake. Jane goes into the kitchen and comes out with a masterpiece. It has multiple layers, all decorated to look like a dress. On top is a crown. Jane places the cake on the table.

"I know you didn't specialize exactly what you wanted for her cake, but this just felt right. A princess cake for your princess." Jane looks nervous that I might not like it.

I pull Jane into a hug, "This is perfect! You did an amazing job!"

Out of nowhere Max appears at my side and is trying to pry his fiancé out of my arms. "Hands off the baker; she is mine." Everyone laughs at Max's horrified expression that Jane was being hugged by a man who wasn't him.

"Calm down, Max; I was just saying thank you."

Chloe comes over, sees the cake, and starts to jump up and down with excitement. She throws her arms around Jane, who is now being pulled in for another hug. I look over at Max. "Do you have a problem with this hug?"

Max starts to mumble under his breath. And my loud laugh that escapes at his expression is not helping his sour mood. I am pretty sure he wanted to flip me off, but thought better of it with all the kids present.

We sing Happy Birthday to Chloe as she blows out her candles. I lean into her, "Did you make a wish?"

"Yep," and she pops the 'p' for extra effect.

"What did you wish for?"

"I can't tell you, or it won't come true. And Ralph, I really want it to come true."

The way she says it and the look in her eyes makes me want to keep interrogating her until she tells me. I will make it come true; no matter what she wished for, I would make sure of it. Everyone crowds the table for a slice of cake, ruining our moment.

I would say the party was a success. The Thai food was a hit. Everyone left, and all that remains is our main group of friends. Phoebe is passed out cold, cuddled up on my chest. Lola is in a similar position, sleeping on top of Noah. It all feels routine, like we have done this dozens of times before and we have, the only difference now being that Chloe and Phoebe have joined the group.

"Oh, Chloe, I am sorry, but we can't watch Phoebe on Saturday. My ever-helpful husband volunteered to go see my family this weekend. I am sorry." Emma mindlessly rubs her belly while she shoots glares at Noah.

"Wait a minute, you asked me to set up one more weekend trip away before the baby comes."

"That was then, and this is now. A girl can change her mind. I would rather help Chloe out this weekend."

Noah mumbles under his breath that he hates pregnancy hormones. Then looks at Emma, "Do you want me to cancel our plans, dear?" The way he said 'dear' was more annoyed than I think he even meant it.

Chloe interrupts them, "Don't do that. You guys go have a fun weekend. I just thought Phoebe would have more fun with Lola, but she will have to survive her mom all day."

"What is going on Saturday that you need a sitter?" I ask.

"I need to run up to the city to pick up some orders I placed for the cabin. I also have a long list of items that need to be checked off while I am there. It will be a long day between the drive up and back, then all the running around. But Phoebe is a great little assistant, and I am sure she will do great."

Now I am annoyed, "Why didn't you ask me?"

Chloe looks around the room at everyone before answering, "Ask you what?"

"Why didn't you ask me to watch Phoebe? I have the whole weekend off."

"Why are you mad? What single guy wants to get stuck watching a baby on his weekend off from work."

"But I am not S-I-N-G-L-E am I, Princess?" That was a little too excessive of a growly grump answer even for me, but does she really think of me that way?

I can see it in her expression the moment it dawns on her that we are having this argument in front of everyone. I should let it go and talk to her about it later, but I am too far gone at this point. "Do you not trust me with Phoebe?"

Chloe stands and moves toward me, and sits in the chair beside me. "Ralph, of course I trust you. This is new for me. It has only ever been me and Phoebe, I am not used to having a guy step up and want to help me."

Hating that we are having this conversation in front of everyone, I ask her anyway, "So, can I watch Phoebe for you on Saturday?"

"Yeah, Ralph, that would be great. Phoebe would much rather be with you instead of stuck in a car all day."

The moment we are sharing is interrupted when Henry leans over and whispers to Bubba, "I think we just witnessed their first fight."

Bubba replies as he clutches his chest, "Our baby boy is growing up so fast."

I shoot a glare there way, not that it does any good. They keep the teasing going the rest of the night. Chloe stays close by until we all decide to finally call it a night.

"Thank you everyone. I can say that this has been the best birthday I have ever had."

The girls all descend on Chloe, offering hugs and making plans for another girl's night despite the protests coming from Max in the background. We get kicked out and are told to go home. Everyone else offers to stay and help clean up the mess.

The drive back to Betty's is quiet. When we get there, we go through the motions of getting Phoebe inside and changed into her pajamas. I am still impressed that she can sleep through being stripped down and dressed in pajamas without waking up. Chloe picks her up and places her in the crib. We both just stand there at the side of her crib, staring at her.

I whisper, not wanting to wake Phoebe, "Did you have a good birthday, Princess?"

Chloe looks up at me, "It was the best, thanks to you."

I lean down and kiss the top of her head, just enjoying this quiet moment together. I look around the room, noticing how bare it is. "Don't women usually go crazy decorating baby rooms? I assumed you would be worse, seeing you are an interior designer."

"Yeah, I would love to give her a pretty room that is all her own, and one day I will. Don't get me wrong, I am grateful that Betty had space for us to stay with her. The process of getting back on my feet is going slower than I thought, but when we can afford to move out, Phoebe's room will be the first room I do."

We just keep standing there watching Phoebe sleep. An idea popped into my head that I can't seem to shake. I would need some help from the guys to pull it off. Chloe interrupts my plotting when she asks, "Can you be persuaded to stay and watch a movie with me."

"Yeah, birthday girl, I think I can be persuaded."

Chapter 32
Ralph

"When you roped us into this little project of yours," Henry uses air quotes as he says the little project, "Is this what you had in mind, man?"

Harrison mocking shades his eyes, "The color is really bright. Did you do that on purpose?"

I am starting to freak out a little as I step back and look at what we did. When the idea popped into my head to redo the room for Phoebe and surprise Chloe, this is not how I saw it going. All the guys agreed to show up and help, except Noah, who is out of town with his family. Ginger also tagged along with Harrison. She has been distracting Phoebe all day so we can work on the room.

Max joins in with his thoughts on possible demise, "Jane is really attached to Chloe and Phoebe, so if this goes south and you guys break up, we are team Chloe all the way."

"Guys, this is not helpful. Is it really that bad?"

Ginger wanders in at this moment, "Oh wow, that is bright," she notices my face fall more. "Ralph, it is bright, but Phoebe will love it. Before you start beating yourself up, let's get the whole room put back together with her furniture and the items that you bought. Betty and I have opened everything and removed all the tags, so it's all good to go."

"Thanks, Ginger; at least I have one good friend." The guys all start to laugh and make more jokes about my ultimate demise when Chloe, a professional decorator, sees what I did.

The weekend that Chloe and I were snowed in at the cabin was when I went crazy and ordered anything and everything to do with ducks. It has been sitting in my garage ever since it arrived. I kept telling myself that I needed to return it, but I never got around to it. When I approached Betty with the idea of decorating the room for Phoebe, she was all on board with the idea.

Betty and Ginger have been a great help in distracting Phoebe all morning while we painted the room. I paid extra money to get a child-friendly paint that is supposed to dry in a few hours and has no fumes. While the paint dried, the guys helped me put some furniture together. Phoebe already had a white crib; I just added a few additional pieces. A white dresser that can also be used as a changing table. There is also a glider with an ottoman. I had to buy it when all I could picture was Chloe rocking Phoebe in the chair. Then there are rugs and a tiny Phoebe-size bookshelf.

Betty is currently feeding Phoebe dinner while Ginger is helping set the room up. She was right that the room needed the furniture in the space to help lessen the bright yellow walls.

Bubba is currently arranging the bookshelf with all the new books I bought. "Okay, I am going to say it if no one else is going to say it. This is the weirdest thing I have done on a Saturday in a long time."

"I agree, the duck theme is weird. Why not hippos? They are totally in right now." Henry's obsession with hippos rivals only Phoebe's love for ducks.

"Jane has been blowing up my phone, wanting pictures of the room, ensuring I will spend all tomorrow listening to my fiancé's rant about wanting babies. So, thanks for that, Ralph."

"Okay, I can't take it anymore. I thought you wanted a family. Why do you freak out anytime Jane brings up babies? I think you are hurting her feelings." Ginger is the youngest in our group, and Max's baby sister, but her age does not lessen her fire when speaking her mind.

"Did she say that? Did she say that I was hurting her feelings?" Max looks like a kicked puppy at the thought of hurting Jane.

Ginger doesn't look like she wants to answer her brother's question, so she avoids it, "Max, seriously, what's your deal?"

"You guys will think I am being a big baby if I explain."

"Oh, Max, too late. We already think you are a big baby without knowing the latest reason. Might as well tell us what you're thinking." Bubba says as he pauses, shelving the books. Everyone chuckles at what Bubba said, knowing there is some truth in it.

"Fine, I am selfish, okay. Are you happy now? I have waited forever for this girl to come along. I just want some time where it is just me and her. I want time to travel and spoil her. Of course, I want kids with Jane, but I also want her all to myself for the first year or two of marriage."

Ginger walks over to her brother and puts her arm around him, "Max, have you told her that is what you are thinking?"

"Not exactly in those words, no."

"What is it with the King family members? Maybe it is something in the DNA; Ginger is not great at communicating either." Harrison realizes his mistake the moment he utters the words.

"Bro, I am not in a relationship, and even I know you just stepped in it with your girl." Henry is shaking his head at Harrison in disapproval.

"Sunshine, that came out wrong; let's focus on Max and how he is a big baby."

I can always count on my friends to get distracted easily with any random topic. Max's inability to talk to Jane about how he has been feeling has done a great job stopping the constant jabs at me for my paint choice.   Harrison is also in hot water with Ginger, which is great news. We are able to finish the final touches on the room with no other comment on ducks or yellow paint.

Everyone heads home, and now all there is to do is wait for Chloe to get home. She has texted throughout the day and called a few times to check on Phoebe. She texted a while back, letting me know that she was going to be home soon. Phoebe and I are watching her princess movie with the bears. She is curled up on my lap, randomly growling at the screen as Chloe walks through the door.

Phoebe lets out a happy scream at the sight of her mother. She climbs off me and bolts for Chloe. Chloe looks tired but equally happy to be home. Chloe bends down and pulls Phoebe into a hug. The way they are acting, you would think these two had been separated for weeks, not a day. Pheobe is the first to pull back "Hi, mama".

"Hello, my sweet girl. I missed you so much today." Chloe proceeds to shower her with kisses that cause Phoebe to break into giggles. When Chloe stops, she looks at me, "How was it? I have to say I am impressed that you bathed her and dressed her in pajamas. I tried to get home sooner, but the roads are a mess."

I want to go to her and shower her with welcome-home kisses, but I am too nervous about what is hiding behind the closed door down the hall. "I am glad you got home safely; we missed you too." I am just standing there like an idiot, rocking back in forth on my heels with my hands shoved in my pockets.

If Chloe thinks I am acting weird she doesn't call me out on my behavior. Phoebe ends up being the one to throw me under the bus. I am trying to work up the nerve to bring up the room when Phoebe wiggles to the floor and takes off down the hall toward her room. She is wicked smart and knows something happened in there today and has hated not being allowed to enter. Chloe laughs at Phoebe pounding her fists on the door as if she thinks it will open the door.

"What in the world is she doing?" Chloe starts to walk toward Phoebe. Chloe reaches to open the door when I stop her. "Wait!"

"Ralph, what is wrong? Phoebe is probably just wanting her duck or blanket."

"I need you to promise not to get mad. No matter what, please promise me that."

"Ralph, what did you do?"

"I had an idea, and it kind of snowballed into what happened behind the door. I just need you to keep an open mind, please."

Phoebe does not have the patience for any of my stall tactics. She continued to hit her pudgy fists at the door. Chloe reaches for the doorknob, and I send a silent prayer to the girlfriend gods that I can keep mine after she sees the room.

The door slowly opens, and there is less than five seconds of peace before Phoebe loses her mind with excitement. She runs into the room and spins around in a circle, trying to take it all in before falling over. I start to worry if too much excitement is bad for kids. Phoebe gets back up and starts to explore her new room. The one not saying anything is Chloe. She is looking around the room, taking it all in, and her silence is killing me.

"Chloe, please say something. At this point, I will take anything. You can yell at me if that makes you feel better."

"Ralph…" It comes out a whisper and then we are back to silence. She makes her way over to the glider chair and sits down. This is not going well at all. Phoebe is sitting on her duck chair that I placed by her new bookshelf. She looks like she is on cloud nine. At least, I won over half the women in my life and made them happy with me.

"Princess, please say something. It is just a little paint and a few things that I thought Phoebe would enjoy. It really is not a big deal." Chloe looks like she is about to say something when Phoebe comes up to me. She takes her normal position of hands up in the air to let me know that I need to pick her up. I lean down and scoop her up.

She puts her hand on my beard and looks so serious as she says, "Ank oo, daddy." She then throws her arms around my neck and gives me the best hug. It almost sounded like she was trying to say 'thank you, daddy". I am guessing that is what Chloe thinks, too, because her eyes look like they're about to bulge out of her head.

"Did she just call you d-d-daddy?" Chloe is stumbling over the word herself.

"No, I think we misheard her." Phoebe wiggles and wants to be put down. As soon as her feet hit the floor, she is off to explore again.

"Listen, Ralph," Chloe is talking to me but staring at Phoebe. Her voice is off. She sounds so far away even though she is right in front of me. She takes a deep breath and continues, "It was so nice of you to do all this for Phoebe."

"But. Is there a but coming?"

"No, I am grateful you did this all for her. It was kind of you and way above the call of duty."

"I am confused. Your words are telling me one thing, and your face is saying another. I know the paint is a little bright; I can fix it."

Chloe offers me a sad smile, "Listen, Ralph, I think it might be time to end our little arrangement. Maybe the fake dating has gone too far. We have had some fun but I think we have accomplished what we set out to. I don't think Betty will bother me with blind dates anymore."

I can't believe what she is saying. All because I picked the wrong shade of yellow. "Chloe, I know I should have asked you about the room and not gone so overboard. There is nothing that can't be undone or scaled back."

"Ralph, this is not about the room. I just think it is time to end this fake thing between us."

"Is this because Phoebe called me daddy? She has been with Lola a lot and probably heard her call Noah that. It is just a word. She doesn't understand what she is saying."

That was the wrong thing to say. A tear rolls down Chloe's cheek. She tries to wipe it away, but I still see it. We continue to stand there, staring at each other. She is the first to crack, "Thank you for watching her today; it was very helpful. I was able to get so much done." Just like that, a mask of indifference is thrown up and she is hiding behind it. "You are probably itching to get out of here. You have been stuck here all day."

"Please, Chloe, don't do this…". I am not above begging if I thought it would do any good.

"I appreciate all your help. I should probably try and get this little one in bed. I can walk you out."

I have been such a fool. How could I let myself fall for the one woman that has told me from the beginning that she would never love me. My chest feels like it is cracking wide open. I need to get out of here before I lose it. "Don't bother; I can show myself out." As I turn to go, she calls out after me.

"Have a good night, Ralph. Thanks again for your help."

I run into Betty on my way out. She doesn't have the normal twinkle in her eyes. She looks sad. I am guessing she overheard the entire conversation. "Betty, let me know when it would be a good time and I will come paint the walls for you." I sound like a caged beast; I need to get out of this house before I lose it.

"Oh, sonny boy, you will do no such thing. That room is perfectly lovely, and I bet Phoebe lost her mind with happiness when she saw it.

Now, for the other one, she didn't mean anything she said; she just needs time. That ex of hers did a real number on her and her heart. She loves you; she is just scared."

"With all due respect, Betty, from where I was standing, she didn't seem confused. I need to get out of here. If you change your mind about the paint, let me know, and I will take care of it." I grab my coat and head for the door, silently praying Chloe will run out to stop me, but she doesn't. I close the door with more force than I meant to.

Chapter 33
Chloe

I feel like I am holding my breath until I hear the front door open and slam closed. Ralph is gone, and I have no one to blame but myself. I crumble to the ground, the floodgates burst, and the sobbing starts. I am freaking out my daughter, and I know I am, but I can't seem to stop the hurt that is flooding out of me.

"My sweet child, what have you done?" Betty's voice is not full of the usual humor. She comes into the room and takes a seat on the ottoman. Phoebe is offering me ducks and hugs. I take a few deep breaths, trying to calm myself.

"Ralph and I broke up. Sorry about the room, please don't be mad. Ralph had good intentions." The sobs are starting to subside, and the hiccups are taking their place. I have always hated that I was an ugly crier.

"Don't you dare apologize for this room. I love it. And that man of yours has more than good intentions. He loves you and Phoebe with everything he has. I know you fiercely protect your heart but what happened here tonight, well sweetie there is no way to say it, except you were the one in the wrong."

"You are wrong, Betty; he doesn't love me. I know he is fond of Phoebe, but that is not the same as love. We faked our relationship so people would stop setting us up on blind dates. I am sorry we lied to you. At the time, it felt like a harmless lie that would hurt no one."

"How did that work out for you? From where I am sitting, it looks like your little lie hurt you and Ralph something fierce."

"I messed up." It comes out as a pitiful whisper. "I knew I was in danger of loving him. How can you not? No one has ever treated me the way he did. I was fine when I thought that it was only my heart that would be broken when he left. I thought it was worth the risk. It all changed tonight with the room and Phoebe."

"Now that man organized a work party and picked everything out in this room. You are telling me that you hate it that much? It's quirky; I kind of like it." Betty looks around the room, assessing all the details.

"No, I love the room. It screams Phoebe in every little detail. Phoebe came up to him and called him daddy. That is the problem. I thought my careless actions of falling in love with Ralph would only affect me, but that is glaringly obvious how wrong I really was. Phoebe loves Ralph with her whole heart. What happens when he leaves? I knew I was risking my heart being broken, but now Phoebe is at risk. I can't have that; I need to protect her. That is why I told Ralph that we should end our fake relationship." It feels good to purge myself and tell Betty everything. I am hoping now that she knows, she will understand why I did what I did.

"Oh, child, I love you, but when it comes to matters of the heart, you are dumber than a box of rocks."

"What?! Maybe I didn't explain it right."

"No, sadly, you did. I have been on this earth long enough to know what real love looks like. You might have entered with thought it was fake, but the only ones you fooled was yourself. That man is a good man. He loves you and your daughter like nothing I have seen before. Ralph is not your ex; he was not going to leave you. Not all men leave."

Betty doesn't give me a chance to disagree with her. She stands and leaves the room without a glance back. No matter how broken I feel right now, I am still a mom, and right now, I need to pull it together for Phoebe. I wipe my face with the back of my hand. I go to her crib and grab out her favorite duck and a new fuzzy yellow blanket. I scoop Phoebe up in my arms, and we settle into the rocker.

Phoebe must know I need a quiet moment to rock her. Phoebe snuggles in, and we just rock. I am not sure how long we have been rocking when I notice that Phoebe is lightly snoring. I kiss the top of her head and lay her in her crib. I back out of the room quietly and close the door behind me.

Utter exhaustion falls over me. This has been the longest day. Even though I was more productive than I thought I would be in the city today, it didn't stop me from wanting to be home with Ralph and Phoebe today. I hurry, wash my face, and crawl into bed. I reach for my phone, which is plugged into the charger. I don't know why my stupid heart was hoping that there would be a text from Ralph and disappointed when there was none.

I keep replaying the words Betty said to me. As I finally start to drift off to sleep from sheer exhaustion, the thought pops into my head: what if Betty was right, and Ralph could love me. I dismiss the idea when I remember he walked away from me tonight. He just walked away.

Chapter 34
Ralph

My phone has been vibrating like crazy from the charger on the nightstand, and until this point, I have refused to pick it up. The only one I want to talk to is not texting me.

After I left Chloe last night, I came home and drank what felt like my weight in whiskey. That is what to blame for me still in bed at it being noon. How could I have been so stupid? I fell for the one girl who told me that she never wanted to fall in love again. I have never felt this type of pain before. I can't get my mind wrapped around the idea that Chloe and Phoebe are not in mine to love and protect. The phone starts to vibrate incessantly. I grab my phone, wanting to throw it against the wall but think better of it at the last minute.

I click open the text app and find the guys have been relentless with texts being shot back in forth.

Bubba: Ralph. I know you think I am a gossip. And I am; that is how I know you need friends right now.

Harrison: I can't believe you finally admitted that you are a gossip.

Noah: I am proud of you, big guy; it is the first step in admitting the problem.

Max: This is an enjoyable start to my Sunday

Henry: This is all great stuff, guys, and Bubba deserves it all. But is anyone else curious about what the gossip is that Bubba knows or why Ralph needs friends?

Bubba: Just for the record, Stella is a bigger gossip than me, and you guys never give her crap for gossiping.

Max: Because she is terrifying, that is why.

Bubba: So you manly men are more afraid of a chick that is five foot nothing over me who is six foot five?

Noah: Yes

Harrison: Yes

Max: Yes

Henry: Yes

Bubba: You are all pathetic.

Harrison: Ok, let's circle back to Ralph.

Bubba: Ralph, come on, man you need to respond, or we are all going to be on your doorstep.

Noah: Bubba, if I have to involve the girls to find out what the problem is, I am going to be annoyed.

Bubba: Noah, if that is your scary principal speech, it could use some work.

Henry: Bubba! Focus on what is going on.

Bubba: Last chance, Ralph, and then there is no stopping the intervention.

That is the last text. I decide my best option is to put them out of their misery so I can go back to bed.

Me: Chloe hated the room. Phoebe loved the room. Phoebe called me daddy. Chloe broke up with me. Now, we are all caught. Don't come over. I am hung over and not in the mood. I am likely to shoot and ask questions later.

Noah: This is not great. I leave town for one weekend, and you guys let everything fall apart.

Max: How is this our fault?

Henry: I told you that you should have gone with hippos.

Harrison: How is that helpful?

Bubba: How is any of this helpful?

Bubba: Ralph tell them about the fake dating. You need to tell them about you loving Chloe and Chloe loving you but being scared. We need the truth this time if you want our help. And FYI she did not hate the room. She loved it.

I can't help but respond, even though I said I wouldn't.

Me: I was there, I would know what she thought of the room.

Harrison: She told you she hated the room?

Me: Not in those words. I could tell.

Henry: You are a lot of things, friend, but psychic you are not. Unless you ask her and she tells you that she hates it, then you don't know.

Noah: What about the fake dating? What is that about?

I have lost all ability to keep this to myself. I want to tell my friends and move on with my bachelor life.

Me: We came up with this idea of fake dating to get everyone off our backs about dating. It was all fake.

Max: I am going to call bull. We saw you guys together. That was not fake.

Me: Sorry to burst your love bubble, but Chloe does not love me. All FAKE.

Henry: We have known you too long to believe that. You love her. And she clearly loves you.

Noah: What is the problem with Phoebe calling you daddy? You have been more of a father figure to that girl than anyone else.

Bubba: Why are you fighting this so hard?

Me: Would it make you all happy if I told you that I fell in love with a woman that told me she could never love anyone ever again. I was a fool to believe I could change her mind. So now I love whiskey.

Me: IF I mean anything to you, please leave me alone and give me time. I am fine. Everything is fine.

Max: You are not fine!

Noah: We can't walk away when you need us.

Harrison: You are stuck with us

Henry: we are going to get you through this

I power my phone off and throw it on the bed. I roll over and close my eyes, hoping the pain will ease if I can fall asleep.

Chapter 35
Ralph

It has been two weeks, and it is not getting better. Estelle threatens to quit if my mood doesn't improve. At this point, I don't care, I will let her quit. The guys have been relentless in trying to get me to hang out, but my stubborn streak is stronger.

I am trying to shut all thoughts of my girls out of my mind while working. It is the only way I can get anything done. At night, when I am sitting alone in my house, the silence is suffocating. There have been so many nights I drive over to Betty's house wanting to barge in and demand Chloe hear me out. The only thing stopping me is, not being able to take the rejection one more time.

Two weeks have passed, and it still feels like last night; my heart was broken. I am currently sitting at my desk trying to concentrate on the quarterly budget reports that the mayor requested last week.

"Well, well, my big brother is alive?" I look up to see Lara strolling into my office like it was her office.

"What are you doing here?"

"Wow, you are more salty than I thought. Listen up; we have a lot to talk about, and you are not returning my calls or texts. You left me no other choice than to sneak an attack on you at work."

"Ever think I didn't want to talk to you?" Am I being a jerk? Yes. Do I care, not so much.

"I am going to cut to the chase and get this over with. You and Chloe are idiots. There, I feel better now that I said that. How about you?"

"I don't want to talk about Chloe." My sister doesn't deserve me being a jerk to her, but here we are, with me being a jerk to her.

She softens her tone; it almost sounds like pity, "Ralph, I know Dad did a number on you. I know you felt like you had to shoulder the burden of his secrets all on your own."

I am speechless; I thought I was the only one who knew. I don't know what to say. So, I just sit there and continue to listen.

"I am sorry, Dad was and still is an awful human being. But don't you think you have let his secrets take enough from you? I know you have never wanted to date because you were afraid of turning into him, which is insane. I will deny this outside of this office, but you are one of the best men I have ever known."

"How long have you known?"

"About Dad?"

I nod, wanting her to continue explaining.

"It was the summer before I went into high school. I overheard you and him arguing. You told him that he needed to stop sleeping around. He said stuff not worth repeating. After that, I started to notice the excuses he made all the time. I put two and two together. I am sorry I never spoke to you about it, though."

"Lara, I don't know what to say. I am sorry you found out the way you did. I tried so hard to shield you from it."

"That's the thing, big brother, I don't need protecting now or then, really. What I would like, though, is to see you happy."

"Lara, don't start. I can't talk about this. I feel like I am barely holding on."

"Sorry, not sorry for the info I am about to unload on you. Don't be mad when you hear everything I have to say."

I do not like where this is going already, and she hasn't said anything yet.

"So there has been a massive plot to get you and Chloe together. Your friends could see you were in a bad place, and I think the word they used was grumpy. Betty knew Chloe needed someone like you. Really you needed each to learn how to love together. There has been so much meddling going on, I am having a hard time remembering it all."

"Try," is all I manage to growl out.

Unphased by my attitude, Lara launches into all the scheming, "One example would be the cabin remodel. It was Betty's idea to remodel so I could hire Chloe. Betty even called gramps and let him know about 'operation help the idiots find love'. I know the name is lacking, but it really explains the process we are all entrenched in. What else? Oh, Stella did not have a date that stood her up the night of the auction. It was always the plan that she would trick Chloe into coming. Betty was never meeting random guys off the internet to set up with Chloe. I knew Chloe was going to the cabin that first weekend; I also knew you would want to see it one last time before the project started, which is why I told you when I did. Now the getting snowed in was mother nature helping the cause out."

"I don't know what to say."

"Ralph, be honest, do you love that girl?"

"Yes, and it terrifies me. She doesn't want me, Lara. I tried, but she still sent me away."

"Ever think she is just as hurt and lost without you? I have never met two more stubborn people who are perfect for each other.

"What are you saying?"

"I am saying that girl is so in love with you, but sometimes we let fear rule how we live our lives and the choices we make. Did it ever occur to you to ask Chloe how she felt?"

My head is spinning with the thought that there is a chance that Chloe loves me. I jump out of my chair. I have given her enough space and time; that's over with now. I round the desk and headed for the door.

"Where are you going?" Lara yells after me.

"I need to ask a girl a question!" I yell back toward her.

Lara catches up to me in the hallway, "She is not home. That was what I came here to talk to you about, but I got distracted by informing you of all the ways you are clueless."

"Lara, I am running on limited patience. If you have a point, I am going to need you to get to it, fast."

"The work at the cabin is all completed. Chloe has been up there on-site working for the past ten days. She texted me last night and asked if I could come up today to do the final walk-through." She pauses, waiting for me to say something, but I just stare at her. "Can you go up and do the walk-through? And if I don't fix this thing between the two of you. A lot of hard work has gone into making this happen."

"Wait, she has been at the cabin all by herself that entire time?"

"Yeah, she said she needed to finish the final touches, but if you ask me, she is hiding. What are you going to do about that big brother?"

"I am going to get the girl!" I turn to leave the station when Estelle stops me.

"Seeing I have been instrumental in the success of 'Operation Help the idiots find love,' I already have your calendar cleared for the next few days. Good luck, boss!"

I want to stop and ask questions about the parts that she meddled in, but the desire to get to Chloe and Phoebe is stronger. I yell back at her as I am leaving the station, "I would be lost without you, Estelle!"

I have a plan, and although it is crazy on every level, I have never felt more right about it too. I jump in my truck, needing to make one stop before I head toward the cabin to get my girls.

Chapter 36
Chloe

I lay Phoebe down for a nap so I could finish up the last-minute details that need to be done before I can hand the keys back to Lara. My car is all packed and ready to go back to Betty's this afternoon, I am just missing a few things that Phoebe is using for her nap. They will be easy enough pack when she wakes up. The last ten days spent at the cabin have been amazing and also torturous.

It's hard to escape the memory of a guy when he is everywhere I look here. There were so many times in the last two weeks I found myself wanting to call him and text a funny picture of Phoebe to him, but I always stopped myself. I know I screwed up, and my freak-out session ruined everything.

Something Betty said really hit home for me. Ralph is not my ex. It is simple but true. I can't expect Ralph to behave the way my ex did. I want to go to Ralph and apologize, but the hurt that was etched on his face that night still haunts my memories and stops me from reaching out. I am a coward when it comes to love, and because of that, I have lost the man that owns my heart. Maybe it was always meant to belong to him.

Phoebe has been missing him and asks for him all the time. Sometimes, she will ask for her "grrrr," but more often than not, it is daddy she asks for. Even if Ralph never wants nothing to do with me, I hope that he would be willing to try and be friends for Phoebe's sake.

I have run out of distractions to keep my brain occupied as I wait for Lara to arrive. I really hope she likes what I have done here. I hear Phoebe calling me from the other room, so I take one more look around the room and stand to get Phoebe.

While I am packing up the remainder of Phoebe's items that she used during her nap, I can hear someone in the great room, "Lara is early, Phoebe. Should we go find her?" I never know how much Phoebe can understand when I am talking to her and how much she considers as mommy babble. Either Phoebe understood me, or she heard someone, too. She stands and waddles out to investigate. She is sporting her fuzzy yellow duck backpack proudly strapped to her back as she walks out of the room.

I grab the diaper bag and look around the room, Ralph's room one last time before turning off the light. I couldn't help myself; when we came back to stay at the cabin, I purposely chose his room, wanting to be close to him. I hover in the darkened doorway of his room, not wanting to lose this last connection with him, when I hear Phoebe unleash a scream. I take off running in her direction and come up short when I see what caused her to scream.

Ralph, not Lara, is standing in the middle of the great room. Phoebe had already made her way to his feet and was demanding to be picked up. Ralph obliges my daughter's demands, scooping her up. The scene threatens to break the floodgates open. These two love each other so much. Phoebe has her pudgy arms around Ralph's neck, squeezing tight. He is holding onto her equally as tight. All I can think is I need to fix what I have broken. We are meant to be a family.

Phoebe finally pulls back. I can only see her profile and the way Ralph has her in her arms. Even with only her profile, I can tell she has a giant smile on her face. The room is so quiet as if no one is brave enough to be the one to break the silence. My sweet daughter is the brave one to speak first, "Hi, Daddy."

The mountain of a man before me looks like he is close to losing it with the sweet, simple words that Phoebe spoke lingering in the air. He finally speaks, "Hi, tiny princess. I have missed you. Do you want to play with some new ducks I brought you? I have some business with your mom." How Phoebe missed all the new duck-related toys that were piled on the couch is evident that she would rather be in Ralph's arms than with ducks, which is a first. She reluctantly allows him to put her down but is still watching him to make sure he does not go too far.

Ralph turns to me with an expression on his face that I can't place. It is not lost on me that he just told my daughter that he only needs to conduct some business with me. The crushing feeling inside me threatens to take me out. Of course, he is here to do the final walk-through, nothing more, nothing less. I take a deep breath, trying to find the strength to get through the walkthrough as fast as humanly possible.

"Okay, where would you like to start the walk-through?"

"No," he growled at me.

Phoebe has her back to us, preoccupied with the new toys, and I can hear her letting out her own tiny growls. These two and their growling. I shake my head at him, "No, just no? I need more words or grunts to put together what you want."

"You," another growl.

"You want me to pick where we start the walk-through? Fine, let's just start in the room we are currently standing in." I am doing a fantastic job avoiding eye contact at this point. The intensity coming from Ralph is too much. You can do this, Chloe, just talk fast, and then you can leave. The internal pep talk is not really helping.

"Stop."

"Okay, caveman, I am going to need more than one-word responses. Would you prefer to do the walk-through on your own and email me if there are changes you want made?"

"No." He takes a step closer to me.

"Oh, you are so frustrating. What do you want, Ralph?!"

"You." That growl was louder. What does this man want, and why does he keep saying me? We just stand there and stare at each other.

He finally speaks, "Do you remember the game we played that weekend we were snowed in here?"

"Yes, we played twenty questions. Why does that matter?"

"I want to play again. Right now."

"What are you talking about? You want to play a game. Don't you want to see the cabin?"

"No, I want to play the game."

"Fine, what do you want to know?" There is no reason for my attitude, but it surfaces all the same.

"Do you hate the duck room?"

"What!? We haven't talked in two weeks, and you want to know if I hate my daughter's room that you selflessly created for her just to make her happy. That is what you want to know?"

"Yes, answer my question."

"You drive me crazy, you know that, right? No, Ralph, I do not hate the room. I love it as much as Phoebe does." I stop myself short before I tell him what else I love.

Ralph's demeanor shows its first crack when a small smirk escapes momentarily at my response.

"Next question, are you still scared?" I want to correct him and tell him it is my turn to ask a question, but I don't because his question has me reeling. Am I scared?

I look down at the floor wishing it could swallow me whole and this conversation would end. It also occurs to me that I have spent the last two weeks wishing I was brave enough to tell Ralph the truth. No matter how things play out this afternoon in this cabin, I want to leave with no regrets. I need to be brave and tell Ralph the truth, no more hiding. At some point, tears started to flow down my cheeks. Ralph comes toward me; he gently wipes them away. He is so close now when he asks again in a whisper this time, "Princess, are you scared?"

"Yes."

"Tell me."

"Ralph, I thought I was protecting Phoebe. It would kill me to see her heartbroken. She has only ever known me as a parent in her life. I freaked out when she called you daddy. I want to give her a whole family, but life is messy, and I want to protect her at the same time. I don't know how to do both."

"I am not him, Chloe; I am not your ex. I could never hurt you or Phoebe."

"I know that now, I was just slow figuring it out." He leans in and sweetly kisses my forehead.

Phoebe starts to call for him as she is waving something in her pudgy hand, "Daddy, daddy, ook."

I turn my back to them so I can wipe my face and try to find some composure. I look up and see the Big Bertha staring down on me. If I didn't know better, the moose is smirking at me. Great, now dead animals find my hot mess of a life amusing.

"Princess, I have one more question for you."

I know I owe him answers, but what is the point? Where is this going? I turn around to find Ralph on one knee with the box in one hand, reaching out toward me. Phoebe is just standing there watching, trying to figure out what is happening. Get in line, kid, we are all wondering that.

"Princess, I have made some mistakes with you. I never should have suggested the fake dating idea. I never should have let you doubt for one moment how real this is for me. I love you…" he pauses, looking like he is picking the right words, "like crazy. Princess, I love you like crazy. I am never going to walk away from you and Phoebe. You are the pieces I have been missing my entire life. I might not be her biological father, but she is my daughter. I want to adopt her and make it legal. I want the house full of daughters that look like there beautiful mother and sons that are growly and protective. I want a whole life with you. Princess, I need you to marry me."

I want to laugh at the way Ralph said the last few words. It sounded less like a question and more like a command, which is kind of perfect for the man I equally love like crazy.

I move closer until I am standing right in front of him. "Ralph, I need you to know something. I love you like crazy, too. I knew the minute you left two weeks ago that it was the biggest mistake of my life. I will probably still have doubts and worries and make mistakes."

"You bring me your doubts and worries and mistakes, and I will fix them all. I am in this for the long run. I want this life with you. Marry me." As he says the last part, he is sliding a ring on my finger. The man is nothing if not confident.

"Yes!" How could I answer any other way?

"Yes?! Really? You can't do takebacks; my ring is never leaving that finger." I look down at the ring for the first time; it is breathtaking. It is a princess-cut diamond set in a platinum band.

"I can't wait to marry you; I love you so much, Ralph."

"Funny you should say that…". Ralph trails off as he bends over to pick Phoebe up.

"What does that mean? You have a weird look on your face? Almost like you are scheming again."

With a smile bigger than I have ever seen on his face before, he asks, "Do you trust me?"

"Of course!" With no hesitation, I can say those words.

"Great, we have lots to do for this all to come together."

Chapter 37
Ralph

The last twenty-four hours have been crazy trying to get all the moving pieces to fit. As soon as Chloe agreed to marry me, I didn't want to waste any time. I wanted to be married. I knew from previous conversations that Chloe didn't want another big wedding. When I came up with my big idea she only hesitated for a moment.

We sent out texts to friends and family asking that everyone meet us at the diner for dinner on the following night, which is now today. I called ahead, and the owner was more than willing to reserve the back room for the large group that we were expecting. All we said was that we had an announcement.

I also called in a favor with a friend of my gramps. His old judge friend was more than willing to come in on a Sunday morning to marry us. I never pictured myself getting married until I met Chloe. So having it be just the three of us, the judge, and two random court employees we begged to be the witnesses seemed perfect. Chloe cried during our vows, and Phoebe giggled.

I was also able to get the paperwork started to adopt Phoebe. The only good thing Chloe's ex ever did was terminate his right to Phoebe. It expedited the process for me to adopt. The judge says in about 30 days, we will all come back and sign the paperwork to make it official. But I don't need a piece of paper to tell me that the little girl in the back seat is my daughter.

We are sitting in the car, getting ready to go in. I reach over and grab Chloe's hand, which now has my ring on it, and intertwine our fingers. "Are you nervous, Mrs. Boswell?"

"No."

"Okay, just because you became a Boswell doesn't mean you can do the one-word answers; that's my thing."

She laughs, and it is a beautiful sound to hear. "Of course, husband. No, I am not nervous. I am happy, so very happy."

"Me too, Princess. Should we go in and watch them all freak out at over our news?"

"Yes, I can't wait to see their faces."

I grab an equally happy Phoebe out of the back of the car, and we make our way into the diner. I lead us to the back room that I reserved. We arrived a few minutes late. I was hoping that everyone would have arrived and we would be the last.

We enter the room to the loud craziness that is our friends and family. Lola is the first to notice us, and she screams across the room to Phoebe. "Hi, Bee!"

Phoebe responds, "Hi-Lo". Everyone swoons over the cuteness overload.

"What's the big announcement, kids? I am not getting any younger." Betty pipes up from her spot between Bubba and Henry. I laugh at the view of her sandwiched between those two.

"Okay, pipe down, and I will tell you our big news."

Lara interrupts me from where she is sitting with her family, "Is this something you and your friends normally do, have dinner to announce you are dating someone? It is kind of weird, big brother."

Chloe tries to muffle her giggle but fails, and I shoot her a glare. "Sorry, babe, keep going, tell them."

"Anyways, as I was saying, Chloe and I got married this morning at the courthouse." I hold our joined hands up in the air and turn my wrist so everyone can see her ring.

"I cannot believe you called that, Betty." Bubba groans.

"Pay up, boys, you never bet against a gambler. You lose that bet every time." Betty is looking pretty proud of herself as all the guys are reaching for their wallets and throwing money in her direction.

"I can't believe we were taken to the cleaners by an elderly woman," Henry mumbles loud enough for us all to hear.

"Estelle, pack a bag; I hear the call of a casino in our near future."

"Betty, you don't have to ask me twice."

"What is going on?"

Noah is the first to offer an attempt at an explanation. "We all had bets on what the announcement was. They ranged from dating or engaged. The crazy one counting her money is the only one who said you would show up married."

"I really want to be her when I grow up," Stella admits to the crowded room.

"Congrats, kids. I am happy for you. I am assuming you have plans to take my new roommates away now that they are legally bound to you. Just do me one thing, Chief."

"Name it as long as it is not 'a get out jail free card', and I think I can make it happen."

"Leave the room yellow. I like it."

Everyone erupts in laughter and jabs, flying back in forth in a teasing nature. I am proud to say that Betty is the one getting the good jabs in. I know everyone is about to descend on me and my wife, and I need to tell her something before they do.

I turn so I am facing her. "Princess, I love you like crazy."

She smiles up at me, "I love you like crazy too, husband."

The End